I0638585

Age 16 and above only

Copyright (c) 2012. Tn Odu. Nigeria's Phantom Publisher.
Published by Phantom House Books, Nigeria
118 Obafemi Awolowo Way, Ikeja
Lagos Nigeria 999999
in conjunction with Amazon Createspace PoD,
7290 B. Investment Drive, Charleston, SC 29418, Copyright ©
2000 - 2011, CreateSpace, a DBA of On-Demand Publishing,
ISBN-10: 978-51078-4-1
ISBN-13: 978-978-51078-4-5
www.phantomhouseafrica.co.nr
[international dialing code:] 23481 3954 0895

It's harder, nowadays, to try and convince the people folk. Why reincarnation is such a big deal is really silly talk. If it is simple for a living person to die, why is it hard for a dead person to live?

We don't speak of such idiocy in Africa—life and death being such a simple cycle. If you're the type who comes and goes, you'll figure *ko matter si wa nkan to nro*[x], though I do remember the earlier times when life was much simpler; the troublesome few who thought they could make you go and not come, or make you come and not go. They were the crazy ones. The really crazy ones. On one hand, immortality is a gift. On the other, well...who would ever give it up for you?

Author's note:

It is no false statement that what an elder sees sitting at the base of a hill goes beyond what a child can see standing at the top of a mountain. I am that child for the one thing working on this title has taught me over the years is how we patronize and truly undervalue the elderly. I, myself, never fully comprehending or appreciating the value of the gray hair until now, so my first respects i pay to my elderly buttresses, first to a distinguished professor, one whose patience and experience fortunately trump my misgivings and oversight about pre-colonial Africa, and to 'my granny', his lovely wife for her generosity and hospitality over the years. I hope my ramblings in your home have not caused you any distress, but I could not ask for more excellent neighbours. I'd also like to acknowledge the family of lawyers, the Oladejis, for their rare insight and spin to the Abiku mythology, especially Elder A.A. Adedeji and R. A. Oladeji, as much of it and hearsay has found its way into my title.

As for my much younger buttresses, much appreciation to the Alates, especially Toyeeb Alate, the Okemes and the Urhobo union as well as my first and second readers on Facebook, and to my proofreaders for 'blazing' through my first draft. Only the Loas know where I'd be without you guys.

Most importantly, i love my family, the special three in my life. All i know is all this would have not been possible without you.

I'd like to take this time to remind everyone that this is a work of fiction, a kind of escapism into a fantasy world so to speak, so in no way should this fantasy replace real events.

Thank you and enjoy.

Tn Odu.

IN MEMORY OF
Nene Onoieshapornake Amajatoja [nee Akpobaro]
Love you and loving you always.

7

abiku

16+

Otito Ioju

[The Truth Has Eyes]

possession

African exorcisms! Everyone knows we hate exorcisms. We don't miss the bonfires, or the ash paint, or the heated oil, or the notorious branding rod—a thing prepared to just shy of a thousand degrees to singe your flesh, if you're a spirit child that is. That's the whole ritual by a local medium, although if you're really serious about the whole shebang, a few clever looking amulets dipped in white goat blood—or is it black goat blood—to scare us away is an impressive ruse. However, if you are the showy type, and want to go a little overboard, like the Kiki lunatic carrying out this exorcism, you can throw in an entertaining frog dance to make all the women confident I'm not coming back again. Who knows? You could get lucky (but we know, he knows, and they all know it doesn't work). It's never worked. Even if they killed me before sunrise, I could be back by nightfall. I always come back. We owe it to everyone. I owe it to myself, in a way, being my duty. It's just that singling out a female from this rare and enticing congregation of potential mothers from the Villages of the Hill makes such a thorny pick. Someone new would be nice. Someone nice would be new too

Ishaporke village. South of the Hill.

It wasn't normal, and rightly so, with the birth mark she had; dark lines forming a dazzling mosaic if you caught the patterns just right, marks she was born with, marks they all knew, marks they were afraid of. All of them, afraid of a 12-year old child, or a nine thousand year old spirit, whichever way you'd prefer to look at it.

"Curse you, you defiant spirit of return," the spiritualist said vehemently and spat to the floor. She watched him wave his hands about our face and dot our forehead with ash water from a calabash. She was alone in this body, but that was what he thought. Truth is, one is hardly alone in a cult of the dead, or dying, you see. Our siblings were of the special sort. We could visit our body anytime we wanted, especially whenever we felt we needed each other's company—and I can't think of greater a time than this. A flaw in a way, since that was how she got caught. Or how we got caught. Still, there is little we can do about it. Our rules never change.

"Back to the underworld I say!" he screamed at us, probably trying to intimidate us and see if we would shrivel in fear and cowardice. He wasn't your typical 'kola-chewing, don't wash my face, teeth, or armpits' sort of spirit medium. He was a cowry-bewitched yuppie; young, more refined in a way, having a chewing stick stapled to his cheek, and a live snail strung around his neck—and with the misguided enthusiasm with which he carried on this ceremony, I'm guessing one acquainted with that new horseman school inside the bushes. Lately, the new folks have had a way of making the revered less reverent. A sad price to pay for stupidity though, for every sapient spiritualist knew not to confront Abiku—and for good reason, our spirits they knew to be bolshie, truculent, bigoted, morbid, petty, and direly resilient. In sum, we're deemed a dangerous relentless evil, yet, this one takes her on, and in his someway twisted ken of logic, to serve as a forewarning to us all. The daring klutz.

"abo we da tewe, me ka nyajo wo[1]," she threatened, but a threat stemming from fear; the fear of the impartial hot-rod soon to come her way. An experience she was to share alone. I didn't say a word, and the yuppie ignored her same. Although he, on the other hand, knew his time for gloating would come. Without a word, he shoved cowries into our mouth, and she frowned. She spat them out, but it didn't matter. In this part of the world, cowries were intended to be a sob to Cerberus. It was his way of soliciting the help of the higher spirits, trying to bribe them with human money so that they would keep us bound in the other world. At least for a while. A world he now chooses to call

---

the underworld. Silly really. It'd be nice for him to know the irony of it all, however this plays out. The irony that the Loas he prays to are the very spirits who send us here in the first place. The higher spirits send us over and over again because we, notably she, are the incarnate and shed more blood for them at child birth than their worthless human money could bargain with in a lifetime. It's trivial when you don't know the rules, you see. Or understand what you're doing. Why in the world do they pay this sapling?

"Return! Depart," he said, spitting out commands and acting all tough as he gave an ornate calabash to our mother; a woman naked by his feet and on all fours like a sucking pup. She was all broken up and teary-eyed. All torn up inside. Even for us, people-folk were hard to understand. She had five girls already, yet her husband wanted more. She wanted more. It was too much fun watching her blossom in hope of a male for every new child. So, she could cry all she wanted. We had no plans of ever letting her go; even if death did do us part.

The spiritualist picked up a calabash of palm wine. Now that was important. That alone was like holy water. One sprinkle and the worthless spirits might consider his plea and mess with my schedule a little. He made his libation; even sprinkled some right across our feet, but what took us wholly by surprise was the chink of the 6-inch terracotta calabash over us! He broke the calabash right over us! The charlatan! Oh for the first time tonight, I felt blessed my head belonged to someone else. I could have sworn a tiny fragment of calabash wedged its way into her skull. It was most excruciating watching her buckle from the pain (we don't feel pain on the other side, so we dread it coming here), so if we've done anything of note, it'd be having saved the soul intended for this body from a life of pain.

This charlatan was spontaneous and unpredictable; his blow sufficient to make us violent and summon a rain of threats, but watching our sibling shudder and stammer incoherently for a minute or two there found us begging to be left alone—an error she quickly corrected. Her head did splinter from the burn of blood and alcohol, but she was the toughest of us all. Her resolve alone was as water to limestone, though it did boost his ego to see a tear roll down our eye. He chewed the bitter stick with pleasure then whipped her, whipping us with gin-soaked fronds from a kernel tree (the very kernel tree they had tied her up against). Its fronds bruised a little, but he wasn't going to whip her to death with palm fronds—that was clear as dawn, although a playmate of hers did clubber her once scores of a lifetime ago (that was with a stone if I remember). She got to return the hand in his passing. Still, I'm not sure he was happy he died her grandfather. No. This charlatan was full of surprises. He was bound to have something else in store for Abiku and our special mugabe of rebels.

The spiritualist spoke to the women and they came to smear off a part of the blood, oil and ash he'd rubbed on our body. This special ritual was only for the women from the Villages of the Hill, grandmothers and mothers of child-bearing age. They were all as naked as she was, so no one was ashamed. This was a naked girls' party. Only the young spiritualist was the male invited, and the only one wearing something too. However, in the stylish way he painted his head, he looked more a girl than the rest of us.

"As soon as Abiku returns to the ground, Abiku returns ash and not dust as told. So this time around, how will Abiku repay what Abiku owes," he now sang to us, and I have heard that rhyme before. Finally, we've come to it.

He picks up a snail in one hand and the red-hot iron rod in the other. This wasn't going to be any more pleasant than it was the last time, so she struggled, but the tree wouldn't budge. No tricks allowed. He had had her encumbered, so not even the tree ants would budge in aid. Now he waves the rod in front of us as he prays to the spirits, before baking the guiltless snail he'd once tied to his neck in its shell. Although the smell of barbecued mollusc was enticing to us, all we could think about was the hot iron glowing ever more menacing. I could still remember the last time one of us got burned. Morbid and tied to a horrible fate, she did. It was gruesome. Being burnt by fire hadn't changed a bit—and with every inch the rod drew closer, even I could feel it.

We closed her eyes to embrace the pain, but it was not as we'd expected. He didn't brand her deeply in the chest as all his predecessors would have done, which was the typical ritual and what was to be done. Instead, he chose to brand her callously across the head! He had intended it to hurt like hell (and it did!), but to me pain wasn't all it meant. It had meant a whole lot more. A scar across the head is a hard thing to hide, you see. So, he hadn't just branded her, the charlatan had practically stamped her soul!

Oh she rages wildly, and out of control, almost like a rabid dog. "This one, I'll leave!" she lashes out, "but you! You!!"

Still, less fortuned to finish that threat, she succumbed to the haemorrhaging and savage head burn.

"Never give birth," I had said in solidarity, only to find my words tumbling out of her mouth as she smouldered. Words I hadn't noticed we'd meant until now, and the first in a trumpet of threats from us all, taking turns in a declaration of war. It was then he heard us. Nonetheless, the more we fought for her the more we spilled fermented wine across her head burn. The sting alone was enough to calm anybody, so we silenced ourselves to allow her breathe. Oh, death would be a relief! Or maybe not, when I noticed the look of insouciance in the young spiritualist's eye. There was more.

"I'll kill you—and all you love! Because—I—am the incarnate," she dared to finish as the young spiritualist bravely told the women to leave and I knew her time was up. He was seeing this through, to the very end—I arriving only after he lit her up like a candle (because the tree had been doused in red oil, you see), but nothing of import really since he was not in the least attentive to our cries for help. Or our half-hearted pleas of innocence. In a stroke of providence, she'd suffocated from the fumes before he torched her alive, but I'd like to consider this entire charade as counting home the Ayo seeds. Who goes home with game, you see, is only decided after we've had our chance to clean house.

Over time, we (and I must emphasize a very special we and not just plain ordinary you) have grown inured to the infinite and inconceivable ways people let us go. Some do it calculatedly. Others try the subtler Machiavellian approach. The pitiful ones beg and play it safe, waiting for us to come to our own demise, but some people, just a daring few, do it viciously with barefaced intent. It's a popular rumour Abikus have a way with scars; that singeing an Abiku could mark her in the next life, but torching an Abiku would render her (or his) spirit bodiless in the afterlife and thwart any future attempts to come again. However, only a bold few dare the wrath of the unknown and actually attempt it, but is it even possible to kill a spirit? One should always ask oneself. For one thing we all must accept, a constant they always fail to acknowledge, is whatever ways we died, whatever ways our parents and friends decided to let us go, the result was always same. We always come back. Nothing ever works.

vultures

Know this, a handful of people are born vultures. Born with the gift to divine the future. Some feel the guess coming. Others see flashes in dreams. The stronger ones have it in more profound ways like trances and epileptic seizures. Hypnosis is a common phenomenon—if you're of the occult. An enviable gift, it is, despite the channel it travels. One we would greatly appreciate, and would spare us the expense of an untimely end. Unfortunately, it is to the same degree a rare gift. Not every person or creature carries it, save the elect few it is usually wasted on (blessed for no reason by Powers they seldom appreciate and forces beyond their cognizance). More intriguing, is that it's usually encountered in the least suspecting vessels—even a foolish vessel could be it. You see, the Niger Cameroons was a dense forest of wet green trees. It was not the kind of place one wears a white uniform on a wet morning, whatever the hurry, but we've lived long enough to also know people are born stupid. Living people that is. Born naturally that way.

"Reverend, I am relieved you agreed to come with me on this escort. I had almost concluded you wouldn't come," the captain said with a rueful voice.

Captain Ted Book hadn't been to confession or mass in weeks, excluding the number of times he'd arrive late. The Captain had practically grown up with the queen's army. Tall, confident, and rumoured to have outgrown his ranks. It was also rumoured this petty detail in Africa had more to do with Ted's charges of insubordination than the regular posting. His tall and confident figure didn't help dispel the rumours either, on the contrary, they escalated them—tucking even newer rumours day in, day out, under the tight black belt and the imposing Seal of Her Majesty's Navy sewed on the black hat he hardly took off. Littler said, Captain Book was a man made and shrouded by rumours—neither did the captain care a day to address or deny the rumours, nor did the middle aged priest in the captain's company know Ted to be a deeply religious man.

"Don't punish yourself, Ted. Self judgment only brings condemnation," Reverend Benedict preached softly, with a rosary in one hand. "Besides, why wouldn't I come? I see this as the answer to my prayers to spend a little more time with you. For my prayers for you and the fort have intensified since I heard the rumours," the priest added, one eye peeled, in a manner less of a remark and more of a question.

"Disregard the spit of the boys, Reverend. The men will always find ways to amuse themselves and pass idle time. Even if it's at the expense of their Captain, I'm sure you know that," Ted answered coolly, and tipped his hat to allow the brightly burning African sun warm his face.

The reverend sighed, "that I know well."

Both the priest and his Captain could speak and act freer now. Father Matthew Benedict was a sensitive priest and spoke with a believable voice. He was equally compassionate too. A man who believed everyone was destined for Heaven. It was just his job to show them the proper path, although it hadn't seemed the horse he rode had any intention of trotting the proper path. Her Majesty's Graces had a compass of their own. A gifted mind for their own direction. The reverend's horse had wandered off the bush path, running the reverend and his clothing into the dewed blades of the monstrous elephant grasses congregating across what was the vast African landscape. Every brush against his priestly attire left a stain, and along with the stain, came the lady bugs and caterpillar eggs. "It's disregarded then," Reverend Matthew said as he tried to pamper his horse back in line and shake the bugs off his robes.

"You still haven't gotten the hand of picking your horses, Reverend. That's Zachariah. He doesn't do straight and narrow," Ted laughed heartily on watching the reverend trying to coax the horse in futility. "Besides, the morning dew soothes the horse. It's probably going to run you and your cloak through every blade of grass between here and the docks. I fear you would have fared better in your confessional vestment."

"Want to lump me in the same boat as you?" Father Matthew let escape through his teeth, gritting as he struggled with the reins of his steed, "You're the Queen's man, whereas I'm a man of the Church. There's something wrong with me wearing black immediately after Sunday's mass. Unwritten yet wrong."

The Captain set his hat in place and reached to end the priest's suffering, and the priest heaved relief the minute the captain tugged Zachariah back in line.

"Thank you."

"It's the least I can do, Reverend, having come all this way with me," Ted answered, searching out a spare rope and strapping the reverend's horse to his. "But I'd suggest you raise your cloak knee-high, else your priestly vestment will bear semblance to something off the Sistine chapel by the time we arrive the docks."

"Not to worry, Ted. I can handle a little dirt," Reverend Benedict replied, taking a swipe at the most reluctant of bugs adorning his cloak in a rich array of spots and colours. Unfortunately, all the reverend did was help smear the stains. "What I can't handle is leaving my legs bare to the bite of those African adders your boys keep talking about back at the fort. Vicious little critters, I hear."

Ted Book swat a scourge of mosquitoes off his face. "Nasty as an adder's bite may be, Reverend, I doubt your robes will do more for you than fend off mosquitoes," the captain responded casually, fastening his belt after this morning's large meal (a meal that helped it skip a buckle), and then took the moment to watch the dense continental forest surrounding them palpably give way to less dense bamboo clusters—vegetation distinguishing of the riverside.

"It's amazing the wonders this new continent has to offer, Ted," the reverend said, watching a horde of mosquitoes hover over his delicate head like a miniature tornado. More mosquitoes only meant one thing. They were steadily approaching what they had ceremoniously christened The Docks. The bald priest tried to dissuade the mosquitoes from using his head as a dinner banquet by swiping at them, but the more he swiped at them, the more aggressively the mosquitoes came at him. He turned to the captain in frustration, "Ted, why would you invite me to The Docks absent your boys?"

The reverend's question had come out of the blue, and it would have been one powerful enough to see both men beneath the hooves of their stallions had

Ted not been in strong command of their horses. When the captain had regained balance however, and the reverend felt secured enough to speak, he prodded still. "Ted?"

"Word from the mainland arrived last month. It's why we are headed for The Docks; to pick up the new medical personnel for the fort, a doctor from the mainland and a young nurse from the Cape."

"Lovely! That is exciting news. It brings relief to know I can finally take my hands off standing in for the last medic," Father Matthew responded, totally exhilarated. "I must confess there was a time I was a bit reserved working the sickbay. Not wanting to take ill myself. You realize it means we would have more time to work the school then? I've come to notice we do better having the villagers come to us, than when we go to them," the reverend added, and a little too suggestively too, but everyone at the fort, including the reverend, knew the captain to be a man of few promises, and of fewer kept.

Ted Book didn't say a word. He was miles away in thought, perturbed and apparently oblivious.

"You still managed to dodge the question, Ted?"

"What question, Reverend?"

"Why we are alone?" Reverend Benedict asked up front. "Is there something you want to share with me, alone? I suppose a sin to confess?"

"The young doctor coming comes in company of a nurse," the captain answered coolly, trying to act indifferently. Unconcerned.

The reverend raised an eyebrow. "Alright. So a young Miss it is then?"

"I don't want the men to see how I fare around women. I don't know why, but my tongue deadens when I look into the eyes of a woman. Especially the much younger ones," he said, using his hat to shadow off a greater part of his face. Or the ignominy that was slowly revealing itself as a red blush across his face.

Now it was Reverend Benedict's turn to laugh. "And what makes you think you're the only man with that problem, Ted? I was married once, you know. It should come second nature to you. You're a brave man."

"No. You misunderstand me, Reverend. It is not a feeling…My mind blacks out for a second. I mean it goes b, l, a, n, k—blank, and then my tongue staggers along. It's very troublesome. I just don't know how to relate with women," Ted grumbled under a lip. "Even more annoying is whenever I try to push myself, I always go overboard."

"Then that's a peculiar problem, Ted. I could say a few Hail Mary's on your behalf?"

"You might be amused now, Reverend, but I don't

think you'd appreciate the humour when the time comes."

"I must say for a tough biscuit I never anticipated this side of you, Captain."

"—exactly what I am wary of," the captain mumbled and brought the horses to a still. They had arrived at the marshy 'rooty' banks of the Niger, and from where they stood, both the captain and reverend could make out the figurehead of the Lady Anne. It had arrived. And, they had arrived. In a stroke of sarcasm, the ship's hoisted figurehead was the figurine of a woman. "She will be the end of me, Reverend," the captain confessed, "the end of me."

Discombobulated by the old man's reply, the Osivie stood tormented by the challenge. The new Horseman's school was really turning their world inside out. The Osivie was the head chief of this village and water tribe, but he was only as powerful as the very old man in his company saw fit, for the Osivie's jurisdiction was also confined to the boundaries of the water tribe; the water tribe being neighbours to the other villages of the Hill (one of which is Kiki, the old man's home village).

"The coconut tree does not bend to the wind unless it is weighed down by fruit. Oghene$_2$! And here I was thinking they were only out to get us. They mean

^{2}god

business," the chief laughed heartily, "so nothing for me today? Not even one ritual or something? Biko[3]. This is not a likely comeuppance."

"No, but it is I who believe the godskins. Their foreign insight soothes me as the wild plantain provides shade for the delicate banana tree," the old man refused.

"Your people salt everything before eating, so why the attitude? One does not buy the garri then request the peels, so why the change of heart? Why now?" the Osivie asked with a smirk, not buying this new stance from the accredited spirit medium. Not one bit.

"Even if the peels come free, one must buy it from another who knows how to make it into a concoction," the old man retorted and wisely. "Seek counsel with my village or Ilu-Sango to know I no longer entertain such request, Osivie. I no longer entertain such requests o, Osivie!"

"Come in and let us break kola to titillate the tongue and offer palm wine to the Loas so my words do not weigh on you," the Chief suggested, for the old man was bent over. So bent over was he that the Osivie stood twice the height of a man that could pass four times his elder. On getting inside, he opened his mouth, "besides, only the masquerades know how they summon the spirits without talking," he said, having spotted his wives wandering aimlessly by his hut about the time he said this. They had been wandering aimlessly, or maybe with intuitive purpose.

"It is as we say, the tuber must quickly learn to spread its thighs to embrace the stone, or fold it and die. That is the way of the woman."

"So I have unwittingly made myself their stone enemy? Anyway, you see into women far better than I will ever be able to."

"My days have long ended. And I am glad. I have resigned myself to enlightenment. As the case with your daughter. She's bound to imbibe the secrets to the godskins and their strangeness," the old man said with a fond smile. Finally, a smile that showed promise.

The Osivie decided to adopt a lighter approach. "I personally pray she comes upon the mystery to that polished water-stone they bring on occasion. The water in the calabash is still the water in the mighty river."

"Of course. The priestess takes from you and has me. She will. It is as they say, only the tapper knows how he mounts the palm without hands."

"As do you when you part the cowries," the Osivie praised again, now eulogizing the old man in an attempt to meander the medium to his earlier request. "You know you're never wrong."

"You're trying to push me, Osivie. You know well what happens when one pushes an old man. I must inform you the Kiki have invited another to do their rituals, and investigate this Madness we are having. So allow me to break my kola in peace. A kola you are yet to offer, oniovo[4]?"

The Osivie laughed heartily at the man who was now only a shadow of his younger more energetic self, "Oracle, you will not blame the rooster for singing his song even at odd hours." There was no use pursuing this any further, so he requested one among his many wives to search one among his many huts for special tributes of kola and fresh wine. The village wasn't poor, which in truth was one of many reasons the Ishaporke couldn't afford to be sick. Even if every other village was.

Welcome to Her Majesty's British Cameroons," Captain Book stuttered in a voice very unlike him and much too hoarse to coax anyone as their visitors approached. He knew to correct it, so then demanded with a sturdier more confident voice, "I'll have your boxes now," he said, addressing the young Miss heading their way. The young woman was walking over bamboo and sapele planks strung up with raffia; planks neatly and cleverly distributed across the Delta's mud and filth to firmer grounds.

[4]brother of the same mother

Almost all the sapele trees and bamboo in the vicinity of The Docks had been hacked to stumps to lay the woodwork correctly. The visitor was wearing expedition clothes; a pith hat to save her face from the scathing heat, a frizzle blouse toning down the size of her breasts, a pair of rigid eyeglasses strapped around her neck alongside a brightly coloured neckerchief, but more conspicuously, she was wearing male shorts and footwear acclimatized for such a climate, yet they had been shorts and footwear that covered less than a fifth of her long velvety legs— shorts improper for a young woman. Confessions the captain couldn't bring himself to confess. Still, Ted couldn't resist the urge to say something. Anything to fill in the gap before it came to handshakes. So since her hands were occupied, propping weighty luggage against her belly, the captain offered his services again, "May I have the box?" he asked, now asking where once he'd demanded.

The visitors paused a moment when they got off the planks, finding it a tad awkward to hand over their luggage to the uniformed yet restless stranger requiring their attention at the end of it. They had travelled in with bags and metal boxes, stainless steel boxes, but as it now appeared, much to the chagrin of the captain and his priestly companion was the unexpected presence of her own companion. Her dark-skinned African companion!

The African stood brazenly by the young lady; properly, be it a faux pas, dressed in expedition clothes, and standing a bit too close to her for comfort. The captain's comfort. Most disquieting, was her manner in squeezing the African by the fingers!

"It's my meaning if you wish—if you so desire to— to hand me—me your boxes—I meant the box—" Captain Book stuttered incoherently, submerged under a tide of thoughts and trying ever so hard to wiggle off the images moulding in his mind.

Reverend Benedict gently lifted a hand over his face. The gesture wasn't an attempt to shield his face from the brutal sting of Africa's yellow sun because the priest could spot a coming debacle. Whatever was happening here, today, was obvious for all to see, and the reverend felt no one in the world could save the situation at hand.

"Well—if it is—your desire then," the woman stuttered alongside the captain, half-confused, as the early introduction was beginning to run aground too quickly. The reverend noticed she had been sweating by the neck, so he got off his horse seeking to salvage the ebbing dialogue.

"I see you are getting acquainted with the swathing heat and mosquitoes," Reverend Matthew said, approaching both visitors with a carry-on water bag. "I'm sure you'd like some spring water to cool off?

Although it's warm, it should save you from the heat here in the Niger. It's dehydrating."

The young lady responded with her first smile. She had freckles across her cheeks, and a very brittle nose. The priest handed her the bottle.

"Thank you very much, Father, the mosquitoes I can bear," she responded, in turn handing over her steel boxes to the captain and of her own accord, sizing up the bald priest. He seemed a centimetre shorter than her, and still had some hair. It may have been hardly conspicuous hair, but hair nonetheless. Probably light auburn hair. Whatever was left of it ran along his neckline. She drank off the cap, giving what was left of its contents to her caramel-coloured companion. Rudely, the African dropped his bags at Ted's feet to drink from the same cap!

Stupefied and discombobulated, both Captain and priest spoke not a word. The Captain did flinch a little, but it probably would have been inappropriate to say what was lingering at the back of his mind. Even the reverend had nothing to say. It was just another odd period of silence punctuating the introduction.

"Forgive my manners, Father," the young Miss apologized softly, picking up on the oddity. "I've been around men for so long I've picked one or two of their horrid habits," she said light-heartedly and Father Matthew tittered generously.

"Then you will have no problem living with the men here."

Her smile broadened by another inch.

The priest offered her his hand, genuinely intrigued by the young woman, "you must forgive the candour when I say the captain and I were expecting quite a different sort of compan—"

"Did anything happen to Dr—Dr—Dr. Cambridge on his way?" Ted cut in brutally, and stuttering at a complete loss. "We had been expecting a doctor from the mainland, and a nurse from the Cape," he added rudely, sizing the ebony man foot up. He hadn't the slightest idea who the African was and why he was here? Nor could he tell if the ebony man was educated, bond or free? But, drinking from the same cap as she was bound to stir some fracas back at his fort.

The young woman shook the father's hand, as a man would, and offered the same hand to Ted. "I am he. Or she actually," she answered wittily, "Dr. Elizabeth Cambridge from Oxford," she added, introducing herself, and turning to the ebony man, "and this is my apprentice nurse, Un'ka Matulu. He's one we schooled from the Cape. He speaks Bantu, has steady hands, and his wee comprehension of English is just about adequate. As is my grasp of Bantu. We've been working together at the Cape for a long time, and the Admiral thinks he might be invaluable to you in helping ease relations to the Queen's army here in the British Cameroons," she said, holding Matulu by the biceps.

"Captain Ted Book of Her Majesty's Royal Niger Company," the captain said, finding it incumbent to introduce his duty in full and working up a tolerant smile as he sized up the African. She noticed the epaulettes. "This is Reverend Father Matthew Benedict. Reverend Benedict is of the church of Canterbury, and has been assigned by the Church of England and Her Majesty the Queen to oversee her affairs in the new protectorate here in the British Cameroons," he said. "But I doubt if your bondman will help. It means little to the locals if he is not from around here," Captain Book said smugly whilst taking her hand, which by a sad turn of fate made him drop the steel box in his other hand. The box's full weight crashed down on his toes, but Ted didn't flinch. On the contrary, the captain smiled with ego. He just smiled it off as he let go of her hand.

"I think you're mistaken, Captain. Matulu was never bond in the first place," Miss Cambridge retorted politely, but with an unsteady cheer. "As I explained to you, he is quite a skilled employ."

"You pay the aborigines?" Captain Book flinched.

His reaction had her perplexed. "Yes, in kind, we pay the indigenous," she corrected slowly, or rejoined, bearing now an incandescent smile, "but I fail to understand what you mean Captain by even such a question?"

The reverend interjected to sort out the fray. "Any referral from the Admiral is fine with us. To be honest, we are fortunate the villagers here in the West are of the gentle and welcoming kind," Reverend Benedict announced, trying earnestly to start things off on proper footing. The priest turned around and offered their horses.

"No," Elizabeth Cambridge declined, hesitant to accept the reverend's warm-hearted gesture. "These are your horses, father."

"Take them. No problem there," the captain responded quickly, examining his feet and the weight of the steel luggage resting heavily upon them (the blood in his toes now coursing to a rhythm solely their own). Oh, the captain didn't shove the box off his feet as everyone would have expected. No. He just ignored the pain and looked at The Lady Anne, flagging the ship's pilot with his hat. "We own the horses that arrived with you today," he said, and rather painlessly, amid the hundred pleasantries he exchanged with the big boat's pilot. He cupped his hands, "Ahoy! You can send the horses down now Pilot!"

Reverend Matthew and his new ebony acquaintance helped the doctor up the captain's horse, and then the priest saw Matulu to his own horse.

"This is very generous of you, Father," she said, even as the priest went on to help the ebony man up the other horse.

The ebony man sought to return the reverend's water bag, but Father Benedict no longer had any use for it. "You can keep it, Un'ka. I'm guessing you'll be needing it," the priest responded, before proceeding to offer kind advice on Zachariah. "And never take your eyes off this one," he rubbed the horse, "she's a wild one."

"Much thanks—thank you," the nurse sort of mumbled, pruning over which words would rightly apply even as he struggled to hold the horse steady.

"We navigate by the hill," the reverend said to them and pointed across the horizon. A forest-laden hill just peaked above the trees.

"We use the hill because the bush paths are tricky," the captain concurred, seeking to impart a word of warning to the newbie doctor. "They might seem to be here this minute, but give it a day or two and they vanish to the rains—although I doubt it'd be of help my telling you this, for when you're in a rainforest you're in the rainforest, not that you'd spot any darn hill," Ted chuckled, but no one laughed. The Captain worked his throat, and grew serious. "So if you're not accustomed to the use of a compass, I'd advice you stick with someone who can," he said and turned away, but to a harrase of horses running down the boarding planks in what seemed like a stampede. Everyone made room. Everyone save the captain whose legs had been grounded by luggage, but luckily for Book, the standard officer's training included how to think on one's feet, so Ted Book narrowly escaped becoming horse fodder. As for the steel boxes, the horses played Who Can Kick Farthest with them, knocking them about the docks, leaving them muddled with a chocolaty dressing of mud. Quite the misfortune.

"Oh my!" the young doctor panicked, but held her lips.

Her apprentice nurse, in reflex, attempted to get off his horse, but the captain courageously got to his feet and flagged the ebony man to remain on the horse.

"Sorry Captain!" the boat's pilot bellowed from the starboard, "'hadn't known you were still by the loading planks," he'd remarked, a rhetorical ring underneath though.

"A simple mistake," the captain hollered back, seeking his hat amongst other things misplaced, flagging the boat's pilot only after he found it, though the pilot didn't care for his response unloading more horses the moment the planks to The Docks were free.

"Ted?! Are you all right?" Father Matthew asked.

"Everything's fine, Reverend. I'm fine," Ted answered with a false smile, trying to act unaffected and unperturbed by the mud on his uniform. Or his pride. The nurse stubbornly got off his horse to aid the captain with the muddied boxes as the captain wiped off what he could of the mud stain.

"Don't worry, Matulu. I can handle it," Ted protested and waved the African man off, horrendously mortified by the incident. He looked sheepishly to the young doctor, "I hope you carrying nothing fragile in these boxes?" he asked, pacing among the horses and seeking to gather and clean up what the horses had misplaced.

Miss Cambridge hesitated to answer. The female doctor pointed at one of the boxes, "ur...just a balance and an expensive...well, kind of...a very sensitive microscope," she admitted, anxiously chewing her fingernails, having not known how more tenderly to put it.

Her ebony apprentice mumbled something in Bantu in a bid to help, and help with a box in particular, but his was an overly generous attitude, and the last straw—one sufficient to uncap Ted's bottle, so in the pulse of the moment, the captain shoved Matulu aside, brushing him off with a cuff to the shoulder. "I said I could handle it, Bantu, or whatever codswallop your name is!" he protested loudly. Regrettably, his words hadn't come out right, and the blow he'd given the ebony man, a blow too sharp to justify.

"He only offered to help," Elizabeth argued from up her horse, quite upset, even as Reverend Benedict stood by speechless. He was at a loss for words at the captain's misconduct. And, as if things couldn't get any more awkward, Ted Book couldn't bring himself to apologize to the ebony man for his gross lack of tact, but that was a character flaw having little to do with the dark colour of Matulu's skin and all to do with the sure-fire colour of Ted's ego.

The African quietly returned to his horse, a burn stemming across his shoulders, as Ted reorganized the cargo and put everything in place.

"Great. Make me the enemy," the captain mumbled, pursing his lips as he led the group away silent as the devil's darning needle. There was no way he could ever make this up. This day was already turning up a horrible disaster.

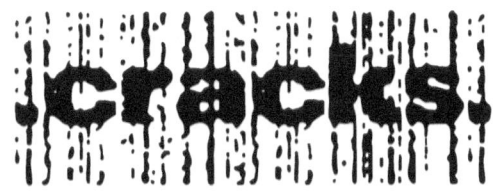

cracks

Now the trait of a fort is its ability to protect (not much can be said for Fort William though), named a fort but garrisoned by hardwood posts and a wiry mesh. In many places, Fort William was open and uncompleted. By the captain's description, however, she was miles from unsafe—and wasn't open to the South! Whatever that was supposed to mean. She was fortuitously barricaded by a cover of trees and a perennial water stream against its rear, he'd explained, although he had to confess she was not impenetrable to the aborigines, or to overzealous French scouts if relations degenerated to zero. Nevertheless, since the Niger Cameroons was new turf to the captain, it was no place to base his security or the lives of his men on trust and good will alone. The Captain had raised an outlook at its North gate. The tall security post was manned by two of Her Majesty's soldiers armed to the teeth, with a spot-on marksman having some kind of firepower pointing down at them from what could pass as the eye of the contraption—although in the eyes of Miss Cambridge, what this contraption looked like was one atypical looking telescope hinged on some kind of swivel (a big one). The more senior of the officers were clad in hats and white and black uniforms, similar to the captain's, and held a matchlock, while the younger officers were dressed in plainly white uniforms and shorts and worked the heavier instruments. They peered down at the visitors as Ted waited by the gate. Elizabeth smiled at the soldiers in shorts, only for their response to return at lightning speed. It would appear she was to be the only female at this fort. A situation that came with the usual quirks.

"I have never seen one of those before?" Elizabeth Cambridge said, referring to the telescope pointing down at them from the outlook above.

"It's a custom powder gun. The first of its kind," Captain Book explained nursing a smug smile, this was his chance to organize himself after today's early debacle. "A necessary evil," he added stopping his horse, as well as the long line of Her Majesty's Graces tethered to it.

"A gun? Is a gun necessary?" she asked curiously, and the captain returned a blank expression. "I had meant is a gun of that size truly necessary?" she intoned, and this time turned to the reverend, "Father, I thought you said the indigenes here were of a gentler makeup?"

"Indeed they are," the reverend intoned after her. "I even run a school for the community," he said, now walking his horse beside hers, "but, that's Ted for you. A good soldier, a tough biscuit, and always the

Boy Scout! Ever prepared, even for the uneventful—"

"One can never be too prepared, especially in a jungle. There's another outlook beside the West gate," Ted interrupted, acting half-concerned about the accolades the priest had been hurling his way. He signalled to the senior officer in the outlook above to send someone to open the wrought-iron gates. "I have worked on many fields before. It just happens I see these Africans for who they really are," he added, only to discover the second time today his words hadn't come out right. Ted couldn't avoid glancing at Matulu, who had been helping out with keeping the horses in line (as well as ensuring the safety of the steel box containing the immensely weighty microscope that was much away from the captain's reach now), but Un'ka Matulu didn't act concerned. Neither did he return Ted's glance. He was African, yes, and probably understood that remark well enough for one who's acquired English is deemed adequate by the doctor, but apparently Matulu was more concerned over how the horses and their dark velvety hides fared in the swathing heat than he was about how burnished the colour of his hide needed to be to impress the captain. Ted Book smiled politely and turned away, but now hadn't notice the African return his gaze.

"So how long have you been here?" Elizabeth Cambridge asked, channelling the discussion to more humanitarian talk before the captain could bind the congregation to another ligature of clumsiness and insensitivity.

"I have served little over a decade...some twelve, thirteen years," the reverend said casually, a tinge of pride caught beneath his voice though honestly the priest had tried not to sound that way.

"Wow! So you neither have family nor friends back at the mainland, Father? I doubt any family would allow one stay that long."

"No, and neither does Ted," the priest replied, enjoying the invigorating company of someone new.

"You are a godsend, father. Starting a school here in the heart of nowhere."

"Oh, no...No," Father Matthew declined ever so humbly. "I wasn't the one who founded the school. The Brigadier did. I just warmed to the idea."

"Who is The Brigadier?"

"Brigadier John William Cabot of Her Majesty's 5th Brigade founded this fort," Ted answered deliberately, pointing his eyes in all directions except hers.

"Then he must have been someone to meet. It's lovely what you're doing for the indigenes," Elizabeth added as a compliment; a compliment to whom was anybody's guess.

The captain just sat there after the gates were

opened (apparently the gates were well-greased) because Captain Book had been too preoccupied or oblivious to everything until they called his attention to it, the junior officers lowering their hats in respect as the captain led his visitors in, and to the barking of guard dogs.

"The problem with living in a fort full of men is finding the privacy to use the bathroom," Captain Ted said, acting to address no one but it was more than obvious to whom his word of warning was aimed at.

The reverend responded in her stead, "I doubt she'll be intimidated, Ted. I think she'll be at home here. She's worked with soldiers before so she'll figure something out."

Why the reverend had thought the remark was intended for scrutiny beat the captain. "If you say so," Ted responded irately, and as they dismounted, the officers lit up in awe of the female doctor in the captain's company. More so, in wonderment of her semiliterate companion. Even the dogs wouldn't let up barking. In a way, being able to sniff out the testosterone, and the new number of strangers in the fort, all the way away from their wrought-iron jails. They barked irascibly, the dogs, having intended the threat a dozen barks for every new horse.

Kiki village. Just North of the Hill.

Stupid child. It didn't seem the boy understood much of what was happening to his parents while he attended them. Sprawled across the floor and coasting by the afterlife, they lay. It was night time, and the stupid child was willing to let the fire in the small hut die out. It sent a cold chill down the medicine woman's spine. The elderly woman couldn't refrain from giving the small boy a bitter scolding when she returned to the hut. He hadn't cared if they'd all ended up in 'blackness'. She had been wearing a snail about her neck; a live and icky one.

"The hen is not too busy as to forget its eggs," the elderly woman said to the child squatting and doodling in the dirt. "What is wrong with you?" she barked, tugging the child by the ear whilst trying not to spill the herbs and barks concoction she'd spent the past half hour preparing. "Get out and fetch and fetch more firewood. We can't save them if I can't see what I'm doing, Osate," the medicine woman snarled with a spank to the child's downy rear.

The boy yelped and hurried to his feet. "Yes ma!" he responded politely, dusting the sand off his hands and rushing out.

"Stupid child."

The elderly woman licked her teeth and wringed the concoction across the lips of the child's parents. Perhaps, a little bloodletting would work? Or a little blood from the bloodletting mixed with her herbs and barks? She had also heard a patient urine mixture worked wondrous miracles. The old woman was at her wits end here. None of her practices in healing was working. This disease she knew all too well and cured way too many times, was now all too strange and dodgy as mosquito larvae. Even worse, she had used up all her concoctions and herbs. She hadn't any options left. She just watched them lying lifelessly, deprived of strength and the power to speak. Both villagers were bound for the netherworld like the others (these two not being the only ones ravaged by disease in this small village) for The Madness was spreading and there was nothing else she could do for the Kiki but wait and pray for a break. At least, the jerking had stopped. That was supposed to be a good sign. Still, their fever was on the rise. She was even down to her last calabash of river water, which offered no help at all. The more river water she doused them in, the hotter they turned up when dry. All the villagers avoided this hut like a plague, but the old medicine woman had been consulting with the other villages long enough to know this community was anything but innocent. From what she could hypothesize, the Loas had cursed these people. One way or the other, something—or someone—had gone wrong in the village. She didn't need 20-20 vision to see that, and for her age she had 20-20 vision, but that was before she took the snail off her neck to rub their bodies with. Ever since, her sight had taken a turn for the worse. It also may be why she hadn't yet known both her patients were already corpses.

The child returned with a load of dry sticks on his head. With hands dirty and all, he set them in a pile. After tossing a few dried branches into the fire, the fire blazed and crackled with newly found life. The boy smiled for getting it right and looked sheepishly to the old woman for a glint of approval. Nothing. So, he hurried out of the tent to play in the dirt. The moment Osate's face hit the moonlight outside the hut however, he whispered to himself. "She's a problem," he had said, and with a voice that was strong and feminine. A voice that could have been much older than his.

"I know, but she's old."

"One mango in a rotten bunch that's what she is. Nothing makes her more important. Nothing! You hear me?!"

"Keep your voices down. It's taboo we talk, you know that."

"Why the caution? You caused the last incident," he said, Osate now speaking in a much more masculine voice. "You're the reason i was burnt," stemmed yet another voice from those tiny lips. Osate's voice soon congregating in a legion of voices. Voices deeply agitated by the sound of them. Osate turned to the wall of the mud hut to hide his face, all this time having a conversation with no other person than himself.

"You don't have to make fun of me every time," he answered them, but he could feel this quickly deteriorating into a fight.

"You're weak, that is why you don't listen. You don't listen, that is why you are weak. Traitor!"

There was a black adder by the foot of the hut, a red -bottom diamond-bellied snake, but Osate simply picked up the snake between his toes and gently sent it flying—and flying through the bushes—bushes separating their settlement of huts from the vast open forest. He was never afraid of it, the snake. Or the bushes. Or the dark lonely forest.

"We say come, but you won't come. We say die, but you won't die. You can't even get that done. You know why?—because you're weak! Pathetic little traitor. A bastard and a traitor till the day you come home. Half world lover!"

A tear rolled down Osate's eye. "I do what I can," he argues defensively.

"Ha! He cries. I thought sending the pygmy was bad enough, only to see the pygmy cry."

One of the elderly voices sought to put an end to the row and so snapped in the heat of the moment, accidentally biting down on Osate's tongue while doing so, "shut up! No one needs to make fun of him!" he or she or it had commanded.

"Ye! You bit me."

"Oh stop whining like a human child."

"See! Stay a human child so long, he thinks he's one. He's soft and a waste of time. Isn't that what you said all those times?"

"Yes. He's soft," the voice snarled. It had sounded pissed, so pissed that it wasn't a compliment, "don't make him softer."

Osate's pupils glistened under the moonlight whilst he and his siblings spoke. His eyes glistened like quartz under the crescent moon, the colour of Morion quartz, when a much, much disparate voice, unconcerned to the current spat among siblings spoke, "it's a nice night in the village. How does the wind feel? Tell me. I miss it."

"You can feel it for yourself when your time comes," Osate snapped. In fact, now he had managed to get a number of them chortling. This conservation was but a cacophony of voices wanting to be heard; voices eager to breathe, desperate for a window of opportunity, for their chance at life.

"We will take you if you don't come home," one of

them now said and had said so in the subtlety of a threat. A threat that caused Osate's entire body to vibrate as would a beetle in a man's palm. Even his fingers twitched! Well, his siblings had made their point, it was now his turn to make his.

"It's still my time. If you want vengeance, do it on your own time—"

"The chicken eats the corn without knowing where it's from. Am I the only one listening to this pygmy?" another voice objected, hijacking Osate's lips to do it.

Now, the conflicting opinions and emotions raging on in Osate during this time are mostly expressions impossible to cumulate. Or explicate. Also, his siblings had rapped so loudly in his ear, it was almost impossible for him to hear the crickets chirp. Or the mosquitoes buzz idly by. Or arrange his thoughts properly. Even when he thought he'd heard the old woman calling. "I hadn't meant it like that, but I'm leaving now. I can only help as far as I can help. We don't need to fight to get me to do what you want."

"We don't need you to do what we want. Don't get it in your mind they like you. They don't know who you are because they don't know who you are yet," came his reply in a sea of voices, but when his siblings were eventually done spinning their threats, Osate found himself in full command of his own tongue. A tongue that smart like it'd been stung by a bee. A tongue parched and thirsty from their frenzied sabre-rattling. However, when he turned around to head for the hut, the old medicine woman who had been taking care of Osate's parents jumped him from behind.

"The hawk that hunts flies so proud and high in the sky that it is oblivious that we below, that we too, are hunting," she said in a shrill voice.

Well, she'd ambushed him, taken him off guard, and so he froze solid where he stood, with jewelled eyes reflecting the spirit of the night.

"Spirit! Spirit! Spirit!" she accused him, and accusing him even louder. Too loudly in fact for such a sombre night because the Kiki had no place for spirit children. Somehow, Osate had to have known this day was coming for spirit children, if or when caught, the Kiki knew to banish to the forests in hopes they would die there, to die of starvation, or see ruin at the hand of the Loas in the very least. Or was it more than coincidence, the conversation he had just had? Still, whatever the case, the question was what it always was. Would he bare teeth or would he turn tail and run? Would it be fair to let such an aged heart outlive his? That was always the question. A question the Loas clearly had intended for him to answer.

the indigenous children at Fort William's Mission School were there by no accident, for nothing ever comes free of price. The few of us who have witnessed a good number of communal clashes know how to spot the matchstick buried in the hay. Self-interest is always in everyone's interest. The notion that Her Majesty's largesse allowed for Her Majesty's trained soldiers to sail with Her Majesty's own horses and journey shy of fifty hundred sea miles across the planosphere into the uncharted waters of the Niger just to trade liqueur, mirrors and knives with the indigenous tribes when they got there was too cavalier a thought to be deemed dumb. Who knows? They could throw in some charity work for the peasant children while they were at it (abi?), and enjoy being smacked on the head by the burning sun or at the heels by puny sand bugs just for the love of it? It is as we've always guessed. Human folks are duller than we thought. They know the truth—the Queen does too—and the truth was the British weren't the only ones scouring the Niger's Cameroon lands for protectorates befitting the Kingdom. Several scouts had spotted a regimen flag way out on the other side of the Hill, 84 degrees by compass, and Captain Book had suspected it to be a blue white and red flag. It had to be the French. How close they had come, no one knew, but the French had arrived at the Cameroons as well. There were also rumours that a Spanish-

Portuguese expedition or fleet was on its way from the Mediterranean on errand by King Philip the Fifth—and it was drawing closer every day the captain breathed air. Time was of the essence in discovering the Niger Cameroons, so providentially having a school inside the fort facilitated that essence. Another stroke of providence however, was that the locals had taken fondly to Fort Willy. They referred to it by the name the Horseman School for the Brigadier then had ridden on horseback whenever he visited the settlements, for in their thoughts what possible harm could the godskins bring anyway? What great wrong could they encourage by having such knowledgeable ones around them and their children?

Miss Cambridge's new class left a whole lot to be desired; strung together from cut tree trunks and bamboo for posts, waterproof sacks for roofing, and raised bedspreads to serve as draperies. The multicoloured sheets gave the entire tent a very elementary look, and having just learned Father Matthew's personal quarters happened to be the permanent structure for the entire Mission School, she was at a loss for words. The reverend remained within his living quarters saying his prayers. His living space was cordoned off from the small school by a red bedspread, so Elizabeth waited patiently and walked the length of the small room. She tried not to stare at the children, but it was nigh impossible trying not to stare at curious African children staring stalwartly at her. She sauntered to the back of the class, walled up by hefty tree trunks and bamboo beams, and looked through the cracks in the woodwork to see a chapel. In the chapel, she could spot the serving altar, some manuscripts, and a piscina. A piece of the wood flaked off in sawdust and so she backed away from the eerie wall of trunks. The wood was bad. The African children still had their beaded eyes peering at her, so Elizabeth bustled to the red curtain where she popped her head through the curtains to whisper to the priest, "father?"

Now Father Benedict's meagre accommodation, like everyone else's, was a humbling one. The priest's furniture was scarce—a single bed, one rickety old chair, and a thirty-inch all-purpose altar table (furniture not disappointing for a man of the cloth). The priest was with his rosary and knelt by his bedside, still observing his quiet time. He wasn't of the habit of answering anyone till his prayers were said and his counting done. After that though, he would be all ears, but he did this time interrupt his prayers and attempt to lift himself off the ground.

"Yes Liz?" Father Benedict answered fondly, one month being more than sufficient for the reverend to acquaint himself with the kind, emotionally conscious nature of the home-schooled, one degree short of an Oxford PhD scholar, half Irish, somewhere part royal, gifted knitter and talkative tomboy doctor, who happens to have developed a penchant for Africa's pulpy mangoes.

Good. He was done. Elizabeth came through the red drapery to help the priest up. "Father Matthew, when do you think I can start the class?" she asked eagerly, geared to teach, a manuscript parting her breasts, and a pair of reading glasses parting the manuscript. She helped prop the middle aged priest by the biceps, vigilantly gliding the manuscript over her belly as she did so. When she settled the priest into his squeaky chair, he let out a gentle wheeze taking a minute to catch his breath.

"Easier down than up, eh," Father Benedict remarked, a little sweat breaking through his bald. "Why haven't you started yet? Liz, you can do this without me you know?" he chided her as he put away his praying condiments. He picked up his Bible then one other stationery from the table.

"I didn't want to have to redo anything, so I thought I'd wait for the class to gather," Elizabeth responded, nibbling the butt of her thumb as she watched the priest attend what was left of his hair behind a small mirror. "How's your heart?" she asked concernedly.

"Ready," Father Matthew weaselled under his breath. An answer that had left the doctor contemplating as the priest waltzed through the red sheet into the more brilliant part of his lodging. The children were ready for another glorious day.

"Good 'mourning', Father Mat Hew," the indigenous children sang in a well-rehearsed chorus as their 'godskinned' teacher walked into the small lodge in what was obviously yesterday's cotton trousers; the trousers had gathered dirt by the knees, one or two strands loose by its seams. It still looked interesting enough though for no one had yet figured the animal it sourced from. A knowledge that would prove useful back at the villages.

"This is the class, Liz," Father Matthew emphasized with a short laugh, "but hopefully not for long. I intend this little class swells till all the indigenes are here," he added, before replying the class, "Brilliant! See Elizabeth, I've only been trying to teach them to greet last week," he cheered, clasping his hands together in delight, "but this I know they remember," he boasted and hinted the sign of the crucifix.

Elizabeth watched the children imitate the priest's crossing of the heart, only missing it when the priest signed left and they signed right, and when he signed right and they signed left, but he wasn't one to ask for much. Any response was okay by Father Matthew. That was his heart. As well as it being fragile. Elizabeth watched the sweat building across his forehead, and she didn't think it was due the swathing heat, although this side of the continent was truly hot, and every noon, for the past month, it cooked her in a cauldron. After the children had crossed their hands though, they stared blankly on (the signing of the Crucifix seeming to be a highlight of their day).

"I'll start you, Liz, with a simple scripture reading," he turned to Elizabeth with a sheepish grin, but she still had this probing stare, "my heart is fine, Liz. You worry too much. For now, let's handle this class."

"All right then, Father, but you know I only agreed to this if you'd put as much concern to your heart as you do to everyone else," Liz eased from the side of her mouth, looking nervously at the primitive class and its admitted for the season. The Mission School used tree stumps for seats, so they all stared up at her like blank little zombies, "dnt three naked kids, and one old man, don't qualify a class, Father," she breathed to herself.

"They are not naked. This is how they dress," Father Matthew chortled, "and not as handicapped to teach as you think," he said, taking Elizabeth by the elbow and dragging her to meet the first pupil peering up at them with truly brown eyes. The child looked pretty healthy and well-rounded. "Meet Eno," he said, grinning widely, and putting a hand on the child's cornrow braids. "Eno is eleven."

"Who?" Dr. Elizabeth responded, cautious to the correct elocution of the child's name, and so keeping both hands to herself and across her belly.

"Eno," Father Matthew answered, "it's pronounced E as in Enlist, and No as in Norway. I too had problems pronouncing African syllables myself—" Now Father Matthew chortled again on seeing the doctor unsettled, this time interrupting himself, "come on, Liz. She won't bite." He took her hands and forced them against the ebony feel of the child's forehead, only for Elizabeth to chuckle. The child's forehead had appeared glossy but now felt supple. It was supple and not taut, much to the contrary of what she'd expected. Very different from her leathery skin.

"I've never touched an African—I mean an African child before," she confessed and Father Benedict lit up on seeing the doctor's curiosity ignite like candle wax. Elizabeth couldn't stop caressing the child's face. "She doesn't talk much, does she?" she asked and swept her hands over the child's cornrow braids. The weave was absolutely gorgeous. "She's a beauty. Who makes these?" she asked and the priest made a face.

"Nice, isn't it?" he answered, "No. She doesn't speak much. Not that we'd understand her if she did. I'm happy you realize she is as sweet as a mango."

Elizabeth couldn't help but smile. She also couldn't help noticing Eno's eyes never left her. Not even for a second. Especially fixated on the clothes she wore. Very curious eyes. And maple like Matulu's, as opposed to the conventional sapphire blue on the mainland. This was truly a puzzling continent with more to be seen. The child eyes shone like two little emeralds. A very warm child to look at, and touch.

"Good mourning Father Mat Hew," Eno announced to Elizabeth in the manner of a greeting, the child was either buzzed or confused as to why they were about her, which made Elizabeth giggle.

"I'm neither a Fa…" Elizabeth had sought to answer, but the doctor got the point. She moved her hands over to the child's shoulders. The child was wearing a band of cowries across her forehead and arms, and when Elizabeth looked further, she found several about the child's feet—and they chimed each time the child made a move. Chiming cowries. She'd never seen cowries before. Very unreal to what she had grown up seeing in London. The child hadn't bothered covering her breasts. On second thought, Eno didn't need to since she hadn't any. Yet.

"Cute…quite cute," Elizabeth uttered and Father Matthew proceeded to the next child. All the children wore leather in this class of four, some type of dried hide or scales.

"This is Osate," he said casually. "He's Kiki," the

priest said, feeling up a scar by the edge of the boy's lips. "Both kids actually. They are Kiki," he said, pointing to the marks by Eno's eyes. 3 short distinctive markings.

"Kiki?" Elizabeth queried, raising an eyebrow.

"Yes. Kiki," the priest repeated and circled the child. "The Brigadier taught me that the entire villages in the Niger Area are from very separate tribes, much different from what we have in England because each tribe gives their children a unique identifier."

"So what you mean is they scar their own children?" Elizabeth paraphrased, noticing how deeply the scars had been incised across the child's mouth. "Isn't that barbaric?" she muttered.

"Not as awful as you think," Father Matthew replied excitedly. "Rather fascinating. It serves as a form of identification to the villagers here—some indication to the tribes of what's theirs and what's not. A very useful advantage in times of marriage or war; a tool greatly aiding the Brigadier in his success about this hill. Even now, we don't know where they originated from. The Brigadier once suspected Bantu, which would have made them ancestral cousins to—"

"My apprentice? The Admiral will doubt that," Liz chuckled, and looked down at the Osate child. The child had short, very dark, and oily hair. And, he was wearing goat hide. Or in the least it felt like goat hide. "Is his hair naturally this way?" she asked curiously, watching the glint of the day's sun take after the boy's hair.

"mm hmm," Father Benedict concurred. "All curly and petite. I've come to learn the Africans don't grow long and thick hair like ours," Father Matthew answered excitedly. "Even for a priest, God astounds me."

"What's the matter with him?" Elizabeth asked curiously, noticing the child wasn't really looking in her direction or paying her the needed attention.

"Oh. The child is cross-eyed," Father Matthew answered. "Osate!" Father Matthew called to the boy, and this time Osate appeared to be looking squarely at Dr. Elizabeth rather than at the priest. Father Matthew rubbed the child playfully on the head. "See? Now, he's looking at me," the priest said, driving home his point. "He's is a deformity."

"Strabismus—that's a birth defect even we can't perform corrective surgery on. The eye is off limits to surgery," Elizabeth said empathetically.

"But don't let his disability fool you. Other than that, there's nothing wrong with him," Father Matthew cheered. "Quite an active little boy, he is. And very feisty too, much unlike his tribe."

Father Matthew turned to the last child. "And this, this is Jite. Her name rolls off the tongue easily. She's my favourite," the priest said, and Liz found the child with a rosary in one hand. She seemed to be praying with it as Elizabeth watched, which kind of made the doctor glance at the priest in bewilderment. Father Matthew laughed heartily, "No. Jite's fascinated by my rosary so I gave her one to keep her from breaking mine. I'm hoping the villagers will get acquainted with God, so my job will move on smoother around here though. She doesn't know how to use it, but I've noticed she can count. I only discovered that a week ago," Father Matthew said proudly. "She's been counting in her dialect. Sharper than a canary bird, this one. I haven't baptized her yet, which is why I haven't taught her the words to the rosary, but I'm very excited."

"I'm equally excited for you, Father Matt," Elizabeth cheered. The child was truly amazing. She wore a skin of scales across her breasts and another across her thighs, and also a belt of pink coral beads across her neck and waist. Elizabeth Cambridge marvelled at the brilliance of the snakeskin. "Such art and craft," she said in awe and reached to touch the girl's scaly wear, but the priest shoved her arm much to the left before she could get a feel of the exquisite snakeskin.

"We are not supposed to do that," Father Benedict apologized. "The child's grandfather is called the Osivie by his people. She's an Ishaporke priestess, which means her mother is a princess."

"And all this interprets as don't touch?" Elizabeth inferred lightly.

"Pretty much," Father Matthew replied, bobbing his head like a water balloon. "The Ishaporke are a water tribe. Very close to where we picked you up last month. We know them by their decorative staffs and their priests that blanket themselves completely. A very superstitious tribe, too. They believe in spirits and goddesses and so on. If she touches a non-Ishaporke villager especially a stranger like you with that skirt on, it would portend ill fate to the royal house. And in turn, spell disaster for her people."

"I know you don't believe all that, Father Matthew," Elizabeth responded sceptically, "what I'd like to know is how you did it then? I mean getting this child to be a part of what you're doing here 'cause it pretty much sounds to me her tribe is wary of strangers."

"Patience is a virtue I am well acquainted with, Liz. This child is my road map to winning her entire royal family to the Holy Faith, and by winning the Royal Family over I would have won the entire tribe. So whether I believe in their superstitions or not isn't important to me," the priest stated unequivocally. "Besides we have him. He's always watching her. He's also why I say don't touch," he added, and so he and Elizabeth turned to the quiet, hunched over old man sitting all alone and to himself in the class.

The old man seemed to be asleep, but the moment Father Matthew rested a hand on his shoulders, he flinched. He wasn't asleep. "Meet Paul the Saint," Father Matthew said with an overly generous smile. "Paul's the reason I have the children in the first place," the priest said elatedly.

"Paul the Saint?" Elizabeth repeated, puzzled by the name. "He's African."

"Yes. Quite a name, isn't it? He's been a wonderful disciple for years and my first convert. I have never been able to put a finger on his real name, though. For a bizarre reason, he never tells me," Father Matthew answered and the old man gazed at Elizabeth. He looked straight into the doctor's eyes and made Elizabeth shudder for a moment. The old man wasn't only bent over but had horrible eyes, heavy eyes buried under even heavier eyelids. For a man the priest dubbed a Saint, he looked sinister; he had scars (more like scratch marks) across his face, and even more visible marks across his cheeks. Moreover, his nose dripped blood and wicked plaque overwhelmed every tooth (of his teeth that hadn't fallen off, that is).

"Isn't he bleeding? Why is he bleeding?" Elizabeth complained timidly.

"No, that's only tobacco. The villagers inhale it in the mornings. It's a custom or some kind of initiation or something. He's not always like this, Liz," Father Matthew explained, and only because he had to, for the old man's appearance today was indeed an eerie one. A sincerely gloomy look for a first impression. Elizabeth hadn't hesitated to back up at the sight of him. Something the reverend could completely understand.

"I hope he's not sick," she decried, only for the old man to look her straight in the eyes, again, after she'd said that. "Did he—can he hear me? I think he heard me, Father," she pronounced nervously and Father Matthew Benedict laughed.

"There's no way he can. Not to worry, Elizabeth," Reverend Father Matthew Benedict laughed at the irony of it. "I communicate with him through sign language. Paul is deaf to our words. As deaf as a mole," he said, yet the old man's stare was cold, deliberate, and stayed.

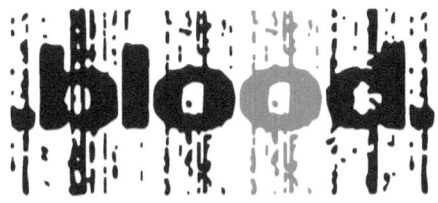

Ilu-Sango village. West of the Hill

"*Ode₅*, no one is innocent. Nobody is who they say they are," Kehinde spoke in the absence of their parents. He spoke coolly, unstained by doubt nor beset by grief. For twin boys essentially raised by the forest, parental guidance and control was shifty at best. The boys were a splitting replica of each other and they weren't lost; only hidden from the religious dogmas ruling the Ilu-Sango. Kehinde counted himself fortunate. The forest was a presence he could count on. Not much could be said about their parents, though.

"Keyin! You leave mother and father out of rubbish talk, especially mom," Taiwo retorted, steamed by his brother's carefree attitude to their current plight. No one stood ever more aloof in thought—and for one who jumped head-first into trouble, Kehinde wasn't one to talk. "Besides, this is all really your fault. You can't bridle your tongue. You cause everything!" he fussed as he sat in the shade of a kernel tree, teed off and anxious. But his tone didn't sit well with Kehinde, it was disapproving and out there.

Kehinde bit his lip, thoroughly vexed. Both brothers had been born seconds apart, only half-a-minute in age between them, but in Africa those few seconds counted for everything. It told of who had the power of say and who had to obey. It told of who had the lion share of everything, and who had to sort out the odds and ends. It told Kehinde as the elder, and Taiwo the younger, even if they'd been born split same in height and looks.

"Ye!" Taiwo panicked as something bit into his fingertips. Whatever it was, it bit angrily. He'd accidentally settled his fingers on roughshod soldier ants; a small army of highly toxic red ants romancing his hand and shooting a fiery sensation up his wrist when he attempted shaking them off. The toxin worked its way into his veins and his entire hand went numb, dying of its own accord. Taiwo couldn't feel a thing wrist down at that moment and Kehinde chortled, not a smidgen concerned, as he attempted to climb a fruit tree. He didn't know what fruit tree this was, but the rains and the heat had arrived so he was certain he'd find something sprouting in one or two places.

"Just keep your voice down, Keyin," Taiwo now cautioned softly, puzzled over how long the numbness was to last.

"Does it matter?"

"So you want to get caught? Is that it?!"

"It beats hiding. I'm not afraid of them!"

"I don't know what you're talking about. Just keep it down," Taiwo muttered as Kehinde clambered the fruit tree irreverently (and noisily too).

"you speak as if you're older than me."

"I am, technically, even if our parents don't see it like that."

"Because you came out first?"

"And I behave like it too," Taiwo said smugly as Keyin smirked.

"You know, if we do get caught then wasting all those years hiding was just stupid," Kehinde remarked thoughtfully, intending to push whatever was left of his brother's emotions off a cliff—and like clockwork Taiwo spat in disbelief.

"*kini isokuso to nso*[6]? Keyin, you didn't mean that. Take that back!"

"You speak as if you do not know it is the coconut who chooses to have its head bashed," Kehinde spat back, nonchalant to his brother's alleged affections and bonds of fealty. Affections didn't count in the real world. He was the only one anyone could count on to see through the murky waters of family, but Taiwo kicked up dirt, beside himself with grief, and stoning his brother whom was already halfway up the tree with a clot of mud.

"Take that back, Keyinde!" he demanded, but now a

[6]What idiocy are you speaking about?

smug smile parts Kehinde's lips.

"You'll regret that! That I assure you, you little runt!" the older brother thundered, coming down from the tree for what was to be half-a-minute of beating when something felt strange, or wrong, and for a moment, just one brief moment, Kehinde was concerned over the welfare of his brother. "dake[7]..." he held a finger to his lips and looked to the bushes after a twig snapped. It was their father, but the odd thing was he refused to come any closer. He was standing a good distance away, keeping a good distance from his sons, watching them argue.

"Eee! It worked! He's here!" Taiwo leaped euphorically, and without a second's thought quickly wanted to meet with him, but sadly it seemed he no longer wanted to meet with them because he backed further and further away into the obscurity of the bushes with every step Taiwo took.

"Wait ode! You idiot! Don't go to him!" Kehinde reprimanded and so Taiwo stopped in his tracks, now confused. "*Arakunrin*[8], what do you want?" Kehinde demanded of their father, a look of distrust about his face, but truly, he had good reason to be suspicious. A certain someone was missing from this picture.

"Baami, where's Maami?" Taiwo asked, but at that moment their father yielded as would calabash to fire.

"Taye, sare[9]! Run!!" he yelled, only for a hunter camouflaged within the low grass to clock him hard on the head with the thick butt of a spear. "Fool's ruined the ambush! Get them!"

Quick to react and light on foot, the boys split, but a lanky hunter jumped Kehinde from the very direction he was running to. "Taye! Help!" Kehinde struggled, trying desperately to wriggle free.

Twins were deemed holy by tradition, but they were holy enough to be sacrificed, so Taiwo tore off a rotting frond from the kernel tree, seeking to weaponize the ant-rigged frond that was three times his size to rescue his brother but before he could launch a swing of it, more hunters jumped in.

"No, Taye mi! They shouldn't take you. Don't let them take you! Run! Run!!" their father screamed, dissolving the little boy's quandary as he fought against their captors. The hunters eventually gagged the screamer and pulled him away, but the message had been received. The Ilu-Sango didn't take kindly to them being twins and there was no way they could escape judgment if ever the serving oracle had proof. Taiwo dropped the frond and took to the bushes.

"Don't run! Help me. Help me Taye!" Kehinde called after his brother. "Help me! They are going to kill me, Taye! You come back and help!!" Kehinde demanded as more hunters encumbered him. He wriggled and fought so fiercely that one or two vines recoiled from the ruckus and smacked some of the hunters in the face. The vines bruised, grazing one of them by the eye while squirting another with tree sap; injuries that made the hunters wrestle the ten-year old violently to the ground and in doing so dislocating his right arm as they bound him up. Kehinde shrieked.

"Sick child," the hunter complained, quick to wipe the sap off his face because white sap was bound to itch.

"Mind what you say," the other hunter who'd nigh been blinded warned reverently as blood oozed from his one bruised eye, "you must learn to fear this child. Where's the other one?" he asked concernedly.

"The other child ran that way," the other hunters answered, pointing further West, "but that one, we can fetch another day," a few of them suggested, content over this catch.

"Don't worry. Just make sure the outcast gets back to the oracle so he can have him prepared for the ritual. I will go after the other one, for of what use is the Agbalumo if it's rotten before the market stand?" he suggested whilst taking the time to find the right leaves to dress his eye. An argument that sounded quite convincing for a moment.

"Agbalumos do taste sweeter when rotten," the

hunter who had sap eating his skin now retorted ambitiously, speaking a little too eagerly to return to the village with just one kid. He jumped into the bushes after the boy's trail before his companions could deter him.

"Just get him back for the sacrifice!" the bruise-eyed hunter snapped at the others, trying to curb any kindred yearning in them for self-glorification. Or mortification. So, they left and the lone hunter went seeking the overzealous ode, arming himself with a bow and just one arrow. He had a name. His name was Makanjuola, dominated the son of Ogun for his tact and skill in the hunt.

I t felt like he heard me, Father."

Elizabeth Cambridge was preoccupied by something other than her conversation with the priest as they made their way to a large cabin on the other side of Fort Willy. It was a cabin built to house all of Ted's younger officers, the Junior Officers' cabin, and like the infirmary she was in charge of, it was filled with double-wheeled cots, horny officers, and no private space. She had a stiff schedule. Usually she would work the officers' cabin after teaching at the reverend's Mission School, which was a fortnightly obligation for her, and which also to Ted's younger men meant rehearsing pick up lines and a lot of fraternizing. Actually,

Elizabeth had learnt to cope with the flirting but it didn't help to see Matulu forever working (and reworking) routines at the infirmary just to stay clear of the captain's officers. Providentially, Father Matthew had sought to do more spiritual rounds about the fort, so this time he escorted her just to check on the boys. They exited the chapel together, going through the training grounds by the Gate as a shortcut than walking the length of the main dirt path running through the heart of the fort.

"I beg your pardon, Elizabeth," Father Matthew responded, noticing the dogs rise at attention in their huge cages. The rapacious lot had spotted the pair coming.

"The old man from the other day, Father. What was his name again? I sort of felt he heard me," she said, querying her thoughts and oblivious to the soldiers up in the outlook with their hats raised to them out of respect for her. She hadn't noticed but Father Benedict was one to notice. He waved to the officers and spent the better half of each minute returning glances and civil gestures. "His name is Paul," he answered, keeping one eye on the dog cages. "Paul's had a notorious past. It took the Brigadier and I a while to actually get to him. Irony is we never liked him at first. Now, he's the only villager who comes to Mass at that chapel of ours," the priest said with a voice rich in gratitude and satisfaction.

The doctor ran her boots along footprints in the dirt made by Ted's early morning parade. "Yes, I noticed he joined us last Sunday. So he's some form of convert?" she asked, slowing her pace and fitting a foot into one big footprint.

"My very first. It's hard to get Ted's boys to frequent Mass the number of times he does. I shouldn't even mention the captain," Father Matthew remarked as they passed the barrack of wrought-iron cages (a resonating growl growing collectively among them). Each cage was massive enough to fit a whole person and being there were more cages than there were dogs to use them, quite a number had been dismantled and laid aside in slabs. Stacked in a pile. One atop the other.

"And what makes him do that?" Elizabeth asked and the priest responded with a short laugh.

"The captain's still fair weather. He seldom shows. Even more these past few weeks with you around," he said flatly, watching her. The young doctor showed signs of fatigue. When she'd offered to assist with the Mission School in spite of her duties, Father Benedict had known it would take its toll. Her face, this face she was offering today, was paler than it'd been yesterday.

"I'd actually meant the old man, Father," she replied, only for a more curious crease to bend her eyebrows, "what do you mean by the captain hasn't been—"

"Witchcraft," the priest steered away the conversation, "Paul practiced witchcraft in his youth. I think it still haunts the man. Sometimes, in the sliver of those moments I get to say a prayer for him at Mass, I feel the uneasiness he feels. The burden of it is probably why he keeps coming. I pray to our Mother everyday he gets redemption."

"Redemption from what?" Elizabeth had asked, and a little too eagerly to agitate the dogs. They assailed her with strident bloodcurdling barks, lashing at their cages to scarify her in a terrorizing display of ferocity. She froze for a moment, dead stiff because it felt like these well-bred dogs could actually take down their cages and come for her.

"Everyone has a past, Liz. I just don't believe they should suffer for it." Father Matthew held her tenderly, ignoring the dogs and suggesting she do the same, so they kept walking.

"It makes me wonder how you do it, Father Matthew?" she asked in awe because obviously she wasn't going to get any exciting answers from this priest, "—crossing cultures and getting to serve these Africans the same way you serve them? I don't think they like that very much."

There was a resounding pronoun in her words. The priest could tell.

"All persons are equal in my Mass, Liz, if we all are going to share the same fate or are going to the same place when our Lord and Virgin Mother return."

"Same here, Father. Exactly what I believe," she chorused, "I do mind the way the officers keep aloof of the indigenes in the fort."

"The same way they keep aloof of Matulu?" the priest concurred, hoping suggestively to vent her thoughts.

"Exactly so! Actually I can understand why they keep off the old man. There's something off about him. Something that gets to me I can't really place my finger on—I don't think he's sincere, Father Matt—but Un'ka, Un'ka on the other hand treats them yet they treat him like a leper. Why do they do that? Ingrates! In all sincerity, we are the visitors. They should know that!" Elizabeth burned, her freckled cheeks reddening in the showing of a little anger.

"There are some who think there is more to you and your aide than just friendship. Might be the reason."

"And what do you make of it, Father? UnKa and I?" Elizabeth asked, looking the reverend squarely in the eyes for an honest answer, but her question didn't surprise him actually, being long in coming and long anticipated by the priest. He was only unsure how she would take his words.

"You've never felt any unease being who you are, Liz. Or about how you feel. And you don't feel any unease being friends with your African. You never have. So for you to feel uneasy over an unborn child made me know straight away he's not your child's father. Yes, I know you're pregnant. I knew the very day you arrived on the ship," Father Matthew answered charily and Elizabeth creased her eyebrows again.

"I don't believe the rumours you read minds, Father," the doctor remarked with what could be a smile.

To the priest's surprise, she'd taken it curiously. "Clairvoyance is but a bridge away from witchcraft, Liz. And we hardly listen to the boys here at the fort."

"How did you know?"

"I might not be the Oxford graduate, but it doesn't take a special degree to notice how you shield your womb every chance you get."

Elizabeth had demanded an answer, but now that she had gotten it, all she could do was slink her head away and suppress a grin. A sheepish grin. "I never realized I was a see-through, Father, and here I stood thinking all men were ignorant."

"It won't be long before he realizes how far gone you are. It's best you inform Ted, Elizabeth."

"You would have me inform the captain? But, he's going to make me leave? He is going to make me leave, isn't he?"

"You might find in the captain more than you give him credit for. As for leaving, I'm not sure you can do that until the ship returns. That means next quarter. It returns every quarter, so believe me no worries there—or here because I'm sworn not to tell a soul unless you are the Man upstairs."

The middle-aged priest had sworn, but only until he drew her cheeks before she tittered. She looked at him with a loving stare and soon they shared a tenuous embrace, not having in mind the company of horsemen watching. Ted and his boys were on their way out of the fort it seemed.

"Neither would he," Father Matthew mentioned to her, nodding away, nodding at the captain on his horse.

Captain Book got off his high horse en passant and humbly made his way to speak with them. Or with her. With someone in the least. He put his hat against his chest and flagged his boys to load up a number of the unused wrought-iron slabs onto a wooden caisson. Ted whistled and Her Majesty's dogs knew to go quiet; trained to do so in the presence of loftier blood. "Reverend," he greeted softly a decibel lower than the reverend was accustomed to. He turned to Elizabeth, but avoided looking the young Miss in the eye, "Miss Cambridge, I had my men prepare you a private bathroom," he spoke with perfect cadence, almost as perfectly as a rehearsed script. Too perfect in fact.

Elizabeth looked puzzled. "A new bathroom, Captain? But I'm fine with the usual—"

"It's a bathroom for you," he interrupted her, fondling his hat and looking to the perimeter. "It was no problem. I had the men knock up spare bamboo and sackcloth. Besides, it's closer to your lodging. It'll suffice for all your needs."

"Captain, I see no reason why you had to go through the trouble of making me a new bathroom, I was perfectly comfortable with the bath—"

"The officers' b—b—bath space is for officers, Miss Cambridge. Your use of the bathroom was only temporary," the captain said, stuttering at first, but speaking quite firmly for a man who refused to look her in the eye. She couldn't understand him. The captain's men were done roping a number of wrought iron slabs unto the caisson as well as the back of some horses, so they called to him.

Puzzled as to why her luxury bathroom took a month in coming or why the captain was constantly interrupting her, Elizabeth opted to ask, "and where is this private bathr—?"

"—behind your quarters," the captain responded

succinctly, cutting her short again, "at the junction between the sickbay and your nurse's lodge. You'll know it when you see it."

"You mean behind the sickbay?—why there's nothing but bush and forest after that!"

The captain wore his hat and made his final pleasantries, "good day to you Miss Cambridge. Good day, Reverend."

"Are your boys going game hunting, Ted, or are you going to visit the settlements?" Father Benedict requested after the captain as he left to join his men, "I was hoping to visit the settlements this week or the next?"

"I'm afraid we'll be doing a little of both, Reverend, so it'll be exhausting for you," the captain declined with a wiry smile and a tug on his hat, now leaving Elizabeth flushed and redder than an overripe tomato.

"Ohh how he gets to me, Father," she stated, flustered as she watched the gates open up for Ted and his men to ride out into the forest.

"Don't take it to heart, Liz. The captain's a special case."

"It's the same place he lodged Matulu, Father. The man's continental! Ted shouldn't have been so crude. If he has difficulty with me, he should be out with it or man enough to say it."

Father Matthew placed a hand on her shoulder as they passed the training grounds and approached the Junior Officers' cabin. "It is his fort, Liz. But, I'm sure he'll warm up. As much as I've come to know Ted, he does nothing outside concrete reasoning. Neither has your African complained over his lodging for the last month. The Captain is probably trying to do what's best for his soldiers by situating your nurse as close to the sickbay as possible."

"And the sickbay being farthest from the camp has nothing to do with it? Listen Father, exposing my aide to the jungle or whatever is out there is not fair and not safe. You know, and I know, the south side is not even protected like he said. Someone needs to tell the Admiral. And, I'm not deaf. I've heard the men talk, Father."

"If I recall, they also talk about you and your aide. It doesn't make anything they say true. Disregard the rumours, Liz. Ted might be as brittle as cartilage, but don't make him up to be a bad man," he counselled softly, but only on holding her stare did he venture to ask, "on another matter, do you love him?" The priest had waited almost a month to ask her, yet the question seeming to pop of its own accord, made him watch her intently.

"Why certainly not, Father! I can't believe you would even ask me that Father Matt," she retorted, walling up her eyes.

The priest responded immediately by flicking his eyes off her frown, "O not Ted. Of course not. I meant the father," he said, flicking his eyes down at her womb, but the doctor refused to respond. Neither did she look at the priest. "Does he even know?" Father Benedict asked, yet another question forcing its way off his tongue, and hoping it sounded more of concern than presumption.

"It was a mistake," she said succinctly, biting down on a lip and looking sombre. "I made a mistake Father. Can we not talk about it, please? Or him."

the little runt cut corners faster than a snake and matched the speed of a grass-cutter! It wasn't a glorious day for the rains to fall, but it came down in torrents, so for a while under the cover of rain, dense undergrowth, and the wet forest floor, Taiwo easily outmanoeuvred his chasers—but, in time, he slowed down to breathe and then stopped altogether, overtaken by grief, unable to forgive himself for leaving his brother in the lurch. All around the rains dripped to the sounds of leafy drums and he shivered significantly from being wet too long. This long bust was now taking its toll as a shoulder of thorns pricked his hand, and quicker than he could think, he let out a resounding squeal. Taye had remained lost until he did. Soon enough, a strange hand grappled him by the shoulder.

"*Mo mu e*[10]," the hunter said, but Taye slipped off the hunter's grip, vanishing beneath a sitting of wild cocoyams growing not too far away.

The uncut foliage of the Niger Cameroons was reputable for its dense bushes and two meter undergrowth, so the broad cocoyam leaves swallowed him up completely.

"Don't make this harder. You think you can run, se?"

The child could make out the figure of the man with the machete from within the undergrowth, so he backed away, roughing through the mud one slow hand a time, but that didn't help for every time Taye rattled the undergrowth he gave up his approximate location. So, he stayed put in the foliage, muscling as much faith as he could to resist the urge to run.

"You're still coming with me," the hunter boomed on learning the child had somehow managed to put some distance between them. He looked to the skies. As a hunter, he had to consider the treacherous convectional rain and the way it put every leaf, every blade of grass, into a dreamy state. It told him one thing as always. At anytime he could lose his catch to the forest and its undergrowth if he didn't heed caution, but the child didn't know that. In fact, he was banking on children being far less witty than the

[10]i've got you

animals he hunted so he decided on word games. "*kokoro to njefo, idi efo lowa*[11]. They may revere you as outcast back at the village, but to me you're just an unpleasant insignificant little insect," he said with a hard voice. "I don't mind dragging you through the dirt and mud at all if that's what you want," he taunted, and squatted into the undergrowth, having been a little hesitant in getting his hands and feet involved at first for everyone knew cocoyam to be a fragile plant—and its stalk irritably unpleasant when broken.

The earth was warm and wet and Taiwo spotted the fallen log of once a mighty pawpaw tree serving as manure for the flora. He lay by the cavernous trunk desperate for cover and camouflage, only to find the trunk's insides occupied by mud, earthworms, and something else—something that wasn't supposed to be there this time of the day. He froze! Petrified to death.

"You are a taboo. I know you've figured that out by yourself. The oracle says you're property of the gods because they don't want you, but even the gods don't want you or why else would they cast you here? Are you listening? Nobody wants you!"

He was hacking down the thick foliage and ripping off seedlings obstructing his view, but all he got were the vagrant sounds of a disquieted forest and the pitter-patter of rain falling. The rains made the loam

[11]the bug that devours the leaf resides inside the leaf

much softer and irritatingly palpable. They clung to his fingers every time and he could see earthworms and the mud homes of insects and dung beetles abroad the virgin soil. "Did your whore of a mother tell you she kept you for her own secret purpose? She never told you what she needed to use you for, did she? Of course not. Dry as a stick that one, but you honestly buy that she loved you? Omo ale[12]. That anyone would have you for sons? I still don't understand why that poor excuse for manhood you call a father allowed himself to be manipulated by her just to keep her happy whilst she cursed the rest of us! What a disgrace!"

Still, more silence, almost as if the child had stopped breathing altogether.

"They say the lice nibbling at a person is found under his garment because I know that if your father had been of proper bloodline like the rest of us, he would have given you up in an instant no matter what your stick of a mother said," he fleered, but was of the mind of giving up on his search when he spotted the child's leg protrude by the fallen pawpaw tree. He blissfully wiped the mud from his hands, and in one hurried swipe, tackled Taye by the foot, hoping to strong-arm him into submission. And so the hunter had the boy in his grasp, that was unmistakable, but he also hadn't seen it coming— the brown-yellow snake that blindsided him from the left, forfeiting the boy's right foot for the

[12]bastard

hunter's left eye. The trauma cost the hunter his balance and he fell flat on his back. Still, the vicious viper wasn't done. It lifted well over half of its weight off the trunk; its marked arrowhead looming over the hunter's other eye like the spearhead of Sango. The aggrieved Gabon didn't hesitate to strike again, and this time striking the hunter's other working eye to put his lights out permanently. He'd never even had half a chance to scream (the large snake's venom quickly bringing him to darkness). In all of this, the child Taiwo managed to slip away, not in the least bitten, not in any way hurt, so how he was able to escape the ordeal, well, is something rather left to the will of the Loas.

mirrors

The world of the living wasn't made to recognize good from evil. Or right from wrong. It just is. But from what we've seen, only two types of believers try to paint life in white and black; the first is your priest, the one who chooses to attach a colour to the soul; the second is a racist, the one who chooses to attach a colour to the skin. It's astonishing, to us, and a staggering lack of insight, on your part, not knowing how you fail to paint beyond the grey into the more colourful sides of what we deem your miserably brief existence. In the end, however, it remains your problem not ours since death as we experience it is the same for everybody. A rule that doesn't change. Then again, maybe the end does justify the means, being in death no one needs more than one colour to paint the hereafter—that we most certainly guarantee.

t he red draperies and white crosses painted over them made the medical tent seem overly crowded and much smaller than it truly was. The cotton draperies also embraced the heat under the slow burn of oil lamps fastened with nails to the skinned tree stems that held up the tent. The infirmary was a large tent set up with foldable stretchers, wrought iron cabinets, and wheeled cots; these collapsible beds a huge inconvenience on a rainy day when pushing wheels over such muddy terrain.

"Help me with this vial, Un'ka," Elizabeth beckoned, under the brilliance of an oil lamp. Its yellow glow having dulled the severity of the stab wound and leg trauma before her. One of the captain's lieutenants accidentally hurt his thigh with a matchlock—his own matchlock. How that happened was left to the imagination. Apparently, he'd sat into it partly inebriated. A true puzzler. She'd stripped off his clothes and laid him bare to his pants. None of his fellow carousing officers objected to that type of treatment (the senior officers even finding it a tad hilarious), almost as hilarious as vomiting inside her infirmary, until the good doctor mentioned using the bone-saw and they sobered up. The lot exited her infirmary after that, one after the drunken other. Although the injury wasn't going to debilitate to that, all she'd wanted was a little privacy and some air to breathe (the air in the medical tent was humid already without alcoholic breaths imbuing the moisture).

Doctor Cambridge handed Un'ka Matulu the vial from a silver tray, but on noticing the great sweat suffusing her blouse the African offered to clean up every apparatus on it. Elizabeth knocked her head towards the vomit across the earth, "Also cover that up for me quickly, Un'ka. I feel like I'm going to puke," she said in Bantu, fixing a wet towel across the sick officer's head before handing the tray over.

"It's the smell you can't stomach," Un'ka elucidated in kind and offered her a mug in return. A mug with no water in it. Or tea. She wasn't sure why he'd handed her the mug, not until she vomited into it after the nurse had left.

"Thank you," she called after him as he kicked dirt over the vomit on his way out.

Un'ka Matulu toddled onto the dirt road with a flask of hot water in hand, about to do the washing when he sensed the dogs barking—and barking at such an odd hour. There was little help he could offer in the tent, so he decided to take a peek (the truth was, for a month since they arrived, the dogs had been going off at odd hours! A time close to midnight. Especially on Tuesdays. Sometimes for weeks on end). He washed the needle and vial on his way to the kitchen from whence he would have a marksman's view of the North gate, and who or what was always responsible for setting the dogs off each night. A company of officers came through, with the captain in their lead, and apparently what seemed more horses than they could ride. One group returned the horses and hauled off heavy wrought-iron stabs from the caisson back to a pile atop the training grounds, while the other group came his way retiring to the knocked up shack of a bamboo cabin made for the junior men. One of them, deciding to take a leak against the cabin when he spotted Matulu, fleered at the nurse, "look, it's the doctor's apprentice! The slave-bone's watching me take a piss."

The other officers popped their heads to take a look. "It's a shame," they all said in like choice of words, "he's just too strong to work those hands as her nurse. We could probably put them to better use."

"—and her to better use as well," the officer taking the piss had interrupted, a raunchy joke to vivify his erection. He raised a hand in salute to the nurse as a jest, but Matulu responded with a stoic smile and less than audible retorts in Bantu. The officer smirked and the others cachinnated making their way back into the bamboo cabin.

After the instruments were clean, the nurse turned to find the tall silhouette of a man on a horse behind him; a dark confident figure staring down at him with a hat in hand. The nurse couldn't tell who it was, when cast against the darkness, but he had one solid guess.

"Where's the Miss?" Ted asked delicately, bringing his horse so close that the mammal huffed down Matulu's face.

"Inside curtain," Matulu responded dryly, keeping

his face from the horse. The Captain walked his horse to the infirmary. He could see the red outline of Miss Cambridge cast against the curtains from the lamps inside. "I hear one of my officers is wounded," the captain spoke without looking at the nurse. "How's he fairing?" he asked from a side of his mouth and Matulu shrugged.

"Soldier inside, doctor inside," Matulu struggled to say, referring the captain to the tent, quickly weary of the English language. As weary as he was of the captain and his high horse.

"Fine is fair," Ted muttered choosing to remain outside the tent and watch the doctor work. He simply cantered away when he was satisfied.

In the time Makanjuola and his bruised eye could catch up, the rains had stopped falling. However, with the way the clouds were set, it was soon to fall again. He quickly found who he'd come searching for because only one body lay lifeless in the sitting of wild cocoyams. In less than an hour, the fool was as squashy as a watermelon; bloated, soft to bursting, full of tissue-water and blood. The body had swollen disproportionately out of shape, was now a site for flies, and foaming in every orifice. Makanjuola cast his wounded eye in a cold gaze about the forest. It was now he realized the forest had eyes—she was watching him.

Whatever be her reason, she was watching over them and watching still. The skies were clearer now, with much sunlight illuminating the forest floor. The only thing clearer were the small footprints he could see that led away from the corpse. He could have chosen to follow it if he'd wanted to, but he didn't dare. Death delivered by venom was considered a message by the Loas; a sigil of their authority and a demonstration of their discontent. So, he armed himself with the dead man's machete before leaving, never touching the corpse or uttering a word.

Now only after he was sure Makanjuola had left, did Taiwo rise from the cover of the leaves; shivering to the cold and not being able to steer his eyes away from the macabre sight. The snake had lashed so ferociously that it hadn't been able to wrangle itself free from the dead man's corpse, or more precisely, untangle its arrowhead from the dead man's eye hole. It lay there, its head still alive and wriggling inside the hunter's skull. It would follow him in death—that was the message. Or curse.

When he came to his senses, however, Taiwo bolted like he'd lost his mind; running in no particular direction with adrenaline coursing through his veins, afraid and haunted by the spectres of his near death encounters—he could vividly see the face of his brother betrayed, he could vividly feel the snake striking at his traitorous heel as he fled, so he scuttled a little too fast for himself and (with his vision impaired from all the crying) hadn't seen the root that caught his foot. The child fell faster and heavier than a bush pig to the ground, his jaw striking the buttress of a stray twenty-meter Iroko tree—Taye felt nothing, absolutely nothing, upon passing out. In another light, for the first time that day, he slept.

to a lot of serving priests, St. Peters was home. Its mighty four walls had fathered most of Matthew Benedict's life as did it father his nascent years of ministry as a sacristan. Its apex cross towered to the London skies but like every other diocese caught in the middle of the Lutheran-Catholic power tussle, its rules of conduct were amoebic at best and a chancy place for a priest to own a wife. A foreign one. Having a woman in one's possession could mean estrangement to the woody towns if one was lucky, or a beheading, depending on who knew what and which side one played politics. And so, like he's always done on the eve of every Mass in London, Matthew Benedict readied the morrow's holy instruments as the sound of thunder cascaded across the cathedral's dome (Oh yes, he was in London) because it must have been raining outside. The vast cathedral wasn't protected from the weather so Father Matthew Benedict (obviously the younger version of himself) readied himself for the cold.

"Where's the sacristan? Sacristan! You come clean out this vestry or I'll get you in trouble," a commanding, but very familiar voice stemmed from the vestry window. Only one woman in his life spoke with that resonating accent—Angela Benedict. He'd named her so to keep her safe because she was not an Englander. Nor was she from anywhere remotely near English culture. Those had truly been desperate times, thinking about it now. Times of weakness (his weakness). As well as immeasurable joy (it made no sense to lie about it now).

She popped her head out of the vestry window again. "Matt Hew, aren't I talking to you?" she now demanded, vexed to the stem.

"You startled me. What are you doing here?" he susurrated, suppressing his anxiety and heading to the vestry. Her being here, here, right now, present with him, felt unnaturally good; so good he realized he was many years his younger, and even had hair! Lots of it! (This kind of amazed the priest because for as long as he could remember, the Man upstairs had more important prayers to answer than growing him more hair).

Matthew Benedict challenged his wife when he got to the window, "Angela!! How did you—you are not supposed to be here! Someone might see you."

But, as always, Angela was young, pretty and uncultured (and had no qualms showing it). "Oh come here. You're so slow," she chided him, popping her head out of the vestry window a third time. Lightning crackled and again another rumble of thunder swept over and down the dome. "Just get in, silly," she drawled, showing the sacristan the door to the vestry. The vestry door had been left unlocked. Unlocked? If it had been unlocked then he was failing at his duties today because it was his job to bolt all the doors to keep pilferers away from St. Peters' swanky cathedral. Anyway, it all didn't matter because he was here to obey her, hurrying in to the explosion of thunder, the peck of a waiting kiss, and the high-pitched sounds of pattering that reminded him of his sack lodge in Africa. Africa? Well, that was odd.

She kissed him, fanning her bony fingers around his haunches amorously.

"Oh no, no, no, no. You are really here to get me in trouble you say?" he accused her, coming to his senses and shearing her hands off his backside. "This is not the time or place. We could get caught."

"O look around you, Sacristan. Home is nowhere," she replied mindlessly, not listening as was her typical manner (and not about to repent of it now).

It was true. Outside the illumination of her words, the priest hadn't noticed his ever-changing environment—from the ostentatious alabaster walls of St. Peters, to the open and eerie jungle of subtropical Africa, and now his humble bamboo lodging at the fort. Even now he could hear the fierce patter of rain upon the waterproof sacks that made the roof of his lodge in Africa when he cared to listen for it. It hadn't stopped raining outside (wherever they were, wherever this outside was) so this, his being with her, served as his cue to remembering (his way out of this formless basket of confusion) because Africa was just one too many a place for the places she knew (the places he'd been to without her present). And so slowly, as an overwhelming flood of regrets came swooping in, Matthew Benedict let her go (now haunted by the exhumation of a memory he'd long thought he buried). "Don't you remember, Angela?" he said to her.

"All I remember is you always coming home late," she complained bitterly, stealing his hands from him and forcing an embrace. "Sometimes too late."

The priest wasn't sure whom he was embracing, but her touch, it was so sorely missed.

Angela frowned upon seeing the clutter across his thirty-inch altar table, as was her way, "you work every day putting everything in that cathedral of yours in place, but you fail to put your own things in place," she complained again.

"—So you don't? You don't remember being so angry?"

"Angry?"

"Yes. With me. For leaving."

"And why would I be angry?"

"I don't understand."

"Understand what? That I love you?" she spoke blithely, more interested in separating the holy stuff from the stationery, and resurrecting the centre picture of the Virgin in the altar, to what he had to say. Asides the fact, the priest couldn't bring himself to say what he was about to say.

"Angela! I—I—I. I let you die," he spurted out, his lips quivering from guilt. "I found your body. I carried it myself."

There! He'd said it. Finally. But on confronting the truth, the priest noticed he became his age. His hands were all gnarled and wrinkly and his bald ran all way through; in a way symbolizing his curse, the burden of his guilt. "I pray to the Holy Mother each day she forgives me. I shouldn't have abandoned you. I left you there because I was afraid that they would find you out," he confessed, but in confessing his supposedly holy white robes darkened morbidly into his confessional vestment. So, he went quiet (afraid of what she might do when confronted with the truth, afraid of the reality of who he might become on confronting his lie), but her reaction was quite the opposite.

"So? I'm here, aren't I?" she argued, aloof to his anguish as she straddled her arms around his neck, taken by some sort of morbid appeal.

"You're supposed to be dead," he stuttered.

"If you say I'm dead, I'm dead. But, if I'm dead who watches over our son? Certainly not one who comes in so late," she added perfunctorily, speaking as one who'd never attached any bad blood to his abandonment in the first place (or one who hadn't hailed all those many curses in a foreign language on him for abandoning her on that plagued island), but her queer answer hit him like a crazed goat.

They had had no children, Angela and Matthew. Actually because Angela had never been able to conceive a child. Something was all so wrong with this blithely engaging young woman standing before him, or was it the spectre who stood to be his wife, that made Father Benedict back away from her. "I don't understand—" he was beginning to say when she hushed him.

"Sssh...Let's not speak about this sour subject anymore. We don't want to wake him up, you know. He might hear us," she said to him softly.

The priest's pupils dilated. "Wake who up? There's no one here but us," he said, but her response, no her sneer, had been like he'd made an attempt at humour. She didn't find it funny. In fact, now it hit him. Now he realized that Angela, his Angela, could never really speak a word in English. Needless to say a fluent phrase. The look on Matthew Benedict's face was expressionless.

"Is something wrong with you? Why are you looking so surprised? Anthony's our son," she chided him, before channelling her attention to more sane matters like the furniture in the small lodge that was out of place. "Turn around and see. He's behind you. You're being silly," she said finally (and offhandedly too) as she fingered at the makeshift drapery behind the priest that partitioned Father Benedict's personal quarters from the small Mission School, so Father Benedict did turn around to see, and when he did, there was movement. There truly was someone there. Someone behind the curtains. Instantly he felt hot, very hot, but not so much as how hot he felt when he spotted tiny toes just under the curtain helm and the small spiny fingers that clung to the red sheet from the other side. His son? The priest's face grew pale. Blanched by anticipation. Blanched by worry. In fact, when he reached for the curtain, he could hear breathing and feel this twitch in his heart. This was no dream.

"Oh stop the silly act and draw the curtain," Angela reprimanded him, storming over and yanking the curtain open. And there, by the entrance to his small lodge, stood the silhouette of a child. She neither looked like a boy and he neither looked like a girl, though Angela seemed to know who he was. Or who she was because she soon grabbed her husband like a deranged woman, "don't even look at him. This one's not ours!" she beckoned him, but it was already too late because now he couldn't stop staring at the silhouette lingering ominously by the entrance. He kept staring at it—at him, or her—and staring awkwardly too, so much that it came for his eyes (the boy, or girl, scrambling towards Father Benedict with the intention of gorging those eyes out forever, offended by them). And it would have, that he felt strongly, had it not been for the blinding light that folded up his dream.

The priest was a man whose eyelids never truly shut while he slept, or so he'd been told by a countless congregation of well wishers, so he was lucky. The piercing shot of light and the resounding roar that woke him up came from the real storm, the midnight storm that took the fort by surprise, bringing him into the thick of the downpour in a deluge of his own sweat. He sat upright on his bed in his cramped little lodge, taking a minute to compose himself and organise his thoughts. It'd been a weird one, this dream. Lucky to have caught his break to reality from a twinkle of the intense lightning bolt that had stubbornly found a way to get to him through slits in the bamboo stems that roofed his humble lodging.

The night was hot, sickly hot, and humid; so humid that the reverend could practically squeeze a bucketful of sweat from his cotton shirt (in the face of the fact that the rain had been falling all night. Rains that did nothing to quench the heat. Rains that, on the contrary, made everything worse, trapping all the heat instead of alleviating it). The prior afternoon had fared better. And if the reverend could have his pick, he would have picked Africa's blistering and dry Saharan day heat over her humid life-sucking night heat any day.

The priest got off his tacky sweat bed to change the sheets, which was about the time he heard the barking. The dogs were barking under the thunderstorm, or after it. He'd made little sense of it at first, looking to his altar and deeming it untidy— untidy enough for the subliminal memories of his wife to gong his dreams, so he sought to put things right—putting right the stationery he'd cast abroad and rearranging other things in place, like furniture, and the missing picture of Mary he exhumed from beneath a grave of fallen books. It was then he made out the sirens. The sirens had been whining under the howl of the storm all this while, but the loud thundering and pit-pattering of rain had drowned them out. He could hear them now. And the more he strained to hear, the louder they seemed to get. The louder they seemed to get, the more lucid the bark of the dogs came across. The priest hurried curiously through the Mission School and onto the dirt road, only to find Fort William wet and abuzz;

with sirens wailing and Ted's officers arming themselves with dogs and flintlock muskets. Father Matthew ran back to his lodge to grab his cloak before hitting the dirt road again—and in the torrential downpour. The priest hadn't cared for getting wet, by the look of things.

t he old man sat in his hut, waiting out the night by reading the heavens. This torrential downpour had only one conclusion, and the Rain God was his conclusion. Sango, in his assessment, was the only God that could poke a hole so big in the sky, its rains would torment the irreverent and leave flashes bright enough to blind the people folk. Oh yes he had to confess, he was no longer the talker, or the practitioner (that was true), now his devotion was to the godskins, but some things never go away. Some things, these things, stay bottled inside till the day one dies. The old spiritualist knew that. He had always wanted so hard to embrace the new religion the new horsemen had spent half his lifetime preaching, but once a man has learnt how to read the signs, it is impossible to turn a blind eye to them. The art of reading the heavens wasn't a secret one. Owed to many years of diligent training and watchful interpretation on his part. So, as always, and as the heavens stretched over him, there was that sound idiosyncrasy distinguishing a baleful sky from a providential one.

Tonight's storm was one of both. Sango was hailing the earth; overwhelmed by laughter. Or tears. Or tears of laughter. Something had come with the deluge, and the Rain God was excited to see how the living would fare. The old man could literally feel this in the dank air as he sniffed tobacco within the entrance to his hut, fingering through his grey and kinky hair watching even more clouds gather—after five exhaustive hours of torrential downpour, of lightning taunting the trees and blinding out the sky in an armour of white, more rain was coming. It was a night of caution. A time of unpredictable outcomes. Or that would have been his advice to the villagers if he was still of the practice (if). Anyway, it didn't matter though because he knew that they would still come for him. Or send someone in their place to press him for assistance. Any assistance.

And that they did.

The word to reach him that very night in the thick of the downpour was that an old acquaintance had just passed, and that she had died for lack of sight in her old age having trampled upon an adder in the murk of night while assisting his home village.

Sadly, things were only going to get worse, and not long by the look of things; for she had been the only other medium investigating The Madness who had not been rendered useless by the affliction.

enerators were expensive to run, but the two generators at the fort were running at full capacity. The Edison bulbs were expensive to have and burn, yet both bulbs installed at the Northern and Western outlooks were bright and burning, facing East and scouting the forest. Ted's boys were on edge and the priest had a hundred questions, but he wasn't the only one—neither were the dogs helping—their olfactory nerves tingling with the sensation of whatever it was that lay hidden beyond the immediate smell of mud, stale wardrobe, and gunpowder. It lurked inside the bushes behind the East perimeter, just stalking the camp. Whatever it was, or whatever it was to be, one thing was sure— it had no intention of leaving. All the captain's officers had their flintlock muskets powdered and stood trigger-ready.

With every bark, each bark a little fiercer, the dogs acknowledged this thing drawing closer to the camp. It was restless behind the fence. One could cut the tension with a knife as everyone waited, the air spiking with adrenaline and testosterone. Ted's boys waited. They waited because they figured if it had no intention of leaving, it had to come out sometime, and so, armed to the teeth load with munitions, they searched for a target under the metal-tasting downpour, any visible target in the forest will do. Anything to kill besides killing time.

Anything behind the fence.

Father Matthew made it across the main dirt road, making it past some of the cabins, and past the public bathroom, but his priestly embroidery gave him up by the kitchen.

"Where are you going Father?" one of the boys in Khaki white stopped him, the others a little too preoccupied to bother about the wandering priest. The soldier had grabbed the reverend by the hand, but his hand was cold and shaky being drenched in the rain. "It's too dangerous for you to be out here," he suggested, but barely looked old enough to be in Ted's army. Even with a musket in hand.

"My son, I need to know what's going on?" he asked and the boy swiped water from his eyebrows and mud unto his shorts.

"I wish I knew, father. Nobody knows. The dogs just went wild while we slept. Something's tried to sneak in, I think." He was quaking now, quaking under the heavy downpour as he spoke, with his lips quivering from being exposed too long. "I don't think it's safe you being out here," he cautioned again.

"I don't think it's an old man you should be worried about," the reverend suggested warmly, holding the young man's hand and warming it up for him. It helped take the edge off.

The young soldier dunked the nozzle of his flintlock

musket in the loamy soil. "The Captain's left the fort to check it out minutes ago. He's out there with some of the lieutenants trying to secure the perimeter, so it might be a while before we're out of the rain. But we have our orders."

The reverend wrapped his cloak tighter, but tighter hadn't turned up warmer because his cotton cloak was all drenched. "I can handle a little rain, my son. Tell me, what are Ted's orders?"

"To shoot if it's on all fours. The Captain is of the opinion its some giant beast. I hear they're hardly out of the ordinary here, these dense forests I mean, 'cause the others, they say they've spotted one or two watching from the trees once."

"How long have you served here, my son?" the reverend asked because he was still a child. In the least he sounded like it.

"Almost a year now father."

"A year? It's hard to believe. I mean I don't see you at Mass."

"I come," he lied while looking the reverend full in the eye, only slinking his head away when the priest looked disappointed.

"I'm going to see you next Sunday, am I not?"

"Definitely," he lied again, but the priest wasn't asking. Not so much as he was telling. The young soldier nodded in agreement, laid flat in negotiation.

"I will keep an eye out for you next Mass," the priest threatened in his own priestly kind of way before moving on. Every one of the wooden posts that completed the East fence wasn't easy to make out at night. And more of its original wiry gauze wasn't in view from where they stood, which was why Father Benedict moved further, further towards the cabin for the junior men, leaving the young soldier with a sigh of guilt and a sour countenance.

The fort's clayey grounds were soaked to spoiling so the priest had to be cautious walking through the mud. He'd barely managed a few slippery steps past the Junior Officers' cabin when he heard Elizabeth call for him, "Father Matt? Is that you between the cabins?"

Goodness! It seemed everyone was out in the rain, though he shouldn't have expected less. The fort's eastern perimeter fenced off the infirmary and Elizabeth's lodging space, so she stood most to be affected (if anyone would be affected at all by all this). Ted's astute response was probably to keep her safe. Aside the fact, there was no way anyone could have remained asleep with all the howling going on.

"Elizabeth," Father Matthew eased his way to her, feigning the impression he originally intended to check on her. "Where's Matulu?" he asked, but asking because Matulu's quarters was only a stone's throw into the bush from hers, yet there she stood, alone under the lintel of her cabin, only shielded knee up from the rains wrapped in a sleeping blanket. She was wearing loose flip flops and white socks. Now muddied white socks.

"Un'ka's at the sickbay. I instructed him to watch the patient just in case we might need to—" Elizabeth had begun to say when she interrupted herself, "why are you out in the rain, Father Matt? You're soaking wet. You should know that it takes its toll on the body. You don't want to catch a cold now, do you?"

"A little rain is not going to kill me, Liz. In fact, I could ask you the same thing," Father Benedict rejoined as he joined her under the lintel of her peanut-sized cabin. She tried grimacing. When that didn't work, she brought him a white towel, warm and dry, to wear from inside her quarters.

"This rain seems to be falling more intensely by the hour. I've never seen anything like it. It doesn't let up. Any idea to what's going on?" she asked, her poise one of consternation.

"It's normal. It's Africa. This is how it rains here in the west," the priest replied coolly despite that the sirens were still running. He didn't want her worrying. "Ted's boys say it's some big animal of some sort. A tiger or chimpanzee or so," he speculated to her ease. It wasn't supposed to be a lie. Just some unconfirmed truth. "Ted's been long out to find out. The sirens are only a ruse. I think they want to scarify it to dissuade it from entering the camp. All the ruckus should be over soon, I promise."

"Oww."

Everyone else looked so frightened.

"So is he going to kill it?"

"I beg your pardon? Kill what?"

"The beast, Father Matt."

"Oh. No. Ted's a trained boy scout," Father Benedict replied, "he respects the animals. He'll most likely scare it away. As you can see, it's not a vast green forest for nothing."

Elizabeth's face lightened up. "I certainly hope he doesn't. I've never spotted live game on this continent. The ones I see are only the ones the cooks serve up dead. Small creatures. Do you think the captain's capable of capturing it? I'd like to see the native beasts up close."

The priest made a warm smile and the doctor warmed up to it. Like salt in rain her fear had dissolved away, so they stood there watching the brilliance of lightning and the cackle of the thunderstorm. The heavens tore at the earth with such vitality, robbing the mud right from under their feet, eroding what it could before the pregnant clouds gave way as it recast the entire terrain in the fort to the desire of its choice. "This continent is incredible in the way it rains," she whispered, watching the rains aggregate in streams across the fort (Noticing now the entire camp was waterlogged). "Am I to worry about mosquitoes after this?"

"It's all clay. The earth swallows up all the water on a very dry day. So if we're lucky, no. You'll see none of this tomorrow. In actual fact, the water's just washed all the larvae away."

The Edison lights came their way scouring the East perimeter as both lights brightened up the forest to its darkest shade of green. Scouting up, then down the perimeter, and then down then up the perimeter. Each light, a brilliant torch, searching as far as it could, but turning up with nothing every time.

Providentially the sky lit up the darkness under a spell of lightning, and that's when in that brief but broadening spark of illumination, Father Matthew thought he saw something stand out in the forest. The head of a child, his fitting guess.

"Did you see that, Liz?"

The priest was pointing into the enshrouding darkness.

"See what father Matt?" Elizabeth asked back. "See what?"

"No. It can't be," Father Benedict mumbled, stepping into the rain and then trudging towards the perimeter without thought or concern to Elizabeth's white towel that slid off his shoulders and into the mud.

"Father Matt, what do you see? I don't see anything," she called after him.

The lights met the priest by the fence. "Is that the reverend?" a crisp voice pronounced from the outlook. "Reverend Benedict, I'd advise you leave the fence please. We still do not know what is out there," the officer blared at the priest. The officer up in the outlook didn't sound commanding, rather he sounded concerned. More irritated than concerned, actually.

The reverend pointed to the bushes and the Edison bulbs swung in the direction he was pointing at. Still nothing. The lights swung back at the priest, in the rain, by the fence. "Reverend, would you please move away from the fence?" the voice objected again, this time it sounded commanding. Obdurately the reverend continued directing the lights to the bushes, and seemed to be conversing with someone or signalling to something. The lights swung at the bushes yet again and patiently patrolled the perimeter, but it turned up with nothing.

"What the heck are you waiting for? Somebody get that bloody priest out of there before he hurts himself!" the voice bellowed exasperatedly, but this time around, when the lights swung at the perimeter, the priest wasn't alone. Father Benedict was clutching the hand of an indigenous child through the fence; a child no older than the children that visited the fort occasionally. The ten, eleven or twelve year old was looking hurt, and seemed to react strongly to the spotlight when they focused on him, so the reverend gestured at Ted's boys up the outlook to switch the bulbs off but they didn't. The mood was one of general shock. Soon enough, the captain and his cavalry rode in from the child's side of the fence, having watched the whole thing from within the forest. Ted gestured at his officers to kill the lights, and they did. They shut off the sirens as well. Elizabeth Cambridge rushed to the fence with towels. The child was darker than any of the other children she'd seen, almost pitch-black in complexion. He had a puffed cheek, a swollen foot, and a dislocated jaw. He could barely talk or walk by the look of things.

ted and the senior officers were back on the other side of the fence before the reverend and the doctor could work the boy through the spaces in the fence and into a stretcher borrowed from the infirmary. Two or three of Ted's younger officers had helped mount the sick boy on the stretcher. Everyone else either returned to bed or to their stations. The child was delirious, his vitals plummeting to whatever ordeal he must have endured, his struggle to have made it this far, a place in the midst of nowhere, staunchly withstood the odds. The child's body was over the daily temperature, and burning ever hotter, even in the eye of the storm. He was near comatose and Elizabeth's first choice was to pump his body raw with dissolved aspirin to combat the high fever. They had to get him out of the rain and to the infirmary as quickly as possible.

"Watch his foot!" she barked at the junior officers impulsively without actually intending to offend them. Still they helped the boy to the infirmary. Un'ka Matulu had prepped a syringe in hand, one that came in useful when he found the crowd heading for the infirmary. The nurse propped the curtains open to allow the officers bring the boy in when Ted and his band of lieutenants intercepted the stretcher—and in the nick of time by the look of it.

"And where are you taking the child?"

The Captain had asked but the brusque manner with which he demanded prevented the younger officers from taking even a step further.

"The sickbay, Captain," they responded even with the storm conniving against their voices.

"You will do no such thing," Ted directed as he

walked his horse between the stretcher and the medical tent, but in fact aiming his words at the doctor wrapped in the white sleeping blanket who was acting like she hadn't heard him the first time.

"But the child has a fever, Captain. He requires immediate attention," Elizabeth stated, impatiently moulding a face at the captain since the rain was overpowering her eyes (and that too was Ted's fault because Ted and his men were standing windward). The Captain still didn't make way. He just stood his horse and she grew upset. "Listen, he might die!" she raised her voice (the belligerent winds granting her amnesty to speak in whatever tone she desired).

"A—A—Attend to him if you will, but not in there, Miss Cambridge," the captain answered succinctly, and he was not alone, his much senior officers gesturing their agreement or involvement in this conclusion.

Elizabeth burst quickly like a gourd, directing her finger at each and every one of the captain's lieutenants, "why? It's my sickbay. And I'm allowed to treat everyone of you in it?" she spat, but they appeared to ignore her rhetoric.

Father Benedict held down her hand and looked up at the captain concernedly, "this child is obviously sick. Is anything the matter, Ted?" he asked tacitly, taking into consideration the presence of the captain's lieutenants, but what the priest hadn't noticed was losing his cloak somewhere along the way. He was totally drenched and was looking unrefined.

"Yes Reverend. The boy's a native and he's sick. As you know, I have an officer in there," Captain Book answered honestly, and soon after fingered the order, so without ado, and without any resistance, the young officers who'd held up the child's stretcher dropped it in the mud, dropping the child along with it, before backing off.

"Asinine poppycock. I'm the doctor!" Elizabeth argued, steaming over like caustic potash in the rain.

"It's pointless arguing with the captain," Father Matthew whispered, putting a hand on Elizabeth's shoulder. He looked up at Ted on his horse, "we need to get the boy out of the rain. What can we do?"

But the fact that anyone would seek permission to use the infirmary made Elizabeth go kamikaze on the captain, "Jesus Christ! God damn you and your high horse, Captain!" she swore and the reverend cautioned her in a bid to calm her down.

Ted hesitated to speak at first, but he spoke nonetheless. "You may say what you like, D—D—Dr. Cambridge, but I have given my orders and I expect to see them followed," he warned, backing his horse away. The consequence of disobeying his orders he aimed more at his officers than at the civilians who were upsetting him, so without losing a moment the three younger officers who'd once helped with the stretcher stationed themselves by the entrance of the medical tent—their new orders unambiguous and stalwartly clear.

All the senior officers trotted off guiltlessly. The Captain also cantered off, but he was affronted by her so he never really went very far.

"Perhaps she can engage my chambers, Captain? He looks like one of my children," Father Matthew lied in a bid to win back the captain's attention.

"Fair," the captain answered lividly, on second thought stopping his horse and turning it around. He cantered to where they stood and stopped close enough to the child. "I'm doing what's b—best for everyone in the f—fort. Even what's best for the def—defiant doctor," he stammered with vexation, thoroughly upset, but he had ridden up so close that water dripped from his horse and onto the child's stretcher. Ted hadn't known this of course, still of the narcissistic opinion he had a right to be angry, but that was the cap to her dynamite. Elizabeth was mad already and so spat at Ted's horse.

"Who are you to say that?! You are no doctor to be giving such directives!"

Reverend Benedict was startled by her fury. "Thank you," Father Benedict said to the captain, and gently squeezed Elizabeth by the shoulders, "have Matulu bring what you need," he beseeched her softly, opting to coax the enraged doctor to the Mission School. Actually the fire in both their eyes made the priest fear they both could tear each other apart, limb for limb, anytime soon. The reverend grabbed one end of the stretcher while Un'ka Matulu offered to help with the other. "Bless you," the reverend said.

Now even though she'd gotten on his nerves, it was a horrible thing watching the man of the cloth getting soaked in the rain like everybody else, and trying to help convey the boy to his lodge. A lodge all the way on the other side of the fort. Ted signalled the men who'd posted themselves by the infirmary, and one of them hurried to go relieve the reverend off his end of the stretcher. On first impression, Elizabeth shoved the officer off his footing and into the mud, "we don't need your help!" she barked. That was how furious the captain had made her, by the look of things.

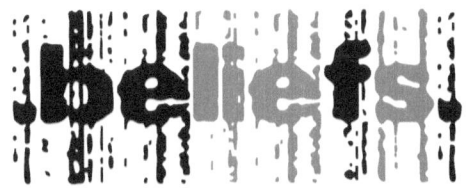

beliefs

River festivals had a way of pleasing the Loas. River festivals and canoe racing had a way of pleasing the people. But river festivals, canoe racing, and the white visitors had virtually nothing in common. Much on the contrary, the godskins were an unpleasant distraction. Their luminous presence tended to rob the attention of the villagers over the sanctity of the festival itself—in the least that was what the oracles purported (not putting into question their overkill skin dresses or the ceremoniously long staffs with jewelled bob heads they trotted out), but since they had raised the young priestess in the image and call of the Ishaporke herself, there was little or nothing they could do about it when she demanded. The priestess had demanded, so the godskins were here as guests at her initiation ceremony, and as long as she abstained from breaking her rites, or performing her royal obligations as mediator to the Loas, the little priestess could show-off anyhow she saw fit (in the presence of whomever she deemed fit). She'd simply chosen, so they were going to leave it at that, but, and a sincere but, the oracles feared if this ceremony was ever to rouse the attention of the Loas, it may be one of lethal jealousy. Why they would fear such retribution?—because oftentimes people forget whom to fear.

the people of Ishaporke had served their guests using the same plate, so to speak—of the visitors willing to eat from the aborigines, that is. It was a base of plantain leaves, not an actual plate, but it did the job for these folks. This riverside festival was a noisy event and the throng was enormous—a congregation of what looked well over a hundred Ishaporke devotees making the mile long trek along the river bank. There were lots of drums, entertaining conjurers, and then amusement dancers celebrating the Loas with miniature gongs tied about their feet, dancing energetically and making their own music.

Ishaporke was obviously the largest and oldest village by the hill, the doctor could see that; outside the stories acquainted her by the reverend. And from what lay before them, this African river tribe was probably the richest. There was a well adorned altar with shiny gemstones surrounding it. There the priest's pupil, or her pupil so to speak, stood beside the impression of a part-human part-python goddess.

"Is he getting any better?" the priest asked the doctor.

"I can't say, father. It's no common fever," Elizabeth answered, examining with askance the mucilaginous fish meal their hosts had served on those broad plantain leaves. When she attempted a bite, however, it tasted soupy, and much to the doctor's surprise worked its way down the oesophagus smoother than the bird meal offered back at the fort. "Which doesn't come as a surprise at all," she added, "it's as you always say, this is no common continent. Matulu has the boy's blood in a vial. I should come up with something before nightfall—if we ever find the time, I mean."

The people chanted pogo, pogo, pogo whenever a race was on. The Captain was a little taken by the intense canoe racing and watched the aborigines compete with one another quietly from the river bank. They chanted as the paddlers raced to a finish. He and five of his senior officers, the other five of his senior officers, (the healthy five) had sat on their horses through the event; not eating or imbibing a thing, wanting to keep their heads clear for whatever reason. Aside the fact that they weren't actually invited. The child had requested the presence of her teacher, but Ted had come to ensure the safety of his priest. Strangely, this part of the waterside didn't harbour any nerve-wracking mosquitoes—a welcomed respite for Ted—which could have been to the fact that the entire area was under the shade of a mighty Sapele tree (point noted) for Ted could have sworn the mosquitoes back at the fort in this bloody season of rain had feelers the darn length of sewing needles! The Captain also noted the old man rarely hung around them today, obviously taken by more pressing matters, matters which kind of seemed odd to Ted because Paul the Saint, Father Matthew, and the Brigadier shared this special bond in language; so Paul was always hanging around, always, no matter the inconvenience suffered. It helped ease the interaction. In fact, the captain who'd come to attune his eyes to the mechanics of local gestures, prided himself in being able to pick up a word or two off the old man's self-coined gesture language. This colourful expression of English when conversing with the reverend, for what it was worth, did go a long way in bridging the gap for the Brigadier during his early explorations here in Her Majesty's Cameroons, and a huge feat for a man who became Reverend Benedict's very first convert. The Reverend, or at least the one who cared for it anyway, also learned to speak back—or finger back, so to speak.

"I prayed for the boy again this night because I feared for him. His temperature shot up. His temperature shoots up at night. I had to throw in more wet towels to the ones you gave me and watch him most of the night," Father Matthew said, catching a few stares from the villagers and noticing fingers pointed at them. "How do you like the gumbo?" he asked downing a sliver of fish with acquired ease, eating with his bare hands as was customary to the people.

"I like the fish better. Only wished I had brought utensils 'cause how do I get to wash my hands when I'm done? Hopefully not in this one?"

"Not to worry. They'll replace this bowl by bringing you another to wash those in, but only after you're done eating."

"Oh good. I was thinking I'd have to walk over to that river to do it."

"not while they are watching."

"Allow me to guess, it's a sacred river isn't it?"

Father Benedict chuckled, deboning his fish meal and picking through the gumbo, "Just know you can't wash your hands in it. Watch for bones."

"Oh I'm done eating, Reverend. 'only wanted to know how it feels like to live like this."

"Hmm, that's rich of you but I fear you'll have to eat everything, Liz."

"Everything? But..."

"Look around you."

She looked around even as she caught a glimpse of the young priestess pointing at them amidst a sister group of girls. All the girls were similarly dressed, dressed in reflective snakeskin and marked off with chalk as the pretty little oracles they were.

"I see no leftovers. And since this is a special

occasion, I don't intend leaving any. Don't want to be the odd man out in Rome…"

"I see what you mean, Father Matt."

"It's also great respect as I've come to notice," the priest mentioned.

"Oh."

"Thank you."

"Okay, but what exactly is this ceremony for?" she asked, knocking her head just in time for the priest to catch Jite show them off to the other girls.

Father Matthew smiled at the children watching, waving generously at them and then saying a prayer for them by fingering a little cross in the air, but they tittered and shied away like the flushed little girls they were. "It has something to do with the changing seasons I guess 'cause each time the seasons change, these villagers are always commemorating something."

Ted and his men laughed heartily, breaking their long streak of silence, same time the people beat their hands in delight and the dancers chimed their feet in melody. They'd come to learn one of the canoe paddlers had stolen first place by breaking the other's paddle. Apparently, cheating was allowed here. Or so Ted thought, for though it had looked like an act of omission, the captain was prepared to argue otherwise.

An elderly oracle parted Jite from her sisters and led the girl to the altar after placing some type of incense in her hands. From what they could make up, when the entire procession heads back to the river village immediately after all the rites and all the blessings were over with, it will be by way of the Ishaporke princess and priestess as lead.

In the meantime, some dancers occupied the reverend and doctor, taken them by surprise by storming them from behind. One of them wiggled her underdressed breasts violently at the reverend and all the captain's men snickered. She then wiggled her breasts and buttocks at Elizabeth only for Elizabeth to be drawn to the dance. The young doctor stood and tried to mimic the dancer and her dance; a hurried rather racy kind of beat. She couldn't fully style to the beat though, but the people seemed to appreciate her for she gathered quite a crowd. And very quickly too.

Elizabeth puffed as she pranced about, taking in deep breaths. "That cross you signed earlier, 'has me thinking these people don't truly recognize what the signing of the cross really means to us as Christians. Do they, Father?"

"I can't understand why do you say that? I'm doing my best—why would you bring that up?"

"Well, it's not really that I'm...I'm actually asking because isn't that like—dangerous? I mean crossing such borders with indigenes could be suicide. I've lived—"

"Suicide's a mortal sin, Elizabeth. We shouldn't talk about suicide."

She took a break from the dancing. As well as a moment to catch her breath. "Oh Father, I'm not one to interfere with your life's work. It's just looking around I get the frightening impression these people take their indigenous beliefs seriously. That's what I meant," she admitted, in some way asking for forgiveness before plunging into another bout of dance.

Father Matt had no quick comeback in his repertoire so he watched her dance without form for a while. "No man having drunk old wine straightaway desireth new; for he saith, the old is better."

"Luke 5. 39"

"Ah...you remember my sermon."

"Mm hmm. Why won't I remember? It's only last Sunday's," Elizabeth retorted while huffing and puffing, taking offense Father Benedict would think her shallow and non-religious—as shallow and non-religious as the captain. She was already sweating down her pits and blouse.

"They don't know any better, Liz," Father Matthew mentioned while he watched Jite and the townsfolk decorate or bless the pagan altar. "Somebody has to teach these people to throw away such trifling idols and serve the real god. Take me for example. The church led me to the light. Now here I am. All the better for it."

"Then you sound as a one who's made this personal, Father. It's no more about Queen and country to you."

"Queen and country? That's Ted's job. To me, more like church and duty," the reverend responded, and about the time a burly and overly adorned middle aged man under the escort of six overly adorned women of different ages split the crowd and approached from the altar, heading as Ted had guessed for the reverend. The Reverend, in reaction, got on his feet.

The burly man greeted the reverend by tapping an ornate staff across the reverend's shoulders, a staff similar in every way to the tail of a black horse, (only God knows what happened to that horse the captain had always wondered) as he and his officers also got off their horses. They all knew who the burly man was. Everyone except Elizabeth, who hadn't cared and kept on dancing. The chief's presence (like iron to a charged magnet) had also drawn Paul the Saint to them. Paul the Saint hadn't come with them to the ceremony (he'd arrived long before they did), but he was the one who'd brought them the invite.

"Your highness Osivie," Ted greeted, taking his hat off and bowing in an overly humble gesture.

Elizabeth stopped dancing on connecting the dots. Suddenly, the stately gems adorning their necks and myriad attires of snakeskin stood out. "if he is the Osivie then he is her—"

"—yes, he's Jite's grandfather," Father Matthew answered briskly, speaking under his breath, and quickly ending her tense before she had the chance to point. "Don't!" he cautioned, "Pointing portends ill luck. The Ishaporke don't like pointers."

"Oh."

there had been a longstanding treaty of peace between Kiki and Ishaporke village, but even when the goats refuse the urge, an ill-timed collision is all it takes to start a fight. This was to be important to the old man, for the fact that the Ishaporke would summon him long before the initiation ceremony.

The oracles of Ishaporke had gathered in a circle as they waited for the Kiki. They hadn't formally been dressed or painted for the ceremony, so upon arrival they went straight to business.

"We've always been a peaceable people, and trading with the Kiki has always been of paramount importance to us, but we want you to tell us the truth. You're one of us. A colleague. We want to know why your people would abduct our people."

The old man's answer was succinct, "no, where is the sense in that?"

"So you deny it? Because we have done some consultations of our own and the spirits don't lie."

"I didn't say that."

"So you don't deny it? You don't deny that your people want to start a war because they think we are poisoning them. Yes? Yes?" they queried eagerly. Almost too eagerly.

"No," he answered succinctly, again, but only because this was beyond any simple answer. He could see the look in their eyes. It was one of bereavement and grief, able to twist any rightly thinking man, so he turned to their chief to elucidate, "Osivie, we've long had peace between our people. I do not know about the others, but I know you realize that we are most afflicted by The Madness. Remember that in times of war and great distress, our people have fought side by side. Even now, we do not blame you for The Madness. We are allies. Do not be hasty to eat the melon because the farmer is at the marketplace. I am yet to figure why my village would even think of doing what you accuse them of. Or why the spirits would say they did—"

"Are you saying the spirits are lying?" Ishaporke's oracles barked at him.

"Because the lizard bobs his head, does not imply he gives his consent."

"You're out of your mind for saying that!"

"Watch your words. He is our friend. He would not have accepted this invitation if he knew we were bringing him here to be interrogated. Or insulted," the chief intervened. "Besides, let him speak for his village."

"But he calls us liars to our face, the same way his people call us murderers to our backs!!"

"I've never heard anybody utter such a thing."

They turned their attention to the oracle, "You do not have to break the coconut to know there is water inside! As if you would admit to your people abducting—slaughtering—our people then hiding their bodies. As if!"

"All I can admit is if you fight them now, they will surely fight you—"

"See. We even see the hate in your eyes when you say that."

"Let me finish! The chaff of suspicion is not easily removed—the fighting, Osivie, I can assure you will not end there. Like kawun, it will remain even to the times of our grandchildren and great grandchildren. The peace we've had all these years against the trees of time will decay to be a sour memory we all know to be false. Is that what they want?"

"You forget that even when the raffia is pulled, its thread will snap someday," they answered in many ways than one on behalf of their Osivie.

The oracle, or former spirit medium, turned from them but only because he had thought this was to be a meeting of friends, of faith, but now could clearly see it was one summoned from the misgivings of distrust. "I speak for peace, Osivie. Now that they are afflicted, and you are not, they will never forgive an infraction. Hopefully, I am not the only man here with the head of reason?"

"You're crazy, old friend, for thinking you can make us the enemy before our chief. We are not the ones who are cursed, but we are the ones going missing! We are the ones whose children are being taken! Admit that if you cannot admit anything else."

"It is for that reason I came. It is for that reason I have honoured this gathering. Even now the Osivie knows I do not honour invitations. No, no longer. I would not have come otherwise. Even now, we eat the preserved fish you sell us. We still have them hanging at our market square."

"What of the Ilu San—" the Osivie had begun to speak, but the oracles of Ishaporke refused to let him speak since they knew the Chief and the former spirit medium from Kiki to be close friends (and to them it was nigh impossible for the chief not to show his bias).

"Let's leave the Ilu-Sango out of this. They are farthest, but his people are closest!" they growled, and so all the chief could do was look overly perturbed by where this was going.

"I realize that also."

"Oh o!" they intoned.

But the old man wasn't just going to stand there and allow his friend to be riled by his counsel of oracles into such a permanent course of action. He had to be wise. He had to be diplomatic. "To speak the truth, Osivie. The Ilu-Sango are an expressive people. If they were doing what you suspect, you won't have to suspect. They don't hide what they do," he said charily, no longer acknowledging this witch-hunting mob. "But it's not us, either. That is your truth."

"If you were our people and our people were your people and one of us was standing there talking to you, what would you do my friend?" the Osivie asked directly hoping for an honest answer; and an honest answer he got, much to the surprise of his counsel of oracles.

"I wouldn't listen," he said.

"Thank you. Now we know you are speaking truth," the oracles said gladly, in more or less the same choice of words.

But the old medium didn't let it end there, "still I would ask the godskins before I act. Let them use their foreign insight because one cannot let the lion arbitrate on what's ideal for the goat. Neither should the goat arbitrate on what is ideal for the tuber. To me, they have nothing to gain and nothing to lose."

"Wisely said. I've always believed they are an enlightened lot. They seem smart and inquisitive. You have spent time with your friends the godskins, no?" the Osivie asked.

"As much time as your daughter has."

"So you know we can trust them?"

"I know enough to know that they can help. They have special knowledge and powers we don't have. They can help settle this quandary between us."

"I agree. What do you think?" the Osivie turned to the once inflamed mob of oracles but they might as well have nodded, acknowledging his soft spot for the old Kiki.

"Okay then, let's settled. Oh provide him somewhere to sit so we can rush this along! He can barely stand as it is."

t he big man greeted the captain and his men the same way, each with his staff to their shoulders, alongside a broad amiable smile. Ted walked to his horse to retrieve some gifts from his pack.

"He is her grandfather, his Highness or Chief, but Osivie is the appropriate title," Reverend Benedict informed Elizabeth, clasping his hands together to greet the chief, but then weirdly signing the cross. He didn't have to, but he did. Father Matt had invented a clever way of passing on subliminal messages.

"And these are his wives?" Elizabeth muttered, churning the words out of her lips on counting their number—and counting over and over again just to be certain she had the right count.

The doctor had been sweating across the forehead and armpits into her blouse, and made up quite the stink when soaked, yet the silken rhinestone blouse she wore for this occasion looked magnificent as it shimmered in the daylight, so the chief took special interest in Elizabeth, greeting her with two taps from his staff and not one across the shoulders as he had done for the men. One of the Ted's officers mumbled something and the others snickered.

Ted returned with a piece of black cloth and handed it to the chief. "Tell him these are yet again gifts from Her Majesty, the Queen of England!" he said and the reverend passed a slack interpretation to Paul the Saint. The Osivie was already elated, exulting over the gifts. Paul the Saint passed on the chief's appreciation. The old man made these gestures slowly, as they had come to know, so they had to endure through it for one hand too far from place would probably rupture an artery in him. Or that's what Elizabeth thought.

The chief found two square mirrors wrapped in the cloth. He smiled generously at the reflection of himself through them and dabbed Ted twice across both shoulders. He flagged his people, and so the natives hurriedly robbed the altar of the half-python goddess off a few cowries and gemstones to hand them over; offerings highly priced among them, offerings that made Elizabeth's eyes light up like two burning wicks on a bed of wax.

The Captain gestured while speaking, "no Osivie, those were nothing more than gifts," he declined, again with the humble bow, but the Osivie and the old man wouldn't let up.

"You have to accept it, Ted. The Osivie shows his gratitude by having the goddess bless you in kind," Reverend Benedict interpreted. "She cannot bless you if you don't take it."

"No. It's important he sees my gifts as gifts."

"He does. Actually, I think he acknowledges them as ceremonial gifts. You have to accept it," he counselled the captain. "See it this way, he wouldn't accept your gift if you can't accept Hers. It's a huge honour."

"I had once thought you cared for my soul, Reverend, and not these puerile pagan rituals?" Ted rejoined as he was forced to take the cowries, and gemstones, as well as tack up his smile to last yet another minute.

"Your soul is in God's hands, Ted. All diplomacy is just means to an end."

"Do let the Osivie know I only accept this gift in the name of Her Majesty the Queen of England!" he reiterated, deliberately laying emphasis on the title of Her Majesty, the Queen.

The chief then stretched his staff to the captain, before turning to his oracles and walking away from the gathered crowd. Paul the Saint gestured they tag along, and they did.

"I'm guessing you understand this fingering thing...I see why it helps now," Elizabeth commented, but the reverend turned his attention to the captain instead.

"The chief says there are matters he'd like to discuss with us—with you in particular. I think he sees you as our leader; a kind of king, like they thought of the Brigadier," the reverend mentioned to the captain.

"That's something you have to find a way to correct,

Reverend," Ted reacted, and uneasily, as he watched the hand signals fly to and fro, back and forth, for minutes between the priest and his fledgling disciple. The reverend's lips pursed in sour grimace. "What? What has he to discuss?" Ted pushed, but the reverend was caught up in a muse so he pushed again, "Reverend? What has he to discuss?"

"The Ishaporke people have not been fitting their numbers by day," the reverend said gravely.

"Beg your pardon?"

"I'm not sure about my interpretation, but I'm guessing what they mean is that their villagers have not been turning up. I think they are saying they go missing—"

"That's horrible," Elizabeth cut in, trying to squeeze her way into the dialogue.

Ted ignored her.

"And?"

"And since no bodies turn up, they know the wild animals aren't doing it."

"Okay? Tell the Osivie I'll keep that in mind. He needn't worry over our safety. We are armed. We'd be careful out there."

"I don't think that's what he wants from us."

"Wants? What is there to want? I don't see the connection here."

"Paul no longer divines for the village, that I know. I suspect the Osivie speaks with us because the villages are unsettled—"

"Unsettled about what? Is there something he requires of us?"

"He says the Ishaporke have quite the record of tying outlaws to their problems, but he's noted all the assistance we've rendered them these past years."

"—well that's something to be grateful to you for," Elizabeth interpolated but the priest simply smiled at her. The Captain ignored he heard that.

"The Chief wants you to use your powers to figure out who is behind their loss," the reverend said.

"Powers?" Ted repeated even as the captain's lieutenants snickered.

"Well, I might be wrong. No, the sign is more or less for you to divine the cause of their loss."

"And how in the world do they expect me to achieve that? I'm no diviner! I'm no god."

"He must mean prowess, if he means for you to investigate," Elizabeth inferred.

"She's right. That's probably the meaning of it. It's almost like riddles sometimes, I mean this gesture language between Paul and I."

"Very well! I'll be glad to do it. It helps keeping an

eye on the neighbours," Ted remarked, now at ease, "tell him I'll be glad to bring these culprits to book in the name of Her Majesty, Queen Anne, the Queen of England."

"Let's not get in a little too over our heads here, Ted. I also believe it will be a good thing to help, but only if we're a 100% certain the other villages have a hand in whatever's happening to these people. We're not a 100% certain, are we?" the reverend responded.

"Maybe so, but the French might. The French affirm themselves in places they are not wanted, Reverend. I hope you have not forgotten they are here also," the captain rejoined before getting on his horse, "the fools are scouting around out there someplace. They'd do anything to leave a claim on our territory but I am not going to wane in their shadow. I'm going to find them. Shoot them if I bloody have to," the captain said with gusto as his senior officers also mounted their horses. It seemed they'd intended to leave the procession.

Elizabeth had noticed the captain wasn't speaking to her, so she walked to meet him by his horse.

"Wh—what is it this time, Doctor?" Ted snapped, already on the defensive.

"I spoke out of turn the other night and I apologize," she said, yet it hadn't appeared like that was all she'd intended to say.

"F—Fine," he said heatedly. "Now w—what is it you want?"

"I wanted to know if you were about to leave—"

"And if I am?"

"You are? Well, I hope not. At least not until the procession is back to the village, don't you think?" she advised softly from his left like they were buddies. Almost as if she'd intended to touch him, but the captain caracoled his horse away from her.

"I have been here way longer than you, Dr. Cambridge. Do not tutor me on how I relate with the aborigines," Ted answered briskly. "But if you'd rather stand here musing over worthless quartz stones than going with the procession, be my guest doctor," he gibed, for she'd been too preoccupied sticking her nose where it didn't belong for her to note the procession on the move. The Captain had spoken firmly. Ted hadn't even stuttered when he said it, apparently still pissed.

now they had the distinguished role of escorting Jite's parents back to the shrine—a large four limb canopy with interweaved canes for a roof. The shrine had beige sculptures and red earth calabashes set across its floor, including an even count of sacred palm-oil concoctions set on separate bundles of fronds and raffia. It was beauty only appreciated by its kinfolk because some of Ted's lieutenants wouldn't even go near the shrine. Surprisingly, differing from the captain's men, Father Benedict wasn't in the slightest perturbed by the religious artefacts at the pagan ceremony. On the contrary, she could say he looked rather fascinated by everything. Even more engaged in conversation. Now, after the painted men had laid their iconic part-human part-python goddess to rest on an altar of kernel shells betwixt their sculptural depictions of deity, the ceremony had finally come to a close. Or the doctor concluded the ceremony had come to a close because everyone was free of duty; the crowd thinning almost immediately, even Ted's men, but that was when she noticed the captain was no longer with them. "Where's the captain?" she asked the reverend, but asking in a rhetoric sense by asking herself because the reverend wasn't at all paying attention to her. So she sorted through the number of blue uniforms he could see on horses, counting through the number that had remained with the procession, the number that had visibly remained, "1, 2, 3..." The captain's men came up short by three. "He's left. The Captain left," she mentioned to Father Matt, but the priest couldn't be bothered, overly caught up in his conversation with the indigenes, trying to discover the significance of each sculpture and their relevance to the village. Or villagers.

The doctor circled the shrine another minute longer, watching the indigenes watch her oddly whilst searching for the captain or his horse. Was it possible she might have missed him? No. The Captain was nowhere to be found. There were no signs of him or the other half of his officers. Somewhere amid the homebound trek, it seemed the captain had grown weary of the lengthy exercise and returned home. Elizabeth walled up her eyes, lipping her way back to the shrine, but that was when it happened—that inevitable feeling of nausea and dizziness. She threw up there and then. Even worse, she'd vomited into some of the red-oil concoctions the Ishaporke people had arranged decoratively across the grounds of the shrine. In her mind's eye, it had been a better option, having resisted the urge to cast her bread upon the chief, the priest, or any of the indigenes around her (although all this had somehow played out differently in her head because now all she'd done was make one big mess). She had made a mess of the ground. She had made a mess of the chief's feet. She had made a mess of the entire shrine!

The Ishaporke as a people couldn't put together a single word, but it was on their faces. Mother of God were the only words that could rightly match the expression across Father Benedict's face.

The remaining three of Ted's officers assigned to watching the doctor and the priest snickered at the messy sight, but then backed their horses into formation on realizing the solemnity across the faces of the entire water tribe. Luckily, their matchlocks had been preloaded with gun powder prior to now; and with just enough to blow a little hellhole in the face of the eventful. As it stood, this was it.

Elizabeth stood at a quandary, unable to apologize for this shocking accident by being at a loss for what to say (even if her mouth lay open). It was open and empty. As empty as a new calabash.

It would be the very first time the captain visited her allotted space, but it was not what Ted expected. Not from a practicing doctor, that is. She was definitely the mole, clean yet untidy, storing all vital medica inside her living space; a few kegs of antiseptics, a pack of syringes and anaesthetics, one heavy microscope sealed inside one steel-cased travel-size box, chewable barks, strap bands, capsules, loose towels—name it, everything taking up space on almost every flat surface available to her. The only free space in there was, of course, her sleeping space where he'd found her sitting (sitting and sobbing) beside a litterbin filled to its capacity. The Captain was not one to judge since this small accommodation was the best he could offer his medics—well, in his defence, he hadn't anticipated one of them to actually turn up a woman.

"She's a woman, Ted—much harder on herself than you might ever be with the boys," the reverend had counselled earlier and just outside her quarters. Nevertheless, they were his opinions of her, not Ted's. Ted walked in with an even mind, taking his time after he stepped in.

"I don't know what happened today," Elizabeth muttered on seeing the captain walk in. She was red-eyed, sombre, scrubbing off the mucus building under her nose, "You all have been working your hearts out here, I realize that. I really didn't mean to—it all happened so fast, I never really—"

"My men are of the opinion you are preg—pregnant, Dr. Cambridge. Are you pregnant?" he spat at her coldly, hacking her apology abruptly without the affectation of holding her gaze.

His question had come suddenly, so suddenly that it had hit her like a bolt of lightning and she just didn't have enough time recoil from it (to arrange a proper response). "I—I'd wanted to—actually when I took up the transfer I'd thought—"

She was stuttering. That was enough for Ted.

The Captain fiddled with his hat, not looking into her eyes again as he prepared to hurl his next question, the Moab of questions, the mother-of-all-bloody questions actually, "is the father of your child a man under my charge?" he asked flatly. And like before, it took a while for Elizabeth to react. When she did, however, she halted her tears and stood to her feet.

"I beg your pardon Captain?"

Her reaction sufficed. The Captain made a full 180 to exit her lodge. "Th—that's all," he stuttered. "I'll have the officers knock up more wood to enlarge your quarters," he said just before he left (leaving her stunned actually).

She'd been belligerent, up to the point she been hard with the captain all week, but to her surprise, in the face of her shortcomings, the captain had been gentle with her. He didn't even accuse her, taunt her, hassle her, like she was used to doing, like she had done to him so many times. No. She couldn't remain inside. She had seen the enemy, and he bore her face. She had to go after him.

"Thank you, Captain," she said earnestly, and for a minute there it seemed like she and the captain shared a moment. Father Matt was present. He was standing just outside her cabin to witness this rare moment. As well as a few of the captain's officers straggling by.

The Reverend smiled upon seeing her upbeat, happy that Ted had handled things well and not inflict more heartbreak to what was already broken. It was a tender moment, but then the captain just had to open his mouth. He wore his hat before speaking, and spoke point-blankly at her, "you don't have to thank me, doctor. Your duty to England is to provide proper medicare to Her Majesty's soldiers. My duty is to ensure hiccups and breaches in procedure don't clog the running of Her affairs here in the new protectorate. I'll request your withdrawal and decommissioning when next The Lady docks. All I need is for you to do your duty for as long as you're able to," he said. Ted hadn't even turned to look at her. He also chose to ignore Father Benedict, who was already beginning to say whatever he felt he needed to say as he walked away.

Almost instantly Elizabeth shrivelled back into her quarters. She wouldn't let Father Matt in. Or anyone else for that matter. Not even to bring in her meal when it was ready.

Only three nights ago, the lieutenant lying in the infirmary had been a change of bandage away from being reassigned to duty. Now, he was dead. No explanations. Nothing. He had simply developed a temperature and faded between the drugs. It all happened so fast early in the day that Matulu just waited. Providentially Father Benedict was the first to enter the infirmary after the long wait, but Ted's dead lieutenant was all he saw. He had come to get Matulu, maybe the nurse could reason with Elizabeth, but this here was a wholly different matter in both scale and consequence. "What happened to him?" he asked, bewildered and curt.

The nurse had fallen asleep against the draperies, but when he stood up it was obvious Matulu had been without rest for hours. His whites were stark white with no evidence of arteries feeding them life.

The priest had to point to the dead soldier again for Un'ka to answer him, "Matulu, he's dead. What happened?"

"Man sick, man die," the nurse said dryly, not breaking a sweat in reply.

"—Man dies," the reverend reprimanded, not certain as to why he was correcting the ebony nurse, "but how come?"

Un'ka Matulu shrugged.

"How would you not know how he died Un'ka?"

The priest scampered over the stretchers. "Okay, can you at least tell me what happened?" he asked a little calmer, pressing his ears against the officer's lifeless body. The lieutenant's corpse was no longer warm, already set in rigor mortis by the look of him. The priest had to force close the soldier's gaping mouth and eyes. As it appeared the nurse had left

Ted's officer the way he died, which wasn't at all the right thing for any nurse to do, but certainly spoke in the nurse's defence in the general light of things.

"But everyone thought he was getting better?" Father Benedict mentioned, bewildered and checking through the curtains to see if anyone else was on their way to the infirmary. As if relations weren't bad already, one of Ted's officers dying under the watch of the African was a keg of gunpowder—a sitting keg of gunpowder under a pack of candles!

"I look. Doctor no come here," Un'ka answered resignedly, a little tousled why the reverend shuffled about the medical tent. The nurse mumbled some words in Bantu, words the priest certainly wouldn't understand.

"Elizabeth was occupied. I mean we were occupied. We had to go somewhere," the reverend muttered hastily. The priest scampered towards the file cabinets as he fiddled through some of Elizabeth's jottings. Ted's boys usually stayed clear of the nurse, but now they could very well have a reason to hang him. He slammed the cabinets shut. Elizabeth had to know before anyone else. "There is no guile in you, Un'ka," the reverend admitted, "just don't let anyone in here, and by anyone I mean not anyone," he said, and just about the time a horse came trotting towards the infirmary. The Reverend's heart skipped a beat. He sprinted out to meet whoever it was (without a second's thought) to keep whoever it was from sprinting in, and in the nick of time too as Un'ka put down the curtains to the medical tent (and quickly), but the nurse had had one solid guess whom it was as he tugged on the curtains. He was rarely surprised.

I hope you're not weary, Reverend. I'll need you and your old translator friend," the captain said, wondering why the middle aged priest manically came sprinting at him and his horse.

"Why certainly, Ted," the reverend agreed spontaneously without having processed a thought. He'd been sweating profusely. "Although I er—" now the priest took time to breathe and think, "on second thought that might pose a problem, considering Elizabeth vomited all over their sacred ornaments."

"Nevertheless, I'll need the old man. I suggest we go visiting the settlements before sundown, if that won't be a bother. I need to get to the bottom of what's going on with these Africans—before this little problem they're having takes a chunk out of me and my fort outside my knowing."

"We should visit the Kiki then. It's Paul the Saint's home village," the reverend suggested, panting heavily.

The priest looked on the verge of collapse, "Fine. I'll have the men bring you a horse." Ted turned his horse away and Father Benedict dropped his hands to his knees in reprieve. He looked to the infirmary to find Matulu watching through a hand wedged between the draperies. The Captain cantered away. "It's good to see you've picked up a sporting habit, Reverend. One is never too old to give those bones a good jostle," Ted said without looking back.

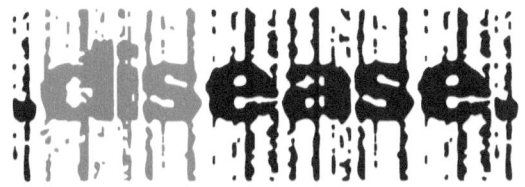

disease

The one the others call the reverend refers to himself as a holy book, and all the other godskins agree. He made a quote from him once and called it sixteen three, but it's not our job to expound on his madness. Or whatever it is he means. Even if we do agree. According to the Kiki, that is. They say we too have signs of our own, but these signs aren't inscribed with ink, or indited somewhere in some olden archive. No. Our signs are inscribed with fear, and blood, indited by word of mouth generations after generations because these Kiki, this village of naturalists with a good history of herbs and at times delusional soothsayers, are rich in our history. They claim to know how our affairs are supposed to work. For instance, they say and we hear that the sun frowns at mothers who uncover their delivery to its naked yellow eye. They also say and we hear that virgins (and this one might have some truth) and first time mothers do not expose themselves at intersections where two bush paths cross. We are known to linger around those intersections, not so sure which way down the paths we'd rather travel. They also say and we hear, and this is most off-the-wall, that falling belly to earth or lying earth to belly is bad for nursing mothers—very bad luck, but who wouldn't that hurt? All we know is nobody wants us for kids just like nobody wants to fall tragically ill; no one, not the Kiki, not the godskins, not even you, which is almost amusing, as if you have any say in the matter.

t he captain could spot the huts north of the hill as they walked their horses up its footpath. Round huts. Huts made of clay. "Can you have your boys put their guns away, Ted? The Kiki are simple folk. You don't want to scare them with your magic sticks," Reverend Benedict said to the captain. Magic Stick being his euphemism to the Kiki of what guns actually did.

Ted fingered the order and his lieutenants strapped their flintlock muskets from sight, "preferable?" the captain rejoined, as calm as a mantis.

"Thank you."

"It never hurts to be prepared."

"Not when you overdo it," the reverend hesitated to say as he reflected over their company of men and the unnecessary accompaniment of ammunition Ted had brought along. The Reverend was not his usual self, the captain caught that.

They circumvented some pools at the entrance to the village; these were round pools of oil in process. Repulsive round pools to be truthful. "You're certain your man will be here?" the captain asked on spotting old women and young children, not wanting to be disappointed after coming all this way.

"It's his village, Ted. He's here," the reverend answered smoothly, and raised his hands in greeting to the women and children working the oil. Ted kept staring at them and at the pools of red oil these aborigines processed by foot, but these villagers welcomed the intrusion, being acquainted with the horseman and his companions. To be candid they all looked the same to them, the horsemen (so it didn't matter if Ted really was different from the Brigadier).

Everyone and everything they saw was in yellow; yellow because it was either soaked in yellow oil or doused by yellow oil. In fact, save the colour of their charcoal, and the colour of their thatch roofs, all was as yellow as a ripe mango. It was genuinely a disgusting sight to behold since red palm usually developed a yucky froth atop the oil after being trod.

A number of the children smiled at the reverend whilst treading. It was a fun time for them. "I must confess, this isn't hygienic. It's hard to imagine this yellow oil ends up so tasty and red when served," the reverend admitted and Ted muted a chuckle as their horses ambled on. "Be kind to remind me to stay off the yam and oil meal I'm offered on next occasion."

"Only on next occasion?" Ted quipped, almost as though the reverend was requiring he do the impossible.

"You understand what I mean. I mean whenever we visit the villages."

"Sure Reverend."

On the other hand, Ted's lieutenants sniggered, sniggering from behind as oil-doused children came running after their horses, "as if he expects more from savage aborigines. Such squalor leaves little to the imagination," someone had said with unabashed sarcasm, but that had made Reverend Matthew stop his horse altogether to put Ted's boys in check, "they aren't savage. They tread oil in the same distasteful manner you tread grapes," he said provocatively before walking his horse, "they do the best they can for a primitive race."

"If you say so, Reverend," the captain cut in as they left the icky sight and the women behind, and cut into the forest towards the heart of Kiki, the village's centre, with an overly generous escort of highly excited Kiki children—indistinguishable one from the other in their yellow paint.

When they passed by Paul the Saint's estranged hut in the thicket of the bushes, then a several number of empty huts along the way, the reverend began to notice the peculiar absence of the men of Kiki (and the reverend wasn't the only one who felt concerned the forest was dank and near dark), even with the midday sun still out there somewhere, but the children straggling along didn't seem perturbed as they skipped merrily through the bush paths, so they continued moving, going past the Kiki's imposing 40 meter trees until they could make out a tree line and then a cut-opening under the forest canopy. Finally, some light. It was when they arrived at the opening that the men found the men. This time, it was the Kiki who had gathered in a meeting; a gathering of bare-chested half-naked elders wearing an adornment of beads and leather (pink beads and dried goat skins), and as the reverend had predicted, there the translator was. Nestled in their centre.

The children scurried away not to be seen.

"We interrupt. If this is the meeting I think it is, then this isn't good. We can't borrow him from this Ted."

"I can clearly see that," the captain answered so the reverend suggested they dismount respectfully, which they did as Ted and Reverend Benedict alone came off their horses; the captain and the priest of the mind if anyone was to intrude this gathering, it should be faces the villagers were acquainted with.

The Reverend approached the Men of Kiki with well -timed steps, as well as overly humble gestures, modalities that were totally unnecessary because the villagers welcomed them by stretching out their hands. Some of them pointing to intricately carved wooden stools, or wooden crickets, for them to sit on. Or squat.

The Captain on the other hand walked through cool -headed, holding his hat to his chest, as the village head, the oldest man in the group (and probably anyone in Africa) stood on his feet. Only a few faces in the group of about 30 old men, a very small number, squinted or squawked as these godskins joined the meeting. They didn't look so delighted having them around (nor did they look healthy upon first glance).

The villagers continued with what it was that had them so occupied, which lucidly was a solemn one. Fortunately, only the reverend would be able to squeeze anything out of this awkward gathering, if they were ever of the mood to share. But soon enough, after about three polite minutes of waiting, the captain's men and their horses grew restless.

"Paul the Saint just told me about some kind of inherited war. A generational war or so," the reverend said coolly after the old man that frequented their Mission School had acknowledged him somehow.

"Okay? That's kind of serious. Is that serious?"

"Actually I was thinking this meeting was about

deteriorating relations they are having with the tribe by the river, the water tribe, but it seems as if something else has the Kiki upset the way they're going."

"What could be more threatening than a generational war at our doorstep?"

"He didn't say. I'm not sure how he figures to handle that if indeed what he told me is true because this could be something else. Something about legless tears or a harvest coming too early."

"Legless tears, Reverend? Do we have a pending war? Or do you mean to tell me we're basically squatting here in the open sun because of some legless tears? What in all bloody hell is that?"

"If I should be honest, I don't know," Reverend Benedict confessed, "It's hard for me to explain, the way they speak is esoteric, but i know it's something shared equally among the villages about this hill. Something like water, but not so much in a good way. It's obvious it frightens them."

Ted watched the gathered assembly of natives with a quizzical gaze, trying his best as the reverend and the Brigadier once put it, to understand societal life and hierarchal organization among the indigenous culture.

"Your translator doesn't look frightened. Sounds like hogwash to me, Reverend," he spat out flatly, growing tired of this smelly gathering of men with flabby breasts.

"It only sounds like that because I attempt to translate. They have this unusual way with language, Ted—sought of a proverbial way," the reverend explained, and a bit too excitedly for Ted's ebbing tolerance. "The dialects in this continent are much harder to contextualize than ours. For me it's just satisfying to be accepted to sit with them, and at a meeting as important as this—I'm still trying to wrap my hand around why they are having this gathering. It's my first time doing this with the Kiki you realize that," the priest said, yet every minute Ted and his soldiers spent waiting oddly on the men of Kiki was another minute the captain knew he would never get back. It was running late, and his lieutenants would vote for a spot in hell first before they'd ever agree to visit the ilu-Sango after sunset.

"Reverend, he is all but hidden from us. Tell them we need him so we can be on our way," Ted pushed impatiently.

"We can't afford to be rude, Ted, not after intruding," Reverend Benedict replied strictly and with an emboldened look for a man of the cloth, but good, the hunch over old disciple inched himself like a tortoise from where he'd been sitting to settle right by them. The Reverend eyed the captain enthusiastically, but then he and the old crow seemed to plummet into another eternity of misplaced dialogue, "he tells me it's something they call The Madness. Some kind of dis-ease. I suspect legless tears is a figure of speech for falling rains or the coming of a curse—but I think I'm failing to grasp fully what he's trying to say."

"I think I've heard enough," the captain retorted. "There is your translator. He's right beside you. Just ask the old man what it is these men in huts have to do with the other men in huts by the river and we'll be on our way. We've wasted enough time just listening to them yak already," the captain also said strictly, seeking to gravitate towards more self-preserving matters.

"I can't just interrupt, Ted," the reverend shot back, but now the captain rudely got on his feet, interrupting the assembly, as he put on his hat.

"I may or may not have promised the locals by the river," he said to the reverend, tipping his hat to cover his face, "but I want answers. So ask him if he would be willing to come with us to visit ilu-sango, since there's nothing left for me here. I will not ask again, Reverend," Ted threatened, and in like manner all of the captain's lieutenants exposed their magic sticks.

"And what do your boys intend to do with those, if I refuse?" Reverend Benedict fought back and Ted fingered for his lieutenants to conceal their muskets.

They were overly excited, that's all.

"Extend them my apologies. You can make it known that I sympathize with their afflictions, but you're our priest not theirs. Your first duty is to her Majesty's officers if you'd rather I reiterate, Reverend," Ted rejoined, closed to discussion. "Our security is what matters. It should come first."

"Very well." Father Matthew Benedict changed his tone of voice. "At least, try to be patient about it," the priest pontificated, and then stood up with the captain for cosmetic appearance. "Always try to be patient. If half the Kiki are upset about something grave, a disease or disaster of some sort, it would be of benefit to know."

They quit arguing and turned to the villagers who'd been gawking with unadorned faces. Ted couldn't repress a smile when the reverend hand-signalled his acquaintance, but rather than give them a reply the old man preferred to deliberate with his kinfolk.

"What are they saying?" the captain asked uneasily because it had been a noisy deliberation.

"I don't know. It was you who pushed."

The moment they reached a conclusion however, all the men pointed farther into the forest. Paul the Saint, like the slow tortoise he was, now got on his feet and crept towards deeper forests. He was to lead the way.

"Where is he going?"

"I think they want us to follow him."

"What about my men?"

"Inform them not to shoot anyone while we're gone," Reverend Benedict quipped a little heatedly before extending his gratitude to the men of Kiki for their assistance. As well as indulgence.

The men responded in kind.

The Captain also forged a smile in appreciation of their... whatever it was they intended to assist them with, and so they smiled back, beaming politely at him. Of them that did actually. He flagged down his officers but the boys on horses simply followed behind, irreverent to what anyone else thought.

"If you never take out time to understand the indigenous, it would surely come at a cost, Ted," the reverend mentioned as the hunched over old man bizarrely led them away into more forests.

"If I didn't know you as well as I do, Reverend, I'd assume you just threatened me. Just like the last time I detected a taint of sarcasm in your voice," Ted said blandly, "In my opinion, you're getting too involved with these aborigines. If you care to hear it."

The old man came to a halt before a small settlement of huts, and the captain grumbled, "what is this about? Why are we stopping?" but he was soon to find out why from the beleaguered look across the reverend's face.

Reverend Benedict spoke as succinctly as possible. "This is it."

"This is what?" Ted Book hadn't anticipated such a response.

"What they've been trying to tell us. The men of Kiki wanted us to see this—the river people, they are not the only ones counting their losses."

"What losses?" the captain asked warily, but not until he caught a whiff of it in the air and spotted what could be the grey putrefying remains of bird-eaten flesh sticking out from one of the endless number of huts did he realize he had his answer. The forest was dark, still too dark to tell, but it seems the old man had led them to the door of death. "You mean corpses?"

*E*lizabeth had exhausted her supplies of hygiene paper. Then and only then did she brace up and make her way to the infirmary. She found her apprentice sitting beside a pale lieutenant; he was obviously dead, his body set like marble and his veins becoming pastel blue. "When did he die?" she asked dryly, pointing at the soldier's lifeless body after spitting phlegm into her last wad of toilet paper.

"Sun come, man die," the nurse answered and got on his feet.

Drying her eyes by wiping them clean with the back of her hand, she sauntered to a collection of supplies atop the cabinets and selected fresh wads of hygiene paper for her nose. "Why didn't you come for me?" she asked and Un'ka opened his hands much in the manner of a shrug, though now exposing a thermometer.

His reply came in Bantu.

She took the apparatus from him and looked at the dishevelled cabinets. "Has the captain been here?" she asked, unfazed.

"No. No Captain. Only Father. Father come," he replied and Elizabeth bobbed her head.

"Father Matt."

She shuffled through the cabinets, doing some mundane reorganizing whilst searching for something—and continuing to search even if all she came up with were already prepared syringes and supply canisters. As well as a bottle of capsules she'd found enchanting (and though she'd hesitated at first, she downed a carefree pill before pocketing the entire bottle). She slammed the cabinets shut, still not having found it—whatever it was that she was looking for. Matulu made more room for her as she rambled her way about the medical tent, sorting through supplies, including the collection of medical apparatuses she'd only recently sacked through, but (finally) she found it! There it lay on the cabinet, being where it had always been if she had only opted to be calm about it. Or ask. She picked up the empty syringe and filled it with air before gesturing her hand over the stretcher towards the lower cots, "help me with him, Un'ka," she requested, and so the nurse saw to the hauling of the torso while Elizabeth struggled with those dead legs. They toppled Ted's dead lieutenant face down for the doctor to drive the syringe into the corpse, even as the air reluctantly passed into his veins. They upturned the corpse and Elizabeth requested Un'ka dress up the body, before sauntering out of the infirmary to tend to her other patient—the little boy who still had a chance at life.

rot. It was a sickening smell; a putrid odour every soldier knew too well, wholly unmistakable, even if the air was stale in such a dank inert forest. These were small isolated huts; huts a good distance away from the other huts and meeting spaces of the Kiki, but starkly for good reason, as they saw, sprawled foot atop foot of each other, putrid and bloated corpses almost whitewashed. Their once coal-black skins now a dull inhumane gray, possibly blanched out by the rains, as the stench of decay fought avariciously to cling to the air. The maggots had made a meal of the bodies. Lizards and birds had made a meal of the maggots, whilst rats and shrews made a meal of dead lizards and birds. The Kiki were dropping like flies and no one had buried the bodies, which came as no surprise to the captain cause why would anyone be willing to risk themselves?

"Virgin Mother," the reverend uttered, seeking out his rosary and symbolizing the cross the moment they had a proper glimpse of what was happening in this isolated arm of the forest.

"So this is The Madness they fear?" the captain pronounced, oblivious to anything else.

He approached the hut from a side, hiding his nose behind the lapel of his uniform. He could barely make out complete faces from any of the corpses in the hut. All their eyes were either closed or eaten, and mouths, or what looked like mouths, stayed open.

They stood there watching the bodies long enough for a handful of villagers, much younger men this time around, to catch up with them.

"—it's some kind of fever that kills," the reverend answered in horror.

"A fever? Is that what it's like?" Ted asked calmly, supposedly undaunted by this despite that they had never ever seen the like.

"I don't know."

"Of course you don't know, Reverend. It's why I want you to ask him."

The old man could tell the godskins were stunned because none of Ted's lieutenants came within 6-feet of the diseased huts. He hadn't expected them to be, but with the way they balked their horses, he knew they couldn't wait to leave.

One of Ted's lieutenants brought the captain his horse, but after having the captain's ear, Ted no longer desired an answer before turning his horse around. "My men say the wind has been blowing southwards for a number of days. I have to agree with them. We must leave, Reverend. And now," he cautioned. And so, more than eagerly, the captain and his boys trotted away, but Reverend Matthew tarried with the people to say a prayer with his rosary for the dead. Or dying. An act that broke something in the Kiki because they soon filled up with tears and came to touch him; touched in many ways by that one gesture. It seemed loss was a language they all understood.

After pacing past the Kiki market square, Ted realized he and his senior officers had left without the reverend. The Captain trotted back angrily, but with what could be the outbreak of an infection or onset of an epidemic at their doors, the captain's lieutenants let the captain go fetch the priest alone.

"Reverend, if this disease is airborne, then I fear your remaining here with the aborigines poses a threat to Her Majesty's commission," he said austerely, even if the priest's mind was elsewhere. Then again, so was his. Unsure who or what was next. "Reverend!!" Ted raised his voice, and immediately the priest returned to his senses. He gestured his leave, and so the Kiki allowed the priest to mount his horse.

By the time the away party returned to the fort, Ted's lieutenant had been dead for most of a day. The lieutenant had also been dressed up for the occasion, laying under a sheet, to make the corpse look warmer (as if only recently deceased) but that was hardly what worried the captain. Ted Book took off his hat, the oil lamps illuminating the grave expression slouched across his face and across the faces of his men. It flickered. A lot weighed down on his mind.

"How did he die?"

"An infection," Doctor Cambridge replied succinctly, sweat building underneath her armpits and inundating her blouse because she was surrounded by a curtain-wide audience of fire-breathing sympathizers. The medical tent was hot as ever, even for a breezy evening, and she cleaned her face using her brightly coloured neckerchief as Un'ka stood by her. He was between her and the reverend actually (the only two who cared for his presence anyway).

"What kind of infection?"

"Gangrenous. Possibly lymphatic," Elizabeth explained, "it was a deep wound. It must have spread through his system from there—long before we could do anything about it I'm guessing. The nodes by the heart would have given out as well. And there's no way he would have survived that."

The Captain had a look of askance. "So it was some kind of fever?" Ted asked but Elizabeth immediately launched a pre-emptive, sharp in cutting the captain off.

"I never said that. It is as you demanded, remember. Neither Matulu nor I brought that child into your sickbay. So don't go accusing anybody of anything. I won't stand for it!"

She was abruptly defensive, laying deliberate inflection on her satiric choice in pronouns, but the assault made the captain miss it. "A—Are you deliberately trying to s—stretch my patience, M—Ms—Miss Cambridge?"

Elizabeth stared him in the eye. "At times fever and delirium are symptomatic of an infection, but a fever isn't what killed him. An infection—that's what killed your lieutenant."

"How is that any different from what I just asked?"

Elizabeth sighed and refused to answer, writing it off as an offense to her intellect.

"Man sick, man die," Un'ka interrupted from where he stood, seeking to put an end to the ongoing argument, but an awkward hiatus punctuated the dialogue as the nurse drew attention to himself— hurting eyes Elizabeth had sought to keep away from the nurse.

Ted bit his lips, "and you want me to believe he had nothing to do with this—"

"Ted, I'm sorry this had to happen. He was one of yours and I can't begin to imagine the pain you feel," the reverend butt in, intending to break the ice and cut down on the stares, "but what I think the doctor is trying to tell us is your lieutenant sustained some kind of infection from the matchlock. It's not sterile as you know. Truth is, we've all had a long day, but with all this tragedy around us, for the sake of our Virgin Mother, let's not end it in unfounded accusations or pointing fingers at one another."

Ted was tense, but auspiciously the priest had been standing between the captain and the doctor. He stood silently while examining the three civilians closely, a stern unquantifiable lingering in his gaze.

"One of ours, Reverend."

"I beg your pardon?"

"He was one of ours, Reverend. On assignment here just like everyone else," Ted corrected tersely.

"Ah. Quite true. I apologize."

"I'm afraid we'll have to bury him tonight. Her ship won't be arriving till the quarter is nigh spent."

"—welcomed news," Elizabeth shot back, pouting her lips at the captain as he put his hat back on.

"I will set up immediately," Father Matthew fawned over the request.

Ted walked away, dismissing the onlookers when he did, so Elizabeth rolled her eyes for Un'ka to drop the draperies behind the captain.

The nurse had no hesitation in doing so.

"I'd best advise you and the captain learn to get along. I do not see the sense in the two of you having to put a knife to each other's throat every time," Reverend Benedict said placing a hand on the flustered doctor.

"He irks me, Father, that's why! Every bone in his body irks me. He just has this way of getting under your skin."

"Still you must learn to be patient with him. Like I am."

"Not everyone has the grace to be like you, Father," she rejoined before requesting Matulu ready the body in time for the caisson whenever Ted's officers felt ready to come for it.

"No. I meant like I am with you," Reverend Matthew chided her. "You have that same grace to be patient with him. We all have grace given to us. Even Un'ka is not far from that good Christian grace," the reverend said catching the attention of the nurse, "if he would give his life to Our Lord, that is. And I think it's good you teaching him a lot about our medicine. A handy catechist isn't bad at all. Did I tell you the Kiki know medicine as well? Paul shows a few of this and that, only his is of the crude sort—herbs and roots and so on—not refined medicine, but really helpful stuff."

Somehow, somewhere into all his talking, the priest had struck a seventh chord because Elizabeth jumped for joy, "you want to know something even better, Father?"

"What is it?"

"You're bound to see this later but come, I want you to see it now," she said, and led the priest by the arms down a very familiar path.

At the lodge, to an empty bed and abandoned clothes, they could no longer find the boy. The little boy they'd rescued barely a week ago. And since the reverend's lodge, which included the Mission

School, was a small one, it wasn't hard to conclude he was no longer in it. That was until Elizabeth spotted an agama slip through the bamboo woodwork, and so decided to pull the sheets from the reverend's bed to try out her little suspicion, but how the ebony child was able to cram his entire body into the little to no space underneath the priest's low-lying bed was remarkable!

The child was in hiding, holding onto himself, withdrawn and shy of stepping out. Not that Elizabeth could blame him, wherever he was from. So she took off her neckerchief and threw it to the boy under the bed; it was still perfumed from what was left of her washing powder, hopefully to put him at ease.

"Hello," she said to the face in the shadows, gesturing kindly to the child by stretching out her hand to him. "Come on," she beckoned.

Father Matthew got on his knees, but couldn't bend over (giving in to a sharp pain stemming from his waist). "Is he under there?" he asked and Elizabeth nodded. The priest waved his hands beneath the bed for the child to see, "hello there!" he greeted warmly only for the boy to drive further beneath the bed, away from his wizened white hands.

Elizabeth laughed. "You're not helping, Father Matt!"

Inching further under the bed to reach for the child

she called to him softly, trying to lure him to her, "come on. Are you afraid? We are not here to hurt you. You don't have to be afraid?"

"Actually, he does. As would any of us if we'd suddenly found ourselves in a strange apartment surrounded by strangers all of a sudden," Reverend Benedict remarked wittily and they both laughed.

"No, I nursed him. If at all, he should remember me."

The priest chose to rise and sit, sighing from the sting of arthritis in both knees, as both knees, he could have sworn, were on the verge of buckling under his weight.

The boy's bad leg had healed as with his cheeks. And since there was a chance the luminous strangers might have had something to do with the miracle of it, Taiwo decided to take the hand of the woman with shiny stones piercing her two ears.

Elizabeth cheered. The child had chosen to emerge only after he heard them laugh.

"See, that wasn't so hard," Elizabeth said with a friendly voice and eagerly pulled him out from under there.

The boy was naked.

She sat him on the bed and sought for a towel. Father Matthew handed her a yellow one. The child also seemed bled out, the cornea of his eyes whiter than chalk so she monitored his breathing because at one second he seemed with them, but the next minute, he was either staring away or staring straight through everything and everyone.

"He doesn't need you to dote over him to be able to tell he's hungry," the reverend observed, also noticing the child's purposeless gaze.

"He should be hungry. He's been asleep 3 days straight. He's also dehydrated," Elizabeth remarked, dousing the towel in water from a rusty metal bucket then cleaning the child's face. "I'm not sure what to offer our little guest. Unless you have something lying around that he could eat, Father?" she asked, half involved in the conversation.

"I don't have anything edible, but the communion loaf. It's the only thing I have in that iron locker beneath my altar stand."

Elizabeth looked to the locker covetously.

"There is a reason I have it in a locker, Liz. You are not actually thinking what I think you're thinking," Father Benedict warned.

"Oh no. That would be terrible. I'm a communicant," she lied, betrayed by her tone but the priest opted to trust her judgment. "Fortunately I still have yesterday's biscuit and that broiled fish served in the morning. The fish is dry and flaky, but he hasn't eaten in days, so I'm guessing he wouldn't mind," she said and smiled at the boy even if the boy refused to smile back. "I just hope the biscuits aren't too old. Or stale."

"We could always get food from the kitchen. Anytime in fact," Father Matthew suggested.

"That is if Captain High Horse allows."

"Stop making him to be a monster, Liz. Of course he'd allow," the reverend rejoined quicker than a catfish.

"Let's hope so, it's his kitchen, you know," she said, now searching for the clothes she had once put on the child (clothes Elizabeth had personally knit together from remnants of old clothes). When she found them and sought to put some pants back on the boy, the child slapped her hands right off. Father Matt chortled so hard, he caught a dizzy spell. It appeared the boy wouldn't allow her anywhere near his privates, now that he was fully awake.

Everything burned to ash, and he along with everything. Everything just fading, fading slowly and becoming nothing. It all burnt, and though it had been a dream, only a dream, the Holy Church considered recurring dreams less-than-ideal omens for priests. It was for that reason, Father Benedict got up earlier than usual that morning to pray at length and cite his rosary longer than he had ever said it. He couldn't remember the precise date when the dreams had started, but they had started quite some time ago. So the reverend prayed for the fort. He prayed for the captain and the captain's men as he'd been doing every day now for weeks. And today, as always, he didn't forget to pray for the captain to see reason.

"You know my position, Reverend. We've been over this several times, it's tiring," the captain said as he mounted his horse and then ordered his officers to open the gates. He was leaving the fort, again, and this time with a handful of officers. None of the seniors. Just the Khaki whites.

"Keeping us from interacting with the villagers isn't helping the Queen's commission, Ted," the priest said, "I haven't been able to follow up with what's happening with the people. Or my disciple. He's important. Your action puts a rift between us and them."

"Your old man is the least of our worries, if he isn't dead already," Captain Book mumbled. "I know my decision doesn't sit well with you, but I do my duty," he said with no compunction. "Besides, I allowed you and the doctor keep your kid despite my reservations about it. Didn't I?"

"I'm asking you reconsider, Ted," Reverend Benedict beseeched with hopeful eyes, "allow me to have either Paul or the children over."

Of the unused pile that had once occupied the marching grounds, only one of the wrought iron cages remained and the captain's boys loaded it into the caisson.

"I don't think there's anything more I can do. You're in my charge, Reverend. My order only stands a while. In time, you'd get your aborigines back. I don't understand the rush," the captain answered snappily as the conversation was swiftly losing its appeal, still the reverend wouldn't let up.

"It's been 3 months since you gave that order, Ted— and you obviously are doing whatever you want."

"Need I remind you that my dead lieutenant could easily have been you, Reverend?" the captain hammered in rejoinder, also intending it be rhetorical.

Still, as always, the reverend was adamant. Rooted to cause.

Ted's boys had secured the wrought iron slabs, so they spent the greater time of their time watching the captain and Reverend slug out this early morning tug of war from beyond the gates. The Captain looked down at the priest and his intractable shimmer of hope. He gave in. "Fine. Find how you can interact with the old man, Reverend, but I will not have him inside my fort—and there'll be no touching," he instructed, before nudging his horse and trotting after his men.

"And Elizabeth? I had thought she would be going with you?!" Reverend Benedict bawled after him.

The Captain caracoled his horse, stopping it just outside the gates, "the Lady might arrive late, but I'm hoping she's arrived already!" he responded after a lean smile, "tell the doctor, she won't be needing my escort. I'll have the men do it when I return. I'm sure she's primed and ready. Hell! I hear she's even packed!" the captain said before riding off with his men. The moment he'd left though, the dogs launched their farce of a growl. The Reverend had to leave the marching grounds for the dogs to cease barking. Luckily, it was the eve before Mass. Matthew Benedict was sure he'd find Elizabeth engaged in her new hobby at the infirmary.

lizabeth was nigh through her second trimester but had spent most of that time hiding behind a huge mechanical tripod. She had puffier cheeks, a protruding belly and podgy fingers. The breasts were a compliment, not that the priest could say, but not all the soldiers eased into the image of her being pregnant. Ted's men stayed as far away from the infirmary as they possibly could and seldom reported sick on account of avoiding the pregnant female. Or her mood swings. Aside the pique they'd nursed against her nurse and the little ebony boy she'd practically adopted into the fort. Inconveniences soon to be rectified if things were to continue as scheduled (the captain and his boys hardly able to wait for life in the fort to return to normalcy). On the other side of the mirror, Elizabeth felt she'd been painted Scottish blue and Irish gold, but as always, she was one to fight back.

The entire tent held an acrid scent when Father Benedict slipped in. The doctor had her glasses on, reading from the giant microscope whilst treating one of Ted's boys for an eye infection at the same time. Matulu stood her eyes and hands. Father Matthew pat the nurse fondly by the shoulder and the nurse directed the priest to the doctor seated at the far end of the infirmary, before flushing the eyes of a remarkably young officer with a squirt tube—a

face the reverend had thought he'd seen before—
only for the teen to be irritated by undissolved salt
in the water and smack the tube off Matulu. "You
don't have to blind me, you bloody aborigine!" he
mouthed off, and Elizabeth, a little frustrated to
take her eyes off whatever she had been working on,
was pushed to threats and witty remarks. The little
man reluctantly lay back down for another saltwater
washing, only this time she'd requested Un'ka
utterly dissolve the salts in a language more familiar
to the nurse.

The Reverend made his way down the tent, past the
cots, stretchers, collapsible tables and cabinets to the
doctor. She had a red keg beside her, a tin-plated
can by her microscope, and mangoes of different
ages on her table (a mango with pits, an originally
green one, and a squashy yellow one).

"Is that kerosene, Liz?" the reverend wiggled his
nose.

"Yes, Father," she answered, not taking her eyes off
the massive cell microscope. "Matulu tells me it
keeps the mosquitoes at bay."

The Reverend moved his ears about for the resident
humdrum of a buzz that eternally dogged the ears,
"does seem to be working, but the smell is just
awful."

She tittered. "A smidgeon of hell in every slice of
heaven. We can't have it all good, Father."

"I know what you mean. You know I just finished speaking with Ted. Why aren't you dressed—"

She took her eyes off the microscope for a second. "This is more than fascinating, Father Matt," Elizabeth responded mindlessly, not having intended usurping the words of the priest mid-tense. "The child's blood cells are very different from the ones we know—even Matulu's." There was a broad smile across her face. "It's crescent-shaped! Very peculiar. This is quite the sample," she stated gaily, delving back into her intriguing world of lenses in lens. "I dare say that all the indigenous people have this blood anomaly. A simple hypothesis will be they respond to illnesses differently to the way we do."

"A noble find then," the priest chimed and could only mould a smile in response to whatever she meant, "still I have to say you don't look at all ready for one who's leaving for the mainland today. Or are you deliberately trying to miss the ship, Elizabeth?"

"No. Of course not. I certainly don't want to miss the ship, Father," she responded as she tore her eyes off the microscope yet another second. "Quite the reverse, I can't wait to share my find with those in London. Imagine the implications for medicine. This fundamental difference in cell structure may well be the reason the child didn't die from that illness. I assure you, Father, they'll be itching to come here," she announced, only to encounter phlegm in her

190

mouth and cough it up into the tin can on the table. Her phlegm reeked. A separate odour all on its own. "You needn't worry—I've packed my things, Reverend. Matulu and I are ready."

"Doesn't look that way," the priest mumbled, resting tenuously against one end of the collapsible table. "I might be old and slowly losing my wit, but I think you want to stay, Liz."

"You want to know the truth, Father? Truth is I'm not so sure myself," Elizabeth answered from the corner of her mouth, "at first, I couldn't wait to leave. I was just plain sick of this fort—the rumours and the hypocrisy, it's sickening, but now, I don't think I should leave this." She sat up straight and unhooked the slide she was working on from the microscope. It held a cotton spread stained with blood. A dry blood sample.

The priest found her dilemma amusing. "Is that's Tony's blood?" he asked.

"Yes. It's the child's blood sample," she answered animatedly, showing off the slide like a work of art. "His cells aren't elliptical like ours. They are more like sickles!"

"Well, this is a new continent. New things don't come as a surprise," Father Matthew said with blasé curiosity then reaching for a mango in the long lull that followed. "Where is Tony anyway?"

"Right here," Elizabeth answered and leaned back for the priest to see the native child squatting by her feet. She tapped Father Matthew's hand on his choice of mangoes, the squashy yellow mango, offering the priest the greenish red one instead.

"Paul the Saint's coming over. Ted finally agreed," Father Matthew swanked and bit into the pulpy aromatic fruit of the tropics. Its insides one of virgin yellowness.

"He finally let up?—that's a victory for you, Father Matt. It's a shame I wouldn't be staying for the welcome party being that this loaded female is heading for the Cape today," Elizabeth said and they both shared a moment laughing. "All I know for certain is I'll miss you. You've always tried to make me feel at home," she added, tearing herself off the microscope—and for the very first time today, the reverend father had her undivided attention.

Demons they were. Yes, that's what they were. No match for mangy dogs. These beings, whatever they were, scattered their pack of hunting dogs as a man would scatter flies. And like mongrels themselves, homed in for the kill. Vicious, unappeasable, strategic, and mostly unseen. Only heard. A flurry of huffs and pulses of lightning always heralding their hunt. As well as that iron insatiable appetite for flesh that dogged the air. They could feel their thirst. A thirst to draw blood. First blood. The gods of the Ilu-Sango must have tipped the day on its head for the hunters were now being hunted (despite that they were strong men). Experienced warriors with sharpened machetes. Men blindsided and hunted by something. The ill-fated. It was certain the Loas had turned their backs on them, being so unfortunate to have chanced upon the lonely bush path to hell, for faster than the rustle of leaves about them and louder than the hooting of the monkeys overhead, they declined in number—the birds fluttering away each time the odds were stacked against them. The heart of their very own forest had given them up, betraying their trust by misleading and tearing them from the protection of each other. She'd become a terrifying place to be as unseen eyes watched them. Covetous eyes. Possessory eyes. Unseen even when the demons came for them. And now, having been torn asunder, knowing they were no longer capable of banding together, the hunters of Ilu-Sango were left to their rogue imaginations. Only one of them outlived the assault, one of them surviving the demented sardonicism of the Loas, the only hunter blindsided by a sturdy branch emerging from the flank of his bad eye. Makanjuola had remained unconscious through the rest of the harrowing ordeal, his very life saved by his bruised eye.

o outsiders allowed. Captain Ted Book wasn't around the fort, but his order stood tall, as tall as the gates and the gauze fence, as a light drizzle wet the fort, welcoming the afternoon and doing what it could to help the sun fight off dusty harmattan winds. As well as mosquitoes.

The Reverend's visitor had come with the children from Kiki, Osate, Eno, but also with an unknown man about half his age; their approach hailed by the tirade of dogs in dog cages, offering death threats the best way dogs knew how.

"Virgin Mother! You came," Reverend Benedict spoke aloud, lighting up on spotting the old villager on the other side of the perimeter looking fit as ever. As were the kids (Osate still slaving under his deformity). The priest reached through the fence to rub the children's heads, beaming with excitement, "and to think I doubted your wellbeing. May She forgive my lack of faith."

Elizabeth Cambridge and Un'ka Matulu came up the marching grounds with their travel boxes, and the little boy they named Tony also helped with the luggage and Matulu's water bag. Queerly, the dogs quieted their barking, choosing to growl as a pool of strangers gathered on both sides of the wire fence.

Now being that none of Ted's senior officers were

up in the outlook today, the reverend sought to seize the opportunity to be decent. The priest called to the one man in Khaki shorts he could spot on high to allow the visitors in, and though the officer stalwartly refused, he later conceded to allowing just the children in. The creepy aborigines should remain outside, and at arm's length— those had been the captain's orders (so as it stood, he'd already stretched those orders thin). The soldier now turned away resolutely, never again to bargain with his soul, as a conversation of gestures now dragged between the priest and the old man. A conversation that left the priest somewhat agitated in the end.

"What's going on?" Elizabeth asked, half concerned as she dropped her bags by the priest.

"He tells me the children wouldn't be coming to the fort anymore. Not after this," the priest answered.

"Well that's not good," she chirped as she counted the travel bags to make sure they were of the right number, now mumbling something to Matulu, who also was dressed in expedition clothes (the very same clothes he'd arrived at Fort William wearing endless weeks ago). "Is it the captain's orders they remain outside?"

"Yes. Paul the Saint tells me it's a living hell out there. They had thought the dry season would help, but it isn't helping," the priest answered mechanically, his lips near dry and shedding (as with everyone else's) but that was due to the disparate change in seasons; Africa's harmattan being austere weather, cold, deprived of moisture, and full of dust.

"Have they come to say goodbye then?"

"Don't know."

"You were expecting something like this to happen. Maybe if we tell them we never truly abandoned them, they might see things differently," she advocated but the priest had become a talking drum, never paying any real attention to her. Or even himself. His mind was already a village or two away, lost, and restless with the villages of the Hill. A people sacked by disease. So Elizabeth turned to Matulu and informed the nurse he'd have to face his demons at the gates since they needed Ted's soldiers to release one or two horses for their trip to the docks. She turned her attention to Eno and Osate after that, as the children rushed to her from within the gates, lunging at them affectionately, having missed them this whole time. She took Osate by his slick oily hair and helped handpick all the foreign particles she could find lodged inside Eno's cornrows—that was until she discovered some of the flaky stuff to be dandruff.

She was already feeling forlorn almost like she was abandoning them (and also like she was missing something). Ah! Yes. The dogs. Strangely, the dogs were no longer barking (at them or at the visiting children), an almost impossible respite, but one much welcomed. A fuller awareness had dawned on Elizabeth, it also happened to be the time she truly took note of the other man on the other side of the fence. The eerie old man had in his company another man. A much different man in age and build. A man eerily unknown to her. A man that had never been to the fort before (for no one had come to visit the fort outside the old man) whilst her stay here, but there he stood fixated on her. Or looking her way. He was lucidly muscular, looking fit and almost unstoppable, like he could snap her dear nurse (who before now had been the strongest man she knew) in half as he would a matchstick, and wearing a distinguishing belt of cowries about his forehead. She watched him closely and the glare reflecting off his bold walnut irises. It was enough to give her the shivers. "Who's he?" she asked the priest from a side of her mouth. "His son? I don't see the resemblance."

"I don't know, but Paul has no sons. They must be fighting the plague together, I think," Father Matthew answered hastily, fumbling in his deep pockets for his rosary. The priest more perturbed than she was used to.

Elizabeth panicked on remembering these indigenes were sick, "Oh my! I forgot about that. Do you think it was wrong allowing the children in?" she mentioned, sampling the eyes of the children and gesturing for them to open their mouths (a tad anxious if it was wise she remain standing so close).

"They sort of look all right to me," Father Matt inferred, but Elizabeth had to rest her palms against their foreheads and napes to test their temperatures before she could relax.

"Well, their temperatures are fine. The children seem fine. Are you sure this disease isn't just a debilitating man-thing?" she surmised.

"I don't know. I never thought to check, but if he says the villages are being overrun by it, it probably means women and children alike. It bothers me Ted wouldn't allow me leave so I can go see for myself," the priest answered sadly at around the time Un'ka returned. As Elizabeth had anticipated, the nurse returned without a horse.

"Just how broad a reach is this—" She had barely begun speaking when Father Benedict reached behind her for Tony, but the little boy wouldn't come to the priest. More curious, was how he had kept his distance from the other ebony children who'd come to be with Elizabeth. She hadn't noticed it before but it was almost as if their Tony had erected an invisible wall just to be away from her other kids. He even flinched upon Father Matt's touch, even when Father Matt caressed him. Even more puzzling was when the priest made their request known to the old man across the fence, the old man and his muscular companion grimaced at the child. Or at least that was what it looked like they did. That alone had been less than comforting.

"He says he will not take the boy," Father Matthew announced sadly, his response coming a second ahead of her asking. "He's adamant he will not."

"That puts a dent in our plans, doesn't it Father—" Elizabeth had responded, hoping to express some disappointment and not express her newly found relief, but then a sharp prick broke her lips and the ferric taste of her blood seemed to trickle from it. She reached to find both lips desiccated by the harmattan dryness, but after moistening them up with saliva she brokered, "you could ask the captain. Don't you think there's something he can do?"

"Outside the mission school, no."

"But why?"

"It'll be asking too much of Ted. Not after you're gone," Father Benedict declined calmly, only now getting to observe how the little boy they'd rescued shied away from the other kids and the village men on the other side of the fence. A very curious thing. More curious to the priest, was how all the visitors had been staring right back at the boy; like they knew something about him, but he decided against jumping into conclusions. Not just yet.

"that's poppycock if it's the right thing to do—and

he should know it. It can't end like this, not having kept him with us these past months," Elizabeth hissed. "I certainly can't take him along otherwise I would've, so we'd never have needed ask."

Father Matthew held Elizabeth by the shoulders, and when their heads almost touched, said to her, "our Lord always looks kindly on those with a loving heart, Liz. I want you to remember that, but if you're looking for someone to blame, blame me. Not the captain. I should have known better. I should have searched out his origins when we found him. It was the right thing to do despite Ted's orders. Now I think we only served to make things worse for this chil—" the priest decided to kill the subject. He didn't want her worrying. "Let's look at what we can actually do, shall we? Do we have any supplies, medical supplies, that might be of assistance? It's the least Christian thing we can do to help them."

"I understand father, but as long as we don't know what this plague is they're up against, all I can offer is blind relief. Besides, the quarter's ended and the supplies we came with are nigh depleted, so it now boils down to you or them," Elizabeth said with a disheartened voice, "hopefully the replacement medic will arrive with enough supplies to last the next quarter, but it's still in the captain's hands and I don't see him having a Christian heart on this one," she said, looking down at the children and feeling helpless.

Father Benedict embraced her as he would his daughter. If he had had any.

"I know the children are fine, so whatever this may be it's not airborne. Maybe not even a contagion," she said as three of Ted's junior officers interrupted them with two spare horses in their possession. The Captain's men stood aloof of the aborigines, but they needn't the captain's orders to do that.

"We could stay?" she offered, now looking to Matulu but the nurse didn't look too pleased. "Okay. Only I should stay then," she rephrased.

"I don't think you can. The three of us are to be your escort, doctor," one of the captain's men chipped in. He was the pursiest of the three in Khaki shorts. "As soon as the captain gives us the go ahead," another said while making a weird face at the children, probably intending it be funny. It wasn't and she drew them even closer to herself, before waving off the bores.

"They're right. You have a baby to think about, Elizabeth. You can't afford to take ill. Not in your delicate condition. And we both know Ted can be as hard as a rock, especially over matters as these," Father Matt admitted expressly, so now it seemed she was on the verge of crying.

"If it will do any good, you can offer them the three packs of pain killers in the fourth cabinet. I also left some ginger roots at the sickbay. It's on the table. I haven't steamed them yet. You need to tell them they'll have to get that done with heated water or ale before they can use it," she said, but on looking at the officers and their smirks she expunged the wetness in her eyes, "the way I see it, some people can get through the day without those."

By now the light drizzling had seized and so the notorious harmattan winds resumed, chilling out whatever warmth functioned of the noonday sun.

"That may help, but the Kiki are naturalists. I'm certain they have more roots than we could give them," Father Matthew said and edged his eyes beyond her shoulders. There was that portentous glare in the eyes of the other man in Paul the Saint's company. The visitor was glowering at the child in his arms, as would a predator, almost ready to pounce. "If I am to return Tony, I'll need to know how to do that," the priest said as he tried walking the eleven year old closer to the fence, but the child shrivelled at being pushed towards the visitors, resisting the reverend with latent force.

"It's okay. I'm here. It's okay," Father Benedict said to ease the boy, still he resisted, actually looking distressed.

"He won't move," the reverend said to Elizabeth and Ted's officers sniggered, but no one had found the humour amusing.

They decided to leave then. "We'll wait by the

gates," they'd said while leaving with the horses.

Elizabeth left Osate and Eno in the hands of Matulu to place her hands tenderly across Tony's shoulders, squatting to match the child's height, "What's the matter? Don't worry. It's all right," she said to him, unable to determine if she was truly getting across, but even while she spoke the Kiki couldn't take their eyes off this boy. It got her upset. "Why are they gawking at him like that?" she complained. "Eno? Osate? What's wrong?"

"I've been pondering over that for a while now."

"Come to think of it Father, I don't think leaving him in their care would have made a good idea after all. We don't even know why the child came to us in the first place."

"That's if he came to us, Liz."

"I don't understand what you mean? In the least, we should return him to who truly owns him, right?" she rejoined, a lot of concern in her voice, so Father Benedict communicated with the old man. It was about time he made a conversation of it. Now when Father Matt finally convinced the hunched over old man to speak with the child, despite that the boy was reluctant to speak back, the old man's voice sounded terse—even for such a discordant dialect.

In the meantime, all this waiting had made Matulu tired, so the nurse gave his legs a rest by sitting on one of the steel boxes. He offered Elizabeth the other steel box, but she declined, her attention focused on the encrypted dialogue between the old man and the young child. Even as the dialogue went back and forth, and aroused interest when Tony was forced to show the palm of his hands to the old man, she still felt uneasy.

"Ask what's going on?" she said to the priest, but Father Matt advised against interrupting.

The child now raised both hands against the fence. The look across the old man's wrinkled face was one familiar to Elizabeth, one the doctor had come to recognize from a sour experience a number of months ago. His face, aside the frown, had displeasure written all over it.

"What is it?" she requested, and now even Father Benedict would like to know, but when the priest requested to know what had his visitors dissatisfied or displeased, the old man refused responding to any of Father Matt's humble gesturing. The only person the old man spoke with was his muscular companion (for he too wore a frown).

"Is something wrong? Will you tell us if we have done anything wrong?"

"He's ignoring you, Father Matt. I don't have to understand Kiki to know something's not right here," Elizabeth said flat out.

Bizarrely, the oily haired boy and the girl with cornrows tore away from her and hurried to the gates; a silent command given to them from the eyes of the strange man in the old man's company. Elizabeth hadn't even noticed the vile scarification edging his lips (the scar being of the same colour to his skin tone) only deflecting light when caught at the right angle.

Ted's officers let the children outside the gates with pleasure. The moment they joined the outlandish aborigine outside the fort, they left. The old man on the other hand had shared a conundrum of syllables before he departed, pointing his fingers at Father Matt, in the likeness of a warning, "Taiwo, ilu-sango, omo ale," he said, words or syllables that didn't make any sense to Elizabeth.

"What just transpired?" she asked, flummoxed, turning to Matulu in curiosity, but the nurse never cared.

"They took the children," Father Matt answered, his confusion also evident, which had her all the more worried.

"Why?"

"I think it's their way of trying to tell us keeping the boy will bring us no good. The child is an outcast from a tribe west of the Hill," he said, pointing in the general direction of the forest-laden hill.

"A west tribe? But I've only heard you and the captain talk of two villages by the Hill."

"There is a third village. Ted and John are the only ones ever to have had any kind of contact with them. They seldom visit it. It's more than a day away." Father Matt turned to speak with the child, but every time he called to the child saying Taiwo, the child responded by saying, "Taye."

"I guess we know now what he wants to be called," Elizabeth acknowledged, but the priest's thoughts grew distant.

"This child came a long way. Only God could have seen him through that distance because I don't think he intended to come here," the reverend said as he handed Taiwo his very own rosary. The child accepted the strange beads with fascination, even if they couldn't understand each other.

"What do you think omo ale means, Father?" she asked curiously, now parroting the hunchback.

"I think it means outcast," Father Benedict answered. "He means to tell us this boy is an outcast. That we are wrong to keep what his gods have cursed—" the priest tried to explain, but Elizabeth wouldn't let him finish.

"that's poppycock! You really don't believe a word of that Father, do you?" she asked (without really wanting to know). "Asinine poppycock!"

Ted's officers had watched what had transpired from the gates. Although they had been too far away to eavesdrop into anything that maybe of use to the grapevine, the captain's men were of the opinion a lot more had transpired than what they had seen.

"Poppycock!"

Captain Book returned with nothing. Save his adventure horde and a sullen mood, he returned with absolutely nothing. The gates were locked down after their return by the Khaki shorts on sentry duty; for dusk was tricky in Africa, the darkness having a-not-so funny way of sneaking up on people. The Captain had dirt on his uniform, so he took off his uniform and suggested the bathroom to all the officers that had gone with him. Predictably, Reverend Benedict popped out of the woodwork (over his concerns for the pregnant female, no doubt), the priest eager to know what, why and when since Elizabeth, and her nurse, who'd been scheduled for a ship were supposed to be circumnavigating the continent by now, but Ted fleered, looking to the evening sky for signs of rain. It was to be a moonless night, dry of clouds and moisture. The welfare of the doctor and her nurse was the least of his worries.

"Ted, your boys didn't do as you instructed them to do," Reverend Benedict said fiercely, heading in a bee-line for the captain's horse.

"I wonder why you would say that Reverend," Ted responded as he got off his horse, a rejoinder unadorned in sarcasm.

"Cause Elizabeth is still here," he advocated, pointing towards the kitchen by Elizabeth's quarters.

"I know that. Not to worry Reverend. They did what I told them," Ted admitted, removing the harness from his horse and giving it one of his officers who'd handed him an oil lamp to help with the swiftly approaching night. The reverend stood by, handicapped by the captain's shadowy response. The Captain also took off his undershirt because it reeked, half-drenched in sweat. "See to it the men bathe like gentlemen before meal," he mumbled to the officer who'd come to help him with the horse before the officer took the horse away. "The Lady never came, Reverend. The Niger must be running low or something, I don't know."

"They will be disappointed. Do you think tomorrow?" Reverend Benedict asked and the captain shrugged, calling for a bottle of water and something to eat. Another officer within earshot of the captain offered his drinking bottle. Ted squirted the water against his face before heading for his bamboo quarters (Ted's quarters was the one structure literally keeping the chapel from sharing the same grounds with the Senior Officers' cabin, and all five of Ted's lieutenants were thankful for that). "How long do you suppose it will take before the tide is high enough to allow them in?"

"Depending on how long these spells last, I can't say—believe me, I am the one disappointed, Reverend," he said and then cursed away from the reverend's ear.

Reverend Benedict pointed again towards the darkness now enshrouding the kitchen; darkness now enshrouding the entire fort. "Elizabeth's been waiting all day, Ted. I won't be surprised if she's fallen asleep or retired to—"

"Let's pray tomorrow brings better news, Reverend," Ted cut in. It was already night time and he was just too tired to be bothered about what she thought, but soon enough they heard scuffling and then the collapse of the bamboo kitchen; the only makeshift kitchen in the fort.

D esperate times call for desperate measures. With over a hundred people dead or dying, this couldn't wait, as those sinewy arms came at him from within the shadows. With what felt like stones wedged around his throat, Matulu heaved and struggled, trying to stay conscious whilst fending off the suffocating squeeze. While groping and flailing with his one free hand, the nurse found his unseen attacker had very short hair. He was also sweating, but for a person who was breathing so heavily down his neck, his assailant's body was cold and dry. As cold and dry as rubber. The kind of dryness one only gets after washing up at the officer's bathroom. Or going for a swim. Either way, he hadn't the time to ponder who his assailant was given those sinewy muscles were in the way of his breathing. The man had pinned Matulu against the ground, leaving the nurse with only two options before he died; either to dig for dirt or grab for hair, whichever made sense (for whether the nurse chose to face death or not this was soon to be over), so the nurse uprooted the man's hair even if that didn't do a thing to tame the beast—whoever this beast of a man was. But then, just when those big stone biceps of his were starting to grind the life from Matulu's body, something in that dark soulless night grazed Matulu by the foot and so quickly working both feet to push the object into his free hand, the nurse sent the tin-plated can flying into his assailant's face and the man groaned. Matulu's relief lasted for three seconds. For three seconds, the nurse reeled back from the jaws of death. A release that felt heavenly, but wasn't enough, for as would a fly to rot, his assailant bounced back from within the shadows, also sending the sharp can flying into Matulu's face. The nurse grunted but then charged like a crazed goat, aiming his arms loosely for a blind target (eventually driving both him and whoever his arms could grapple against the kitchen's bamboo walls), which is why the kitchen's bamboo skewed and then collapsed, the entire wooden structure falling on its side and making a ruckus. Opportunely, a little nail edged from the exposed woodwork and did a good job of lacerating the assailant (a little vengeance on behalf of the fort), but now he went buck-crazy and astoundingly landed Matulu flat against the ground.

With the tin can weaponized in his hands, he straddled the nurse beneath the behemothic impression of his weight, seeking to uncap Matulu's skull when the captain found them. Ted dislodged almost half the man's throat with gunpowder and he fell limp to the ground, ever before the reverend could come around.

"You killed him!" the reverend exclaimed, seeking to aid the nurse to his feet, but the nurse looked traumatized and refused to get up, recovering his breath and reaching for the murderous tin can. His head ached like it'd collided with the axle of a coconut. Upon getting a closer look at the body, the reverend realized he'd seen this corpse before—when it still was a person actually. "And what if he turned out to be one of yours?" the reverend asked rhetorically as the captain went on to stamp out a small fire.

"He wasn't mine. Any of mine would have ended the Bantu with a shot to the head. You know him?" Ted asked coolly, shifting to pressing concerns. He towered over the dead man's muscular build with the lamp, "he's wet," the captain announced, noticing how the earth clung to the intruder's body, "bloody bugger. Must've swam upstream."

"Yes I know the man, but I know him only because he was here today," Reverend Benedict confessed cautiously, before speaking kindly to Matulu trying again to get him up on his feet, but the nurse staggered, still disoriented and queasy.

Ted called and the Edison bulbs flickered on. The lights unveiled the full ruckus. The scuffle had taken up most space as the doctor and the nurse's luggage had been splayed about the place, but now the reverend panicked.

"Un'ka, where is Elizabeth?" was the next thing he demanded from Matulu, but the nurse was of no help; he could only look towards the sickbay, trying to prevent his regnant migraine from downsizing whatever was left of his memories.

The sirens hit and Ted's small army responded, his younger officers lagging only a few seconds behind, as the search began, everyone searching for the doctor, including the captain, who eventually found her passed out just outside the infirmary—her neck collapsed in a very unsettling posture.

The Reverend, on the other hand, and all by himself, encountered Taye also passed out inside the infirmary, but with his hunched over fledgling disciple clutching tightly to the boy.

"This is you? Why Paul?" Reverend Benedict intoned dejectedly, but there was that eerie expression upon the old Kiki's face, as eerie as the bizarre necklace he strung around his neck, and one from which he'd hung a snail (a living moving snail). "Stop this, Paul. Don't relive your mistakes. He is only a child," Reverend Benedict spoke softly and from the heart because the old man was in possession of a large cooking knife; the metal knife morbid and shimmering in the yellow light from the lamps. The child had been dotted from head to foot, ritualized in ink—was it ink or was it oil? Well, it looked like ink under the illumination of the oil lamps. Still the Kiki had a wild look in his eye. One portending something evil. One the priest had never seen before.

"You call this your disciple?" Ted interrupted, making his way through the cotton drapery to find the old man bent over the boy. In a rhythm, the captain's officers busted through the draperies armed with flintlock muskets, now seeming a good time as any to use them, "and what in hell is that crawling up his neck?"

"It's a—it's a charm from his old religion," Reverend Benedict answered glumly.

"—he doesn't appear to be your fledgling anymore, Reverend," the captain remarked on noticing the steel knife in the old man's hand; its stainless steel reflecting off his will to harm the child, but the captain must admit for a people diseased, and a man who would have easily outmatched the age of his father, the hunched over old Kiki was strong, looking all the more menacing now grappling a cataleptic boy in his arms. A stark contrast to Ted's father. A man who had battled acute arthritis and senility before his passing.

"He's harmless, Ted."

"That's not what I see. I see blood. That crawling snail of his is dipped in blood—whose blood is it because I don't see a cut on the boy," the captain stated guardedly. "You caution him. Tell him to put the bloody knife down, and slowly, or he will regret it. I swear," Ted warned. Or threatened.

"I said he's harmless, Ted," Reverend Benedict repeated himself, "he's not going to do anything rash."

"Then why the hell is he in my fort wielding a bloody knife, Reverend?" the captain retorted impatiently, blowing down against the sweat building abroad his breasts because with all the lamps lit the medical tent felt as close to hell as he had ever gotten. Even with his shirt off.

"Whatever it is you think you are doing, Paul, it's not right. Believe me, the Lord doesn't want you to do this," Reverend Benedict beckoned, insidiously inching to retrieve the knife from the hand of his convert. The old man grunted instead, edging the cooking knife against the boy's throat and forcing the reverend to back up more steps than he'd previously gained.

There was now barking outside as one of the captain's lieutenants freed one of Her Majesty's dogs and enters the tent with it on leash. It notched the tension up a few degrees.

"He's frightened, Ted. Could you tell your boys to lower their rifles? I don't want him to hurt the boy," the reverend appealed, breathing heavily now. A little sweat breaking through his bald.

"I don't care about the welfare of your children, Reverend. What I care for is the safety of my men, and your safety. So tell your deranged disciple if he doesn't lower the knife, I don't care how long he's been a friend to this fort, I'll be forced to put him down," the captain answered, as the tent turned into a new world of agitative barking, bragging and growling.

Still, despite the noise coming from the dog, everyone noticed the child hadn't woken up. In fact, having had enough time to strip the child off his clothes, dot him up in blood and what smelled like a palm wine solution, there was whispering that the child was probably dead and this deadlock was a waste of time.

"Please," Reverend Benedict pleaded with them to

be a little more patient, and for an instant, just then, there seemed to be a trace of reservation in the old man's eyes. Father Benedict sought to seize the advantage and beckoned him for the knife, but all he received from the Kiki was a sign of four fingers—a form of numerology among the villagers signifying what was to be a basic offering. Or ritualized killing.

The Reverend heart skipped a beat.

"What is he saying?" Ted asked, his officers itching for some action, when the reverend, against his better judgment, made a poor attempt for the knife, but Paul the Saint slit the child by the throat long before the priest could get to him.

Now almost on impulse, as if on hormones or the smell of blood, the dog in the tent snapped its leash and zeroed in on the only perceivable threat within the periphery of its vision. It tackled the old man, taking him down and there was nothing Ted or any of his officers could do to stop the animal. Nor did they seem to want to. In fact, all they did was bicker with the reverend after that.

ted quaffed down the aperitif and moved on to the bread. The Captain wasn't apologetic in voice, or tone, but that didn't stop the reverend from requesting the impossible. "You want me to unbind him and let him go? Of everything you've ever asked of me, Reverend, why

would I do a crazy thing like that?" the captain belly
-laughed, nibbling the bread and sifting through his
pottage. Ted ignored the potatoes.

"I can't say I understand what has happened to him,
but what I can say is that man strung up out there is
not the man we used to know. Please Ted. It's a very
delicate time for them right now. I know I'm asking
for a big hand here, but we can't risk another strain
in our relationship with the villagers. You know
that."

The Captain's cabin was the only lodge to have
proper dining space; it was a skeletal tent propped
by eight bamboo pillars and a curtain of brown
drapes that separated the captain's more personal
living space from this place. It had one oil lamp
burning brilliantly at the centre of a very long table
made by nailing mangrove bamboo together (a table
for the captain and the captain's men whenever the
evening calls for it).

Ted aimed his fork at a soaked potato. "He was this
close to killing one of your children, Reverend," the
captain demonstrated with the fork before snorting,
"I guess that's what I get for selling knives to
aborigines."

Still, in the face of what was said, the reverend held
his compassionate stance, so Ted stopped eating. He
wasn't so sure he was getting across, "that man
you're so keen on protecting, Reverend, poisoned

your doctor—our doctor! A woman with child! Yes! He did that. Even attacked her apprentice—a man who could have passed as his brother, as you might say. Doesn't that strike you as odd? Hmm? So if you think for one second I'm going to trust a man who betrayed every trust you placed in him when he snuck into our fort, then damn it Reverend!" the captain bellowed, one straw short from losing his temper. The priest was always so forgiving (and to an irritable fault!) so he chose not to look the reverend in the eye when he tumbled the words out, "all these years I condoned these visits on behalf of your pet elephant project and the fact that the Brigadier saw some use for it. Only for him to learn our weakness and exploit it! That's what I see! I don't know why you can't see that—it's bloody frustrating!"

Reverend Benedict stomached the curse words. Ted was upset and rightly so. He could understand that. "He's delirious and could be sick. At least don't leave him out like that all night. It's cold," the reverend pushed and so the captain combusted like flash fire, having had enough of putting up with all this religiosity. Within seconds he was on his feet, "this insouciant obstinacy is what has brought this on all of us! You just said it. We could be sick. All of us. It's the B connecting your nose, Reverend, and you can't see it! Let it go!! If you do not learn to see beyond your compassion here we are all dead! Tell me Reverend, what's to stop your old friend from amassing the aborigines and killing us all? They outnumber us a hundred to one!"

"You're blowing this out of proportion, Ted."

"Am I?" he questioned. "Having a stranger swim upstream and worm his way into my fort with not one of my men noticing is blowing it out of proportion? That was just one man, Reverend, but not any of my men noticed him. Not even one!" The Captain snapped his fingers, "he can have you dead just like that and I'll be powerless to stop him. Oh, it's the real him all right. Your disciple knows what he is doing!" Ted said, taking his seat again and slowly returning to his meal, "—that's if he was ever your disciple. I'm sorry you can't see that, Reverend," he mumbled. The Captain wasn't diffident. Nor had he sounded like it. "I'm trying to keep us safe. I can't believe you'd even ask that."

"I know you do all you can, Ted," the reverend said evenly, exiting the captain's quarters without another word. Whatever crisis was going on with his neophyte was just too hard to elucidate without having the captain undertake the full fourteen years it takes to become a priest.

"The men stay at my orders," the captain said after the priest, shaking his head in congruity. "The men stay," he repeated, affirming his stand in case he hadn't said enough. Just in case.

Since the Edison bulbs had to go off sometime, the captain's men tied the intruder to a stake in the clear of the marching grounds, only then did they leave him in the guard of three men. Still the men built a fire before the sneaky bastard because Africa's harmattan was ruthless and unforgiving at night (they'd been counting on that) and it didn't disappoint as the harmattan engulfed the entire forest in a dutiful haze, but also because they were optimistic the Kiki would survive the night since these people rarely die when you want them to, and so a bonfire burning brightly cocksure made him less of a threat.

"How did it go?" Elizabeth asked slowly, scooting to a side to create room for the priest as he came to join them by the big fire. The doctor was all wrapped in a thick woollen blanket; a mug of hot tea in one hand and three of Ted's Khaki shorts by her other.

Joining the handful of men camped around the fire, the priest felt his heart twitch as he strained to sit. "Ted's a bit unnerved that's all," he answered optimistically, and turned to examine the dart wound she'd sustained by the nape, "how's the neck?" he asked and she smiled weakly. Some of it, whatever the old man had given her, was slow in wearing off and still in her system.

"See. The men made me tea," she cooed, showing off the mug, her voice a little off pitch.

"That's nice," Father Benedict answered, watching Ted's boys shuffle away from her and ease into blankets of their own (now that he was around).

"Does it hurt?" he asked her, making conversation and she scratched the prick beside her neck.

"No, but it itches. Don't worry father I'm fine."

Father Benedict looked up at the contorted face of the old Kiki bound to the stake like firewood for the fire—bound as brutally as his attack had been on the doctor and her aide only an hour ago. "Ted thinks you've been poisoned. I told him Paul isn't dangerous. Just lost or confused. It's possibly some herb. A sleeping root or something. I've known him a long time. I'm sure it's nothing that would harm the baby, or you."

The doctor rested her head languidly against the priest. "I hope so," she said tiredly, "but I've always had a..." she seemed to drift off. "I've always had a bad feeling about him," she said, finding it hard to stay coherent, or keep her tongue properly moisturized, so Father Benedict kissed her upon the forehead as he said a prayer for her. He too was beguiled by everything, though he didn't want to show it. Paul the Saint had been his. These were his people, so none of what was happening was making any sense. It was about this time the priest spotted Un'ka Matulu, only now taking note of the nurse also camped by the bonfire; much away from everyone and having a noticeable gash on his face. The nurse was all wrapped up in himself, keeping to his own blanket while keeping an eye on the old man who for whatever reason almost had him killed tonight. Un'ka was also stringing a red thread around his neck. A red thread having some blackened artefact as pendants. "I pray he is all right," the priest said, noticing the sleeping child was also hugged in the aide's arms. The boy was alive and breathing, but he hadn't woken up yet.

Elizabeth raised her head just enough to catch Un'ka's face against the fiery glow of the bonfire. She laid her head back on the priest's arm, "I've called to him, but...he's not speaking to me. In London...some of the others suspect emotional trauma...to follow physical trauma," she said softly, "but it's speculative research. He'll be fine...He's just doing the dried bat voodoo thingamabob he does whenever he's afraid."

"Dried bat voodoo?" the priest parroted, the words as puzzling to his ears as they were foreign, freshly concerned over whom to pray for. Or what else to pray against.

"Just some native religious stuff, father...The

indigenes at the Cape do it all the time with dead bat wings...nothing serious. Something about an Evil Eye or so...but he always comes around," Elizabeth replied peacefully, making herself more comfortable where she lay.

"Well it's not every day someone tries to kill you," Father Benedict answered, watching the nurse. He stared down at Elizabeth, the young woman utilizing his hand in lieu of a pillow.

When she caught him gazing sympathetically at her, she poked him gently with her index finger. "I said I'm fine...did the captain mention anything about our ship?"

"Ted mentioned something about the tides earlier. He tells me it's the dry season. Says it affects the water here that's why the Niger is a little too low. So it is possible your ship has been delayed. Who knows? The Lady Anne could arrive within the week, with dedicated prayers," he said to her.

The light smoke from the bonfire acted as some sort of insect-repellent because there weren't any pesky mosquitoes or crawling bugs about the place.

Paul the Saint squinted and groaned, the crackling fire smoking his eyes with threads of dry ash.

"Why do you think...he did this?" she asked, referring to the old man tied up barely a meter away from them.

"I don't know, sincerely. I'm at my wits end regarding what would motivate him so. The many pressures bearing on him," the priest answered, and fingered his hands at his former friend, but the old Kiki knocked his eyes away. His body writhing in pain and his eyes giving off water. "The ropes are too tight. It's hurting him," the reverend said, and beckoned to one of the boys by the bonfire. They were young officers already easing up to the manifold uses of one big fire. The pursiest of the three pitched his gaze towards the captain's quarters, and the priest responded with a warm smile. "Just the feet," the priest requested.

On agreeing, the officer got on his feet and loosened the ropes binding the aborigine by an inch or two. Legs only. Still, the old man wasn't responsive so the priest signalled the officer take off the gag as well, which was much to the young man's consternation. After a little nitpicking, the young man loosened the gag and hand ropes just enough, but then returned pigheadedly to the warmth of his blanket (No more favours), but that was enough to loosen up the Kiki, and for the first time in over an hour, he said something with his hands, pointing gnarled fingers at Matulu, or at Taye cuddled in Matulu's arms for the nurse had already fallen asleep.

"What's he saying?" Elizabeth asked dreamily while watching the eerie figure and the long gaze he'd directed at Matulu.

The priest rubbed his palms to keep them warm in the harmattan. "He's only pointing. He's not really saying anything," he answered, laying back to rest his shoulders from this night, but the old man continued to manoeuvre his fingers to the best of his ability.

"Isn't that how he talks?" Elizabeth asked like a number of minutes later, in and out of consciousness, much after she'd supposedly dozed off.

"I'm not sure he's saying anything meant for us," he remarked, he too a little heavy in the eyes, when Paul the Saint started to moan through the gag, so again the reverend requested Ted's boys help the old man become more comfortable (in the least to do it for themselves if ever they intended to get any sleep tonight), but even for a clergyman his demands had reached their limit. The Captain's boys only tossed a few more sticks into the bonfire, but that was all. Reinstating the gag whilst ignoring the reverend, they muffled the old Kiki's bastard cry.

demons

It came in a flash dream. In a flash dream stood the abomination mulishly. Prima di croce santo dei crucifixus it stood. The cross bled having the sacred blood run down. As it should. From the holy wounds of Jesus, abroad the rocks of Golgotha, the blood spread richly. As it should. It came pouring down despite the Virgin Mother's desperate plea for her son and his humanity. As it should. But only to be lapped up by dogs? It most certainly should not! That enraged the priest. Father Benedict clambered over the stones of Golgotha to meet them, throwing sticks, pebbles, and practically anything to ward off the atrocities besieging the holy cross. "Get away! Demons!" he shrieked, throwing more stones than he could remember. And at first, it worked. The dogs backed into the haze enveloping the hills and for a while stood nowhere to be seen upon Golgotha. It was cold and dank up there. The winds were equally merciless. So dank and windy, the priest could practically taste blood in the air. It was about this time he noticed the blood had ceased flowing down the holy cross (congealing into gooey clots and oozing at nothing other than what the priest could describe as a snail's pace), but the next thing he heard was that strident growl. The dogs were back. Unfortunately he was caught between a steep plummet down the rocks of Golgotha or being devoured alive by three of Her Majesty's dogs, wild and unsympathetic beasts, with nothing in hand to defend himself, but that was when the Holy Cross called to him, or he'd thought it called to him, so it called to him again. The Cross of his murdered Christ called to him in a language unbecoming of Aramaic or Latin, but as if that wasn't weird enough when the reverend looked up at it, he found the now Bantu-speaking cross virgin and untouched, not besmirched in any way, and having a reanimated Christ staring right back at him (and boorishly too), evidently not needing any salvation from him or from mangy dogs. These words became tied up in his head; it no longer bled, he no longer bleeds, it no longer bleeds priest—or were they but a few of the many voices Father Benedict thought he'd heard on finding his arms and feet ripped off (with the bulk of his entrails arranged at the corners of his bamboo chapel) in testament to some kind of pagan ritual.

"Mother of God!" the priest sat up in horror, gasping from his heart beating too wildly. He couldn't remember the exact day these night terrors started, a number of months now, but he knew they weren't good for his heart.

The big bonfire by which they'd camped had long gone out and was smouldering, but there was another cry; awake and stirring through the smoke, stirring enough to move him from his blanket. The pellucid harmattan cover mixed with bonfire smoke had little to no visibility. The amalgam was dense; so dense, and so near surreal, Father Benedict might have counted this also a part of his dream if it hadn't been accompanied by a hodgepodge of smells—the unkind smell of charcoal, smoked flesh, and a very distinct smell. A smell the reverend couldn't quite place. Not yet anyway.

The priest's first step into the murk was the boldest, stepping through the moving shadows to where the old man had been bound hours earlier, hoping the stake hadn't given way and the old man seared over a naked flame while they slept. That would be reprehensible. As it would be catastrophic.

He had to feel his way through though, being a moonless night, feeling his way and groping close enough to make twinkle images of the old man from the starlight above. The stake was where it ought to be (that was good), but it was only until he could accurately make out the Kiki still upright and safely away from the smoulder that the reverend relaxed his nerves.

The old man was breathing soundly, but just to be sure a part of his friend hadn't somehow found its way into the fire, Father Benedict felt him over. "I want to believe this is all one big misunderstanding, my dear friend," the reverend said genially, only for him to realize the Kiki had been sweating through the night, which kind of picked at his curiosity because this continental harmattan was nothing but dry air, and the smoke that enswathed them even drier. A strange thing that he could even sweat at all, but it was not until he groped for the Kiki's left hand and it felt as a bundle of wet sticks that he knew something was wrong—the old man's fingers were hard and dripping wet! Actually it had startled him, but not as much as the Kiki's heart-pounding cry right into the reverend's ears when he took the gag of! A long resounding howl like a wolf into the night.

Father Benedict wasn't new to the agony of a soul in torment and the priest could immediately recognize the pitch of pain and fear in this one. Actually the old Kiki had been howling for an extended time now because he was soon out of breath, but the surrealism of drifting to a place farther than the ears could hear help torque a knob in the reverend's soul because everyone in the fort strangely remained asleep. Elizabeth still hadn't woken up from her coma-like sleep, but (she could be excused) her fatigue could be explained. What couldn't be explained was why the captain's boys remained snuggled in warmth, totally bereft of consciousness for the priest could hear their snoring. Even Matulu stayed asleep. It was almost as if a weighty veil had come with the fog, holding down the fort as would a consciousness, when the reverend realized something else moving alongside him in the shadows. Whatever it was, it interrupted his thoughts by moving again and this time the priest could feel something sprinkling (or was it squirting?) against him. He felt like a catechumen being baptized. The shadow moving within the shadows had the smell of blood pit against it, so the priest stepped away in fear (not reflex). Opportunely, he trampled upon Ted's boys sleeping soundly in their very comfortable blankets and that sufficed. Ultimately they got up, and reacted quickly too for right away they resurrected the bonfire, and like a spell lifted, even Matulu surfaced from slumber.

The scene that presented itself was one they'd never seen. Of Her Majesty's dogs, one was loose or had broken free of its iron cage. Whichever the case, the animal had tracked the foreigner by scent and repeatedly tore at the old man's hand until the Kiki had no hand. All this time, it had been trying to subdue the intruder by dragging his hand into submission even when the bonfire came back on, but since the old man was roped to a stake all the beast ended up doing was to tackle him without the finesse of a domesticated canine for Her Majesty's dog had picked the intruder's hand clean; so cleanly it had picked the Kiki's hand to the bone, biting, tugging, snapping and tearing off. Each time, the old man screamed. And even now, his moans were unbearable. Even more, like a consciousness of its own, Her Majesty's canine hadn't cared for the kindled lights (or the audience watching) as it tore through the hand and cast tendon, tissue, and bone about the place. It cast most of what it shredded into the fire because it didn't or wouldn't consume the old man's flesh (almost as if it was avoiding something, or simply because he was diseased or it didn't want to). It looked deliberate and the unparalleled sight kept everyone at a loss for words, or action, nobody able to lift a finger to end the old man's suffering. Aside the obvious fact, this particular dog weighed half a man's weight.

The Captain's more senior boys arrived half dressed to the ruckus, or savagery of the attack, but to spare the animal, they instructed Ted's younger officers to fuel the bonfire (hoping that more heat would dissuade the beast). That didn't work. Neither did it do anything to delay the animal from chewing off what was left of the Kiki's fingers.

The trauma alone knocked the old man unconscious, but Her Majesty's canine wouldn't let up as it drove its fangs into the Kiki's wrist, pulling and gnawing (very well intentionally) like it desired he be awake through the unhurried ordeal. (And that worked!) A bout of pain shot through the Kiki like adrenaline, and he wailed this time, and wailed so loudly, that it drove him into shock, so the captain's lieutenants sought handling the situation another way. They demanded the younger officers bait the dog with whatever they had on them, but none of the boys in Khaki shorts considered that command seriously, pointing out (to their lieutenants in case they'd missed it) two open-tooth fangs and eight razor-sharp reasons not to. Alternatively, they took to clanking and jangling hoping to distract the beast long enough for it to let go of the aborigine, but all the distraction served to do was arouse the captain from his quarters. Ted unloaded a shell into it before his officers could suggest the boys in shorts go for bails of water to douse the animal with, bringing the hesitant hubbub to a necessary halt.

"If it knows what blood tastes like it's only a matter of time before it turns on another," the captain announced as he holstered his pistol, the shrill pierce of his gun enough to rouse Elizabeth from sleep. "Put it away," he grunted, groggy and in a sulk, so the junior boys hauled off the dead animal to give it a burial in the bushes. Or someplace beyond. "I need lights!" he ordered, and his officers echoed those orders up the outlook.

The Captain realized the civilians were up—even the doctor was up.

"What's going on?" she asked from her resting point, but it appeared she had missed the action because everyone else shared this ineffable look.

Ted approached the flames to inspect the damage. "Who's charge? Whose charge was the animal?—and why aren't my lights on?" the captain asked impatiently, examining the mauled aborigine and the hand that was no more. There was no response from the Northern outlook, so one of Ted's lieutenants personally climbed the structure to investigate. The old man stood unconscious, again given to shock, and soon to haemorrhaging if he wasn't treated quickly. "Untie him," the captain ordered, frowning at the officers with sleeping blankets. "You don't look at all yourself, Reverend. Are you all right?" the captain asked, taking the reverend by the hand, only for the reverend to shrink from his touch. The reverend was not himself; almost suggestive of some kind of mental trauma.

"We're fortunate to have you with us, Miss Cambridge. I'd suggest you come take a look at this," the captain said to Elizabeth, and the doctor on getting to her feet, approached the bonfire.

A remnant of what was now the old man's hand had been gnawed to the wrist and bled profusely into the open sand. "Is it life-threatening?" the captain asked but Elizabeth shrivelled away, in a way powerless to question her lack of desire to help the old man. The Captain turned to the boys with blankets, "whose charge was it?" he asked again, but every one of his officers astonishingly seemed to forget who'd returned the dog to its cage last night. The Captain held up a frown, trying to fight off the ignominy building across his face. "You do what you have to doctor," he said to Elizabeth when the Edison lights came on, "—and I suggest you also take a look at the reverend," the captain said concernedly, but with just the right cadence of calm before they could all turn to the priest; not a soul wanting to ask why the priest was all covered in blood, or how he came to be covered in the blood of the Kiki. But, Father Matt noticed even Matulu stared at him funny. In fact, at the slightest whiff of the telling, the reverend lost consciousness (his collapse being proof to how much shock an aged heart could take in one night).

By the third morning, Captain Book was by the marching grounds, surrounded by buckets of water and lather, having his officers wash the dogs and inspect the dog cages. "If you're here about the dogs, there's nothing I can assist you with, Miss Cambridge," the captain spoke aggressively and from a distance when he sighted her coming, making sure his hat was in place by the time she was close enough to be ignored.

"I'm clueless to what happened here two nights ago if that's what you think I've come to ask, Captain. I'm not here about your dogs," Elizabeth responded curtly, intending her words be brief.

Ted grunted and signalled his officers skip the

scrubbing and move on to dismantling the newly vacant dog cage. He noticed her neck injury healing quite well. "How is he?" he asked placidly.

"He's stable."

"I had meant the reverend," the captain rephrased, not intending she get his meaning muddled up.

"I said he's stable," Elizabeth retorted, now moulding a frown. "We moved Father Matt from the sickbay to keep him from those who've contracted the fever—some of your men lit candles in his room yesterday."

The Captain stared away, overlooking the buckets to the very spot where all this menace started. "They respect him. It's expected. How do they fare, my men?" he asked, an uncertain ring in his voice.

"Still how your officers found them—half-conscious and delirious. One of them seems to be paralyzed," she reported succinctly to end the small talk, and so they said nothing for a while.

"Wh—What is it you want?" Ted finally asked, growing weary of her eyes watching his officers dismantle the now vacant dog cage and restack it for use.

"Wha?" Elizabeth muttered, quickly losing track of the question.

Apparently the doctor enjoyed felting and sweating her prunella blouse out in the heat for no obvious reason, so he put it to her out-rightly, and without a smile, as the adolescent rays of the African sun cast a 10 a.m. shadow across his face, "Wh—Why are you here, Doctor?"

"When are you expecting the ship to the mainland Captain?—cause I don't get why you're doing that unless you intend putting a fresh dog in that cage," she had asked, only to have the captain ignore the mindless remark.

"The ship comes when the ship comes. As you can see some of us are as eager for it as you are," Ted answered candidly, and in some way had a smug smile across his face. "We pray sooner than later."

Elizabeth clenched her fists, deciding now was as good as any time to say it, "I'm taking the reverend with me whether or not he beats the coma."

"The decision of who goes and stays is beyond your station, Miss Elizabeth," the captain spat flat out, having intended it be his rhetorical answer to the question she must have forgotten to ask. Ted had dragged her name in a drawl (and wouldn't have done a better job if he had dragged her personally through the mud). "The Reverend only leaves by summons from either Her Majesty or the Holy Church. You're neither both, so I'll take it you don't know that."

"We don't play bureaucrat with a man with a bad heart. As his physician, it's my obligation to make certain he gets proper medical attention. He can't die here your prisoner, Ted!" she declared, grinding her lips and maintaining her stance. Being tough with the captain meant being tough with Ted.

"Are you my prisoner then?" the captain responded cynically and to the audience of his officers because by now the men had developed an unhealthy interest for the captain's cavilling with the doctor. "We have our orders, Doctor. We do what we must. Having served with soldiers, I would think you've learned how this goes—your ship comes when your ship comes, Doctor Cambridge. Be rest assured, you will be the first on it!"

"When that ship comes, Father Matt and I will be on it," Elizabeth retorted and walked away bravely. Standing up to the captain made her tremble. He had that effect on her. He had that effect on everybody—everybody except Father Matt.

"Don't cross me, D–Doctor. Your Hippocratic Oath has nothing to do with me," Ted warned after her.

His officers were done washing down the cages, so he ordered they prepare the iron slabs and load up the caisson for their next trip out.

the first time the priest opened his eyes he hadn't opened them for long and saw Matulu attending to the paralytics in the medical tent, and the little boy helping out with the first aid box. The second time the priest opened his eyes, all he saw were the nurse's dried bat voodoo wings dangling loosely over his head as the aide attended him, so he shut them almost as quickly. The third time Father Benedict opened his eyes, however, he saw Elizabeth beaming down at him like the morning sun, "I was told you were awake," she exclaimed and examined his pupils, "it's great to have you back."

The tent was smaller somehow. Oh. This was his lodge. "I remember the sickbay. How long have I been like this?" Father Matt asked and tried to sit up. Liz gave the priest a hand and rested him against the bed's wooden frame. His things were in place; tidy and looking well spaced.

"You've been unconscious for three nights and two days," she said matter-of-factly, almost as one who'd been counting as she sat by the foot of his bed, trying to mould a frown. "Your heart gave in— though for a while I was starting to fear you had joined the others," she narrated, intending on keeping that frown. She paraded her fingers above his eyes so he could count them. "The Man upstairs must truly appreciate you, Father."

"I see," Father Benedict intoned, "Means today's Monday and I missed Mass for the boys," he strained to say. The priest had phlegm clogging his throat so she suggested he spit it out into the tin can she offered him whilst unpacking a large stethoscope from her first aid box.

"Your dotting parishioners left you those," she teased after placing the snaking object against his breast, referring to the spent row of incense and candles in his lodge.

"How's Ted?" Father Matt asked, finding himself distracted by the slight scarring by her neck.

"High on his horse as usual. He refuses to let you come with me when our ship comes. He'll be glad you're recovered, though," she informed, before grinning, "—dnt I intend to frustrate what he has planned."

"I'm not cut for your hippy language, Liz. Truth is, I've never gotten what it is you mean when you say dnt," the priest growled hoarsely.

It made Elizabeth smile, "you're like a father to me, Father Matt," she said on taking his hand and cushioning it with her bulge of a womb, "so do note that I want you with me when I leave for the mainland. Hopefully you get it now."

The priest cuddled her hands. "Elizabeth, I can't leave. Actually I need the Church's permission before I—"

"Same poppycock the captain said, but your heart takes priority."

"My heart isn't here," Father Matthew replied, laying a hand against his beating breasts before taking her hands into his and reclining both against hers, "rather it's in here, in the hearts of those who love me, so we really won't be separated."

"You only say that to try and make me feel better. On the other hand, what will make me feel better is having you come with me. No arguing," she said tersely, but whatever was preoccupying his mind got the better of him and for a while the priest was lost to the beauty and uncontrolled flickering of the candles.

"How's Matulu?" he asked finally.

"Matulu's not been talking. He's barely said a word to me, much less, anyone, since the incident—" she answered, observant of Father Matthew's shortened attention span. She worried a bit. "Is there something you require Father Matt?"

"What?"

"I mean your look. It's distant."

"Oh, it's my rosary. I'm just trying to remember where last I put it," the priest replied and she stretched her hand over the altar table.

"Taye put it here," she said as she lifted the rosary

to the priest. "He's a sweet kid—tidied your room. Swept it with some special broom he made and then set everything," she cheered proudly. "Look. He even learnt to do your vestments. The ones you piled up," she added, pointing to the corner of the lodge that had once been stacked with bloodstained clothes from three nights before. All that sat by the corner now was a half-used paper bag of washing powder.

Father Benedict attempted to work his feet, "I need to see Ted," the priest said grimly, but Elizabeth pursed her lips and eased the priest back into the bed.

"I'll call Captain High Horse to see you when you're ready," she scolded, "right now, you need to listen to me. I'm your doctor, not your Liz, not your parishioner, and not your babysitter. Your doctor! And your doctor says you need to rest that heart. She's not letting you out of her sight. In fact, if you had only listened to her jibber jabber in the first place, she wouldn't need to worry about you."

"Liz, I remember that night," the reverend said without embellishments, but the doctor was quick to reply.

"How much do you remember because I remember too."

Father Benedict touched his garment, being the very garment he'd been wearing that night, and the pregnant doctor scoot even closer to him, "he's alive if that's what you're asking. We managed to cauterize the wrist to save his arm from gangrene," she said, "the captain had us move him to the sickbay after the horrid assault, which was incredible. I never for once considered he could be so selfless. If the old man's lucky, the wound's not infected already so we wouldn't have to amputate the entire arm," she informed. "You'd have been bunkmates so you could see for yourself, but we moved you here last night to be safe you don't contract the fever from the others."

"Fever?"

"Yes. You're not the only one who's been asleep since that night, Father Matt," Elizabeth rejoined, "some of the sentries we found, I mean the captain found in the outlook, were unconscious and burning up. Yesterday, I confirmed a protozoan in their slide sample. I can't exactly say what it is yet, but it's multiplying and swamping up their bloodstream so I figure it's a parasite."

"We have the fever?" Reverend Benedict huffed in guilt.

"Don't let it trouble you, Father. We've had that fever for quite a while now."

The Reverend couldn't understand.

"Starting with the lieutenant? You remember the

lieutenant, Father Matt," she said, but owing to the priest's ailing heart, she pronounced, "so this has nothing to do with you. Besides, if it's any inkling like what you say is out there, we'd long be dead by now; and I mean all of us, but we're not. See? So it has nothing to do with you."

"But you told Ted his lieutenant died from an—"

"—infection not related to the fever. Yes, I said so, but you'd have to ask the Lord to forgive me; what else would the captain have believed? Even if he had to cook it up? I don't want Matulu living by what's dead the captain has buried, but still he does—oh yes, I heard that rumour," she hissed, "so I wasn't just going to stand there and let his men hold Matulu accountable for something he didn't do. They'd probably bury him there if you catch my meaning."

The priest sat there like he'd been struck by lightning.

"The gaffe is mine really, leaving him alone in the first place. The Captain is such an ass," she remarked but then bit her lips, apologizing for the swear word.

"The rumour you heard was no rumour," Father Benedict confessed. "Linton did die two seasons before you came. He was our last medic. You know I worked the sickbay."

"Okay?" Elizabeth huffed. Wondering why the priest was opening the door to a heart to heart.

"I worked his place because they were my boys too and I their priest. Ted avoided sending the body home not to risk the crew to whatever Linton took ill from, but he did bury Linton by your aide's quarters—it was all bushes then so it was nothing deliberate. There was no way he'd had known you were coming." The protrusion beneath her breasts had grown even more the past few days or months without him telling, "this continent is new to us, Liz. And to you as well. If Ted's boys have caught on something, it could be dangerous considering your baby and—"

"There's nothing I can do about that," Elizabeth interpolated without a note of concern to herself, "without the ship coming, I mean. And since I'm stuck here, I might as well get on with it."

"I pray you don't mean that because I don't think it was coincidence what happened last night," Father Benedict said.

"You mean three nights ago?"

"Uh, where's the boy?" he asked off plumb and Elizabeth shrugged.

He looked persistent.

"If he isn't here—he's probably helping out at the sickbay," she answered softly before asking, "why?"

"Is the boy always in the same place Paul is?" the priest asked, staring oddly, and Elizabeth felt she could paint a frown from the reverend's stare.

"For what it's worth, your eerie old friend is one horribly healthy old man, but yes. Like I said, Taye's probably at the sickbay," the doctor answered tersely.

"So someone's been keeping an eye on him—I mean not leaving him alone with the boy unsupervised?" the bald priest asked and again Elizabeth shrugged. In fact, she chuckled sadly, "I don't seem to understand your meaning by referring to Taye as the boy, father—but I'm not stupid. I'm not going to leave him within the reaches of that old crow. The Captain's stationed some of his men at the sickbay in case we may be in need of any assistance. They take shifts so they can stay round the clock, so your answer's no," she replied and lifted herself to depart with her first aid box. "I had the cook make you soup. I'll have Taye bring it to you when you'r—"

"No!" Father Benedict cut in harshly, but his tone had fallen oddly out of place. Even for a priest. So he chose to speak plainly, "—there's something going on between the child and the old man. It's why I said whatever happened that night was no coincidence," he spoke, almost as if he had winnowed out the words. What was more evident was the priest's emphasis on the child being with the

old man, and not the old man being with the child—
a man who may have attempted to murder her
without batting an eye.

"Are you afraid of him, Father?" she asked sincerely,
an uncertain look in her gaze.

"I'm afraid of what he can do," he answered
sincerely, a very certain look in his gaze.

"But why would you say such a thing, father?"
Elizabeth responded with a second chuckle. Another
sad chuckle. "He is only a child. I don't think he is
old enough to hold a grudge, least contemplate
holding a knife to the old man's throat—but if you'll
have my candid opinion, I'd say that old crow
deserves someone put a knife to his throat." She
frowned.

"I think you should sit down for what I'm about to
tell you, Elizabeth," Father Matthew said seriously
and in a way her frown seemed to dissolve into
nothingness.

Elizabeth sat.

It took a while for Father Benedict to find the
words, but he found them.

"The first time I arrived at this fort, this place was a
little more than the open forest. Brigadier John
William Cabot was in charge of things then. A man
strong and pig-headed, a character he shares with—"
They jointly knew to whom the priest referred, "—

which is strange," Father Benedict remarked, "because John was the adventurer. Ted's not. My goals had been made clear before I came, and though I tried not to drift off my primary assignment, I have also tried not to neglect my secondary assignment as well; both assignments equally dutiful under God. Balancing them for me was the tricky part. The first part of my assignment, the part Ted has come to understand as my primary assignment, was to keep Her Majesty's men in line with their faith while they accomplished their task."

"and what task is that?" Elizabeth interrupted, distrustful to the way the captain ran things at the fort.

"You'd have to ask Ted not me. He seldom talks about our presence here. Neither did the brigadier. Another trait both he and John share," Father Benedict answered quickly, the priest didn't seem bothered by the question nor did her muted curiosity bother him. "The church fears Her Majesty's men would be godless in a new land. Or turn to pagan worship because it is easy to stray away when no one's watching. And so, I came. The second part of my assignment, the part I've come to understand as my secondary assignment, was to promote the church in the new protectorate by any way the Lord and Virgin made way. So, I started serving Mass here. To me, it was the one thing that fulfilled both assignments. And though he was years older than I, the Brigadier applauded the idea and received me well. He even built us that chapel and honoured it with a rood—which then was only a frame of what we have now. Ted built the rest. John was a godly man, and most times wanted me with him on his expeditions. He also sought my advice—occasionally—whenever he was opinionated or confused. He even admitted to his shortcomings whenever he was wrong—"

"One trait the captain is in dire need of," Elizabeth interrupted again, but the priest had come to predict the interrupt.

"A good man—the Brigadier, almost like a father to the men," Father Matthew said with a forlorn look, and Elizabeth couldn't hide a smile.

"What happened to him?"

"He was summoned to the mainland as I hear, after his assignment at the Verde. John's old. He's been too long at mainland to be of any active service now. I pray not dead," the priest answered. "He was fond of taking me to the settlements, like I told you, believing my presence, actually the presence of a priest, would somehow help him do better in reaching out to the villagers. And that, well, let's just say he was most successful with the Ishaporke people. He loved their craftsmanship and the villagers loved him in return—perhaps because he was one to give gifts and spend a lot of time camping around them. Actually, they are nice people as you've come to find out yourself. I, on the other hand, striking a balance, grew fond of the Kiki and their knowledge of tropical herbs and fruits. And believe me that knowledge was worthwhile those seasons I spent working the sickbay—"

"What about the third tribe you mentioned a few days back? The ones you call the Ilu-Sango?"

"John never let me accompany him when he visited the Ilu-Sango. He always said they needed more time to warm up to our incursion into their lands and so on. They are a trust-centred people. And he said that till his decommissioning from this assignment. I just interpreted it as his way of keeping some things to himself. Actually, it was around that time I met, you know, Paul the Saint, and how I got involved in this missionary work. Somehow I saw it all as the Lord directing us to reach out to these strange new people, so I started on my righteous cause. I didn't want to miss out on the opportunity to establish the Church of England here in the new land, and the Brigadier agreed to help with the church work. It was his original idea we start a missionary school, and I run it. Hopefully the villages would open their hearts to our technology, and in the end we would worm our way into their community. He even helped out—once, but then I discovered he just couldn't cut it with the children. Still he helped. Paul, on the other hand, well we hadn't a name for him back then, he opposed our work."

Elizabeth didn't look surprised.

"He opposed us and fervidly too," Father Matthew continued, "was always one to stir up dissension and any form of opposition from among the indigenous. I think he saw us as impostors. Or opportunists. But in the end, we found him to be a grieving young man, that's all, but that had been after the Brigadier and I had grown accustomed to having him around raising hell everyday by our perimeter. It was façade. Truth is, he was miserable before he converted and just looking for a vent, a way of escape," Father Matthew said gravely. "In retrospect, it's funny that I've grown to love him. I think he was miserable then because of the children. He couldn't have any."

"He is impotent," the doctor inferred.

"No—not really, but he clearly chose not to," Father Benedict answered succinctly. "I think I have told you more than once before, Liz, that the old man once practised sorcery. According to him, he was born and trained as a medium for hire—"

"Pretty much what your indigenes are doing to that little princess that used to come to your class—that Jite girl," Elizabeth interrupted and the reverend nodded.

"But the day he had me convinced was the day I

witnessed him drowning a baby," he said, and Elizabeth hadn't noticed her lips part ways. "He'd said the child had to die, and die by a special ritual—the child was his."

Doctor Elizabeth Cambridge hadn't a word to say, but the priest wasn't done. There was more.

"This is going to be hard for you to understand, Liz," Father Matthew spoke cautiously, choosing his words very carefully while treading the emotive line of what was right and what needed to be done. He watched her face contort and lose vitality. "I would have tried to save the baby that day, aside the fact the Brigadier told me not to interfere with the local customs or their ceremonies. Even after that, it was hard for me to understand all he kept telling me. Or the many warnings—believe me if I had been able to save that child that day I would have," Father Benedict interrupted himself on spotting hurt building in her eyes. The ball had started rolling, so the priest forged on. "It's been years since he's changed his ways and renounced his old religion, but I fear I got a glimpse of his old self the night he attacked you. I was right and wrong about him, but now I'm only confused."

"How can you be right and wrong about somebody, father?!—what in the entire world do you mean by right and wrong, Father Matt? Please tell me!" she demanded stubbornly, the hurt in her eyes cogently morphing into umbrage.

"Whatever you think I mean, all I know for certain is that in the eye of their local customs that child and the old man are like wood and wax. They should be nowhere near each other," Father Benedict answered, less sure Elizabeth would buy his words as they stood, words nude of sense or sentiment.

"Why? Because I don't understand."

"Why is what has me, Elizabeth. Why he did what he did that day? After all these years, why would he revert to his old religion? And why now? On first thought, when I saw him with the child that night, I feared Paul had reverted to his troubled life as a medium," Father Mathew mentioned, attempting to take her hand but she recoiled from him, "Elizabeth, I must say something to you. This goes against confession, but I fear the worst if I fail to communicate this confusion with someone else."

The doctor attempted to rise, but Father Benedict caught her by the hand and eased her back to sitting. "This is important, Liz. He killed his child. The woman who was supposed to have bore the baby was by his feet that day. She didn't even shed a tear. I was taken aback, totally. In truth, there she stood terrified when I tried to suck the water out of the child's lungs and hand her baby back to her— I've never seen anything so absurd. So unmotherly.

Yet, she looked so fragile." Father Benedict was teary eyed and hollowed out, but his eyes were very different from Elizabeth's. The loose skin around her eyes were sunken and red like a fiery hearth eviscerating her tears. Not a drop fell in their passionate stare. "But this baby, his baby, was not the only baby he had killed, but according to what he told me in our sessions alone, it was to be his last. So now, all I ask, all that confronts my mind since that night is why? Why now? Because if I know, then maybe, I just may be able to save him."

"You want to save him?" Elizabeth cited, aghast, her face flush and flustered. "What you're saying, Reverend, is that that man—that demon—lying in our sickbay is a baby killer but you still want to save him?"

If Father Matt had felt nothing at all, the priest felt that. She'd never called him Reverend before. Not once. The doctor was set to panic mode and Father Matt couldn't figure the button to calm her down. "How many babies?" she asked, now set to cry.

He had no answer.

"How many babies?" she asked again lifting her eyes to the sack roof ceiling, not willing to have her tears fall while he stared into it. Her battle was fending off tears. And rage.

"You can't ask it like that—the language is brutally complicated. Not all of them were babies. A number of grown children were among them," the priest answered sorrowfully and watched the fire in her eyes sizzle out to a tide of tears. She hurt.

Elizabeth ground her teeth, unable to wipe clean the faces of the cornrow braided children and the slick oily haired boys ingrained as victims in her memory. Innocent faces. Innocent children.

"We all have our demons, Liz. He's had a rough past. Listen to me, it was a life he was raised into as a child. The truth is, these villages see babies or children with questionable birthmarks as something other than babies and children. They take them through a custom, a rite; they call them life and death spirits—have an indigenous name for them if I remember correctly. Yes, abiku. It means the one who breeds death, I think."

"How many children, father? I can't believe you would buy into this! That you would defend him! You're a priest—it's incredulous!"

"First thing I learnt from John when I arrived here is this is not our home. Our rules do not apply here, Liz. It's their home, hence their rules. I know that's hard for you to understand, but you cannot judge people too critically especially when they know not what law they break," Father Benedict answered, "in my life as a priest I haven't seen—"

"How about the universal law of life?" Elizabeth shot back, dropping her head and letting her tears run in rivers of unforgiveness, "why do you even propose we protect him—he is nothing to protect!"

"Elizabeth!! I know you may doubt what I tell you, but you have to let me finish!" Father Benedict raised his troubled cords by a notch just to get her to be quiet. So with the exception of drawing phlegm, she remained quiet. "He killed his own baby!" the priest iterated very clearly and very slowly just so she could get his meaning. "Why would someone—why would anyone do that?" he asked but she made no response. "Like you, I didn't understand it neither the countless times he told me these stories of his past life and how he was raised. I ended the sessions so we could start on more positive things, more constructive acts to his new faith and not focus on the relics of a past gone sour." The doctor either looked attentive and quiet, or pensive and oblivious. She just kept her eyes away. "In all my life as a priest, I have never encountered anything out of the ordinary. We had had to wrestle his sanity past all that mumbo, but even as a priest, as a priest Liz, I was taught to believe that some people are born," Father Benedict found himself at a loss for better words, "—different."

Elizabeth had a disbelieving look strewn across her face, "one night is not the Armageddon, Reverend. You're taking his side."

"There's a whole lot more than what I can tell you,

Liz, but I want you to trust me when I say this—not everything can be understood," Father Matt concluded and decided to get on his feet.

Elizabeth had either forgotten to help the priest up, or just wasn't in the mood to. He took her shoulder but she walked away. "He's a demon, father," she said glumly, wiping the tears that had completed their run down her cheeks. Her lips quaked in rage, and even the first aid box in her hands trembled at the same frequency. She stormed out of the priest's lodge bearing one, solitary, thought. Poppycock!

messengers

It's public knowledge spirits come in different guises to the living world. A widely known ruse is parading as the semblance of an animal, or some being, lurking in the shadows until the messenger can deliver its message. A message meant to be heard, not repeated. Pity the fool who survives. It is for that reason snakes are hated as much as they are revered in Africa being that they carry messages from the afterlife—their venom, the very bosom to the afterlife herself. But for as long as we can remember, the in-betweens, or go-throughs, have always found ways to veil the living from the dead, and hoard away the unpalatable messages our actions preach. And yes, over a successful millennium of years, these in-betweens have managed to check the messenger and the message. Messages about your afterlife. Secrets to life where we hail from. Where you all end up. We can't say that we blame them, however, because none of you is ever eager to know why the dead are so interested in the living, or why you are just as keen about us. We count that as one among the countless scores of secrets people like your mediums and priests who seek to know more hide from people like you who know nothing, for your world, this life, and our world, what you call the afterlife, are in no way distant strangers. Rather, they are like sibling twins that share one placenta. They will always be in conflict. And in that light, no matter the many lies they tell you, is the inherent reason bad things happen to seemingly ordinary people in your world whether you choose to acknowledge it or not.

A coffin-head snake slithered its way beneath the heavy cotton drapery and into the infirmary from behind a cabinet, writhing its entire body against a limb of the wheeled cots, cloaked by lengthy bedspreads spread generously with helms almost grazing the floor. In fact Matulu whisked past it so many times, his carefree warm-blooded ankles entreated a bite.

"Doctor Cambridge!" the captain stormed in, startling the little aborigine, Taye, and sending him scurrying to a corner of the tent. The Captain tossed his hat upon one of the beds, jerking its iron framework off position to allow his junior officers haul in two new patients for her to take a look at. He pointed the junior officers to where the vacant beds were and the men placed the sick lieutenants right by his other sickened officers, before standing aside. "Where's the doctor?" Ted asked Matulu, the captain's heel stationed only a foot and a bite away from the infamous coffin-head, "—and what the bloody hell is that damned thing?" he inquired, noticing and fingering at the charm of bat wings about Matulu's neck, "take the bloody thing off," he demanded, but the nurse would rather keep his charm, moving to finish his injection rounds on a chunk of the captain's time. "Well be quick about it!" Ted grunted as the nurse slowly unencumbered himself from all the clinical kibos and kilimanjaro, but he obviously could have cared less if the captain had brought the entire fort in on a stretcher. "Bloody Africans!" he snorted.

Their temperatures were sky-high and they reeked of vomit; the whole tent in fact; the symptoms having been the same these past days; some lethargic, having started with a little vision impairment; others not so lucky, suffering from acute delirium and extensive muscle spasms; but all of them, without grounds for reason, reacting strongly to light. Or any focused light. In fact, they all hated the sunlight. In a week, the sick had more than doubled in count. Just yesterday, alone, he'd admitted three making the count an even eight for the infirmed.

As Matulu proceeded to get the doctor, wherever she was, one of the men jolted, asphyxiating under his vomit and jerking like a diseased chick.

"Matulu! Come first! He looks like he's in pain. Help him. Help him!" the captain called, itching for the nurse and making way for the trained aide to work some magic. "Hell! Is she bloody helping at all?" he grumbled, on noticing the ever pallid complexions of all eight in the diffused lighting in the tent; sunlight blanketed through double-layered curtains and overhanging draperies.

Coming as second nature to the nurse, Un'ka Matulu calmly turned the lieutenant's head to a side to let the drool hit the bedspread and aid the officer in breathing. He also made sure none of the infected man's juices got on him.

"Thank you," Ted said when the lieutenant lapsed into rest and his breathing levelled, patting Matulu by the waist in appreciation, but also shoving the nurse away soon after, "oh get that grotesque thing out of my sight."

Matulu simply disrobed and went looking for the doctor, as Ted picked a bed to sit on, running his hand through his hair. He hadn't bothered if the comatose old man was laying on the bed he picked. On the contrary, he monitored the Kiki; unconscious and apparently brain-dead by the look of him, his wrist in wraps and wraps of bandage, soaked in a bloody almost near black stain with a strong air of clinical liquid exuding from it. The Captain spotted the ebony child squatting by a corner of the medical tent, but his look stayed expressionless. He ordered his officers outside the tent to go after the nurse, leaving him alone with the child, and the silver coffin-head writhing below. The snake changed wheels; slithering its entire body further away from the captain. Ted poked the old man by his bandages and grimaced when the aborigine's reflexes were that of a cotton doll.

Everyone returned quicker than the captain had anticipated as the pregnant doctor parted her way through the curtains and requested Matulu leave them raised. Just for a while. As usual, she wouldn't have the captain's men inside the tent so they remained outside, following Ted's orders. She ignored the captain as she took the temperatures of his lieutenants.

He watched her work then utter something to the nurse in Bantu, but in a manner like she'd asked for something.

Matulu brought her, her glasses, a needle, a bottle, a canister, and some cotton wool. She pricked their hands, sopped up the blood, and then handed the nurse back the wool. The nurse locked the samples in a cabinet whilst the doctor popped a canister of meds. "The Reverend is awake," she mentioned succinctly, barely a mutter to be heard.

"T—Then he'd be glad to see the fort falling apart," the captain retorted, not having intended a response. "Eight of my officers are sick, and frankly I don't know if I might be next l—lying there next to them."

"Do not blame everyone else for your shortcomings,

Captain," Elizabeth muttered again, slapping the pills into the men's mouth and signalling for Matulu to raise their heads. The nurse did so, and she crammed more than half a dozen pills down their throats before letting them lie.

"Shortc—comings?" the captain stuttered. He gained control of his voice, "my shortcoming is allowing you people do whatever you want in this fort," he rejoined, inflecting his eyes at the child in the corner.

Elizabeth dumped the canister carelessly on a balance when she noticed Taye squatting in the corner. She scowled at Ted as though he was responsible for terrorizing the kid into submission, before lifting the child to his feet and leading him out of the infirmary safely past the big bad wolf. Her little saint headed in a bee-line for the priest's lodge as Elizabeth returned and slipped on her overcoat.

"And just what do you think would happen to us if you take ill?" he asked her. The Captain had intended it be a rhetorical question, but she answered anyway.

"Then you can bury me by his lodge," the doctor retorted, with wit, upon sharing a smile with the Bantu. "Besides, I'm not taking ill until our ship arrives," she affirmed, almost as if she had a lid on this thing. "—that's if the stupid thing ever arrives," she muttered, before having Matulu strip the sick officers off their uniforms.

She motioned to move the wheeled bed, the very one the captain sat on, without even looking at him, so Ted got off the old man's bed, helping her move it; both their legs now sharing an aisle with the coffin-head below, with the snake towering barely twelve inches away from the doctor's calves. She requested two blankets from a stack of blankets, but the captain provided them before Matulu was done stripping down the officers. These had been blankets the little boy had washed, but the captain wouldn't know that. There were many things he didn't know. Nor would he have cared to.

The Captain tacked up a smug grin. "It's ob—vious you seldom care what happens to you, doctor, but have you thought about what's best for your baby?" he remarked, but it had been a remark that had been so off the captain's usual headstrong egocentric self that a teed off Elizabeth slapped him. And with premeditated impulse.

Ted looked at her, no glowered at her, smouldering like a torch, but thought better of it when he saw the doctor shield her face and womb in reaction to his mien—or was it the speedy intrusion from his officers, for suddenly his attention was needed at the gates. In fact, that sort of blew off his tempest. The Captain looked to Matulu who didn't care to look back. "I wasn't going to hit you. Your ship's in two weeks. Hopefully after that, I'll never have to deal with the two of you again," he said to her flatly and stormed out.

Ted had left his hat behind, which kind of was a big deal for the captain even though she tried to ignore it. Elizabeth walled up her eyes and went after him. Her nurse, on the other hand, couldn't have cared less how it all went. Matulu simply returned to duty, closing up the curtains and shuffling the cots back in place.

Reverend Benedict watched the boy stand a third the height of the door, but the moment Taye tried slipping into his room to sit in a corner, the priest sat up—and sitting up was all he did for a while, under the boy's austere stare, watching the kid watch him watch the kid. The boy had Morion-jewelled eyes, pupils pit black, even against the ebony glaze of his skin, and despite they sat less than a yard from each other, a vast rift stood between them—that discarnate awkwardness in eye and body language.

Father Benedict fumbled for his rosary. He'd misplaced it somewhere between the sheets. So taking that for a cue, Taye got up, offering to help, but the reverend halted the child by lifting his hand to the boy's face. The hand had come up suddenly. So suddenly Taye only looked on curiously, now unsure what it was the reverend was fumbling for. When he spotted the glow-in-the-dark rosary between the creases, however, he drew it out to a more than alarmed priest. Taye could only make a smile at the reverend, a patulous smile, and mumble some discordant words before handing over the wax rosary.

Upon taking the rosary from the boy, and feeling those little bony fingers warm to his touch, Father Benedict figured this boy was just a boy. It was time he freed his mind from such idle notions.

"You would think after so many years a priest would be different from everybody else," he said softly to the boy's ear, as he drew Taye to himself, tickling him playfully until they shared a leisurely moment laughing. He mounted Taye on his laps and leaned his jaw into the child's curly hair—the thought of this giggling child, this innocent boy, being a spirit child, sounded ever more ridiculous the more he went over the allegations in his mind. He was a man of faith. Why would anyone, in their right minds, want to tag a child, or hurt any child for that matter, children who are yet unstained by the sins of this world?

Matthew Benedict eased into bed.

Truly, and if the teachings of the Holy Church held true, whatever it must be, be it spiritual in any way, would have had a primal reaction to the crucifix, wouldn't it? In the least, that was what he was taught to believe. Besides, it wasn't like he could spot any birthmarks on the boy. Elizabeth was right. The old man's faith was one with holes, the outcome of which was uncertain.

Matulu had sought redemption from the voices, and with their cacophonous bickering, the nurse hadn't wasted a moment hurrying to drop those newer, bigger, and thicker double-layered curtains behind them before returning to his routines. It was enough time to allow the silver coffin-head snake anchored by the wheels to slip up a leg and slither unto the sheets manoeuvring its way deftly but precisely to the old man's bed. The silver snake settled on the Kiki's breasts, now towering over him (almost brazenly), when Matulu dunked an aluminium tray against the bed. "Imamba!" he exploded, but he had missed, so the snake exposed its black as death coffin of a mouth at him in defiance. Or threat. But the nurse got off another strike, wiping the tray hard against the venomous snake and striking it relentlessly until the malleable sheet of aluminium warped to the shape of the bed frame. He backed away in reflex, not fear, seeking to keep his distance and ponder how many snakes might be loitering. It'd been a pretty long snake, now noticing its silver body dropping the whole three feet to the floor and outthrusting one full end of the sheet. He couldn't see if he killed it (buried beneath his tray) alongside the old man, who was most probably dead, but after an eternity of neither slithering nor struggling, Matulu approached the Kiki to pry out the misshapen tray from the bed frame. He discovered blood upon the sheets, only to discover later that was because he had reopened the old man's injuries for on snapping the thin tray off the bed frame, a very livid snake lunged at him.

Visiting Fort William was a rare honour. Especially if the visitor was the Osivie of the Ishaporke people under the escort of his chalked oracles and two dozen bodyguards. Or snakeskin wearing devotees. The only visit likened to this visit was a time void of the captain's charge—the Brigadier had been host then, and the fort was nothing more than a camp of bamboo sticks and tent pegs. And just like in the last visit, this British fort was handicapped in the welcoming and appreciation of their guests, only this time the captain's pretext would be disease (standing as a barrier), not furnishings, and certainly not etiquette, so such prestigious guests would have to remain outside his gates. All other protocols observed. Ted signalled to the men up in the outlook and they vanished from view. He was also joined by more of his senior officers, stacking up behind Ted in a wall of loyalty to acknowledge the presence of the Osivie, as was customary, rules drilled into them by the Brigadier, though all of the captain's junior officers stayed behind; holding their stations and merrily unbound to the outlandish leanings of diplomacy, or etiquette, the older ones were forced to observed.

"I was beginning to wonder how long it would take before someone shows up for the old man," Captain Book muttered while chewing his lips, "without the reverend, I wouldn't expect this to go smoothly."

He glanced towards the infirmary to find Elizabeth trudging towards them. She was with his hat. "See if the reverend is well enough to join us," he said to them only to notice the reverend by way of the chapel, and in his company the aboriginal boy they'd had for months now—a fortuitous sign, hopefully. A sign that everything would resolve itself.

Elizabeth stood aside with the captain's hat watching the many indigenes by the fence. The younger men looked malnourished and fatigued. The older oracles seemed lethargic and wobbly by the knees. The chief himself looked bleached and bloated, and wasn't properly adorned as the time they'd witnessed his glorious presence. In stark difference to the adults, however, the children looked gloriously healthy. All three of them.

Elizabeth inched closer to the fence just as the reverend got there with the child.

"It's good to see you on your feet and strong enough to walk Reverend," the captain confessed and the priest smiled warmly at the captain.

"It's good to be seen."

"Your man racks up quite the storm I see. I should have paid more attention to what you said."

"—I doubt they are here for Paul," said the priest when he spotted the children of his mission school in the company of those visiting.

"Whom bloody else but the old hobgoblin?"

Now when the reverend attempted approaching the fence, the boy resisted, and had resisted so strongly that the reverend staggered from the boy's tottering. He won't go near the fence. Or them. The Captain took note of that. But as if in response, the cornrow braided one and the skewed eyed boy (both children who frequently visited his fort) lifted their fingers and pointed at this peculiar boy on their side of the fence (almost accusatorily), and then the visiting delegate spoke and nodded in the muffled way people do when they share secrets, so the captain made note of that too. But when their guests gestured towards this boy within the reverend's arms, it would seem the reverend was feeling overly benevolent by pointing back at them (or was he requesting a trade for the other three children outside the fence?) Ted couldn't tell exactly what was going on, but he knew they had enough mouths to feed at present. There was no way he was allowing any more mouths in this fort, even if their entire village was sick or dying. Opportunely, he jumped in when a man among the aborigines coughed; the captain securing the reverend behind an arm and further away from the fence.

"Not to worry, Ted," the reverend besought the captain as he politely removed Ted's arm from his way.

"Mind telling me what's going on Reverend?" he asked politely as he went for the reluctant child, intending to hand him over to the visitors.

"Don't," Father Benedict pleaded, stopping Ted from forcing the boy to them.

The Captain shrugged and let the restless priest and child be.

The Osivie gestured towards all the others in his company and then gestured at the child.

"That won't be possible," Reverend Benedict declined softly.

"What wouldn't be possible?" Ted interpolated, but it appeared both chief and priest hadn't the intention of engaging him in this apparent negotiation. Whoever it concerned.

They gestured an exchange, requiring the curly haired boy and cornrow plaited girl to lean against the wiry gauze, before requesting the child in the reverend's arms. They were requesting a second time. "It is the boy they want," Ted said to the reverend, but as far as he could see the reverend stubbornly held on to the boy. "And why can't they have him?" he ventured to ask.

"This child is not theirs," the reverend answered simply and the captain raised an eyebrow, but the look he found slouched across the faces of his lieutenants was a jaded one. They were bored of this, and so the weariness of caking out in open air quickly caught on.

"Neither is the child yours. The way I see it, they can very well do whatever they want," the captain stated, having pieced together this pixie of a jigsaw.

"The case is not that simple."

"Then simplify it."

"It's not that simple, Ted."

Ted skipped the formalities. "Fine. I'll let you have it your way. They are yours to handle. I'm not needed here. No more children," he said and that was that, walking away with his lieutenants to more pressing concerns, equally ecstatic their current predicament revolved around whom was where not where was whom. It was quite understandable by

Ted to be a ghost to the Osivie whatever the fat man's concerns were. He really didn't care.

The pregnant doctor interrupted him along the way. "You left this," she said and mumbled some hogwash about misjudgement and faith. Ted took his hat without a word, securing it to its rightful place before walking away, simply leaving her standing there as an awed audience ogled at her behind awed eyes. Eno, Osate, and Jite were on the other side of the fence. The children probably hadn't realized she'd been pregnant all this time, so she smiled at them warmly. Weirdly, they didn't smile back. It appeared in the presence of their parents, the indigenous children required permission to smile. Or maybe not. She slid by the reverend to ask, "why would the Ishaporke come all this way? Didn't you say the old man believed this child was of a different village?"

"He is but I've had time to think about it. It is as you said. If we are to hand him over to anybody, it should be his people—the Ilu-Sango," Father Benedict answered. "My predicament is how to put it to Ted. I realize I've asked for too much lately."

The Osivie ignored Elizabeth for reasons best known to him and his oracles. He gestured at the child again but Father Benedict kept the boy to himself. The chief of the Ishaporke reluctantly stretched a hand to Jite, the priestess of Ishaporke herself, still

Father Matt showed no sign of releasing the boy to them.

The priestess herself came against the wiry fence, but that was when one of the captain's boys in Khaki saw it fit to challenge her as he emerged from behind the huge powder gun, venting his strange and dissonant tongue down at her. The child took her hands off the fence. She needn't anyone to tell her that.

The chief of Ishaporke was too weak and bloated to argue, so one of the oracles blew some kind of powder or dust towards the fence before they turned away. There would be no trade today.

Father Matthew Benedict clutched Taye close to himself, keeping the powder from touching the boy. Or allowing Elizabeth breathe it in. Whatever it was. Whatever was happening. It was also quite disconcerting watching the children leave with them. Something was wrong. Terribly wrong. "Why do they want to trade him in for one of theirs?" Elizabeth asked.

"I suppose they've come to misunderstand why we desire the children here," Father Matt replied, equally curious in stringing together whatever was going on with the Villages of the Hill.

"It doesn't explain why they would...don't tell me this absurd visit has something to do with what you told me earlier? If I'm right. Am I right?"

"I'm not sure," Reverend Benedict answered mechanically, his gaze a mile away as an odd feeling went about him. Wondering what other consequence lurked in the shadows for denying them the boy. Or what obscure fate awaited these villagers for not having this boy.

"My head reels that the chief would try to trade his granddaughter for a total stranger. She is his granddaughter, isn't she?" she asked.

"I didn't think you caught that."

"Well I did! I know an exchange when i see one. You still haven't answered my question, Father Matt."

When the priest failed to reply, she grimaced, "—the customs here are bizarre. This continent never ceases to amaze me."

"Hard to believe," Father Benedict mumbled with an unfamiliar smile. "Truth is, I'm going with my gut here."

"You made the right choice, Father Matt."

"Doesn't feel that way. Still not our land either. I fear I'm walking blindly here, John always told me never to interfere in their affairs."

"They looked sick, Father. The boy may be one of them, but it would have been criminal to let these ones take him from us," Elizabeth argued, and so Father Benedict and the child walked away. The Reverend also noticed a skip in the child's walk (almost euphoric), but it didn't come as a surprise him. The less she knew the better, so they simply walked away.

It missed! And by a quarter of a foot! Matulu knocked the bed away in reflex and the eerie old man dangled atop it. The nurse could feel the raw venom tauten his skin as it dripped off the aluminium tray and onto his clothing; for against the misshapen tray it had come crashing. As he scrambled away, the long snake snapped at him repeatedly; striking and missing, striking and missing, one more strike after every failed strike (because the long snake had had its tail caught by one of the cots), and that in a stroke of providence had accounted for the quarter of a foot separating the nurse from the afterlife as the mamba bled from the injury of the weight pinning it down. Matulu held on to the charm around his neck for even more luck, on noticing the wound aroused more fervour and ever more belligerent behaviour in the silver coffin-head. When he could muster the courage (and also when he realized at any moment the silver mamba could break free of its bond), he sent the crumpled tray smack into its head. Slapping the tray hard into it, and over it, over and over again, until this time the coffin-head was dead, and unlike the last time, had no more blood to shed. Immediately, the nurse yanked the draperies back up (every one of them) to let a flood of daylight into the infirmary, exposing any leftover dark spaces. He cross-examined the tent for other surprises. Roaches. Rodents. Any surprises. As a matter of fact, the tall grasses growing behind the infirmary looked all the more menacing now. As do the grasses by his lodge.

He whipped the body of the snake from the bed frame and left it strewn across the floor. Refusing to touch it any longer than he had to. Or unwind its tail caught in the wheel. Just in case it somehow stayed alive.

In length, the coffin-head lay longer than any man head to foot, so Matulu sat on the ground, oblivious to choice, and refrained from moving a muscle until the doctor returned (and it did take Elizabeth a while to return).

When she did, she found him crouched by the beds and immediately became curious over what was going on with the Bantu. That was until she spotted the snake. "Un'ka! Snake!" she panicked, hopping on the farthest end of the nearest bed, but soon enough she realized it was a little too late for jumping around. "You killed it," she said, stating the obvious.

The officers that were stationed outside barged in, a little too curiously, on hearing the panic-fraught female. Matulu ignored them. He just sat in the dirt, watching the mamba he'd crushed. This was the second time, someone, now something, had come for his life.

"It's a long one, Un'ka. How did you do it?—How did it get in here?" Elizabeth asked, even if she knew all too well she wasn't going to get a response from the nurse. He still wasn't talking to anyone. The doctor noticed the tail of the snake trapped, or locked, under the wheel of a bed. It was the bitter old baby killer's bed. She checked the old man for puncture wounds. He was clean. And still unconscious. The Captain's men saw the snake and systematically checked the captain's sick officers for bite marks. No one in the medical tent had been bitten.

Elizabeth hopped off the bed and squatted where he sat. "You saved them. They don't deserve you saving them, but thank you," she said gratefully, "—not that I'd blame you if you didn't," she mumbled, probably joking or probably not, as the soldiers grunted and left the tent. A little while later, she found it impossible to twig how the crazy old baby killer had escaped being stricken. The odds of it!

Captain Book checked on the reverend while he was taking his soup. A little while later, Elizabeth bust in when the child had put the reverend's soup bowl away. Ted, as before, ignored her, but the only way he could accomplish that completely was if he wrapped up his conversation with the reverend. And so he did, "if you are that bent on visiting the Ilu-Sango, I see no better time, Reverend, but I'd advise caution," Ted said, acquiescing to the reverend's request so he could get on his feet. "We'll be on the move any day you say, so take a rest. We have all the time in the world to do that," he said courteously, pitching his hat as he passed Elizabeth on his way out. A smug across his face.

Still it was a mutual feeling, in a way. "Un'ka killed a silver snake in his sickbay today," Elizabeth announced to Father Matt as she tacked up a plastic smile, arching her words for the captain. "He saved them! Nobody was hurt," she sung.

"A snake?—we've never had a snake in there before."

"Yes! Yea long! It's incredible the nurse arrested it. I was about to suggest to the captain he lend a hand in clearing the thick bushes growing behind the sickbay," she said, raising her voice for Ted to be able to hear her all the way away. To her surprise, the captain answered her civilly. All the way across from the reverend's Mission School.

"Fine. I'll have my officers clear the area."

"—that includes the brushes by Matulu's lodge, Captain? I'm hoping your officers remember he lives out there too," Elizabeth opted to add, but he gave no response to her, leaving her wondering if he was still out there. Or was just being an ass.

"Things run a lot smoother when you two aren't reaching for each other's throats," Father Benedict remarked and Elizabeth grimaced. Taye sat himself quietly into the reverend's chair, figuring out from frequent use how to use the rickety device (and feeling quite comfortable using it), but Liz usurped the seat and sat the child across her laps.

"It's guilt. If you want to know the reason, I landed him one across the cheeks—I hadn't meant to slap him," she admitted and Father Matt looked a lot surprised.

"I suppose he didn't return the hand?"

"Strange things have happened over the past few days, I guess," she tittered, watching the child sitting on her laps and running his legs idly.

"You say that but you don't believe that," the reverend chided her, noticing how she was with the child.

"Maybe I should," she confessed jokingly, "I mean everything so far—dogs gone wild—I slapping the captain—a snake seemingly waltzing its way into our sickbay—our overcrowded sickbay without so much as biting anyone—I mean, what are the odds of that, Father?" she commented, easing her back into the chair.

"I am as surprised as you are," Father Benedict answered softly, just having reached a decision about the child. There was a murky line between coincidence and fate. "I've asked Ted for us to return the child to his people at Ilu-Sango. He needs to be with his own for the safety of everyone."

"I thought you said the Ilu-Sango was like the holy grail of villages?" Elizabeth asked, toying with Taye's hands.

"Ted does. Still I'm thinking tomorrow."

"Tomorrow? So soon?"

"Or the day after," Father Benedict answered succinctly, intending to be snappy about the whole thing, for this being a conflict he couldn't fully grasp, he felt it best they stay estranged to it all. Father?" she commented, easing her back into the chair.

"I am as surprised as you are," Father Benedict answered softly, just having reached a decision about the child. There was a murky line between coincidence and fate. "I've asked Ted for us to return the child to his people at Ilu-Sango. He needs to be with his own for the safety of everyone."

"I thought you said the Ilu-Sango was like the holy grail of villages?" Elizabeth asked, toying with Taye's hands.

"Ted does. Still I'm thinking tomorrow."

"Tomorrow? So soon?"

"Or the day after," Father Benedict answered succinctly, intending to be snappy about the whole thing, for this being a conflict he couldn't fully grasp, he felt it best they stay estranged to it all.

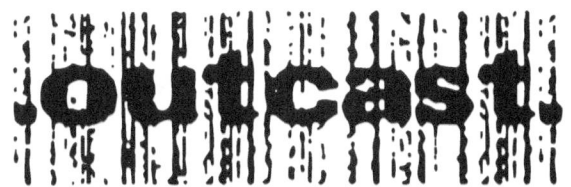

outcast

Vomiting was an everyday experience at the fort; usually at a drinking table, sometimes overnight after a hangover, but most times at the macabre sight of a freshly decomposed wild thing. Headaches and migraines also came with the territory, the yellow sun's scorching impression taking a toll on the soldiers now and then. As with fatigue, which was also a frequent on this new continent. As frequent as the runny noses they've been known to catch on continually dusty harmattan afternoons like today. But losing one's balance, running a temperature, twitching or jerking, or keeling into delirium were more than the atypical returns for serving one's country on foreign soil, Ted feared. Now five more beds had been taken. All in the space of a day! They suffered from symptoms more than fatigue and the white light, making the total number of infirmed a whooping thirteen! Captain Book ordered his officers to machete the bushes hedging the infirmary. If anything came slithering out, the captain didn't want it anywhere near his officers. They brought the last man in last night, so he stood by gormlessly, watching Doctor Cambridge work her microscope and Matulu attend the sick officers in beds.

"If I am to bury them all, I'd appreciate you telling me," Captain Ted mumbled, fumbling with his hat. He didn't stutter. "Nobody seems to be improving."

"Whatever this is, it's spreading fast. I can't truly treat anyone until I have zeroed in on the agent, which eludes me. I'll have to rule it as transmissible if I find no agent soon," she confessed sadly, taking her eyes off the mammoth microscope. "I don't think you and your officers want to be in here any longer than you should," she instructed suggestively, uncomfortable with the number of eyes overseeing Matulu's every move and insertion. "I also advise you bathe and wash those clothes. Un'ka and I would do the same. As should your officers. And speak to the cook, Captain. Almost all camp-related ills are due botulism—"

"Very first thing I—," Ted interpolated, but running out of saliva before he could finish, "he's says he's fine."

"Still I'd like to examine him," Elizabeth said strictly. The Captain felt his meaning upended, but nodded humbly. She looked at the men on beds then looked at the captain. Ted was distraught. "I can give them pills to alleviate their discomfort, but you'll have to realize I'm yet to figure out what we're up against."

"Thank you."

"—uncanny really, the invading protozoan doesn't

look at all active under a microscope."

"I need to know if you will be pulling my men into quarantine?" the captain asked, and politely too, perhaps scarified by the dwindling number available under his charge.

Elizabeth sighed. The Captain was right. "If this continues, we might have to start sharing beds," she muttered, chewing at her fingernails, "but I'm going to see to it we do something about him first," she said out loud, turning her attention to the odd baby killer sleeping soundly in her medical tent and taking a whole bed to himself. She indicated to Matulu to separate the Kiki from the other officers even as Ted Book of Her Majesty's RNC looked on with a weird, but amiable expression about his face.

He placed his hat on, and for the first time, Elizabeth sensed a feeling of kinship exuding from the captain. Ted Book tugged his hat to her and left in a beeline for the bathroom, his spirits uplifted. He also made sure his officers made the trip with him.

When he was done and all but stepped out of the shabby bamboo shack they called a bathroom, Ted bumped into the reverend. Or the reverend was waiting for him.

"I was just at the sickbay. Elizabeth said you would be here."

"Yes Reverend?"

"I was wondering if today will be a good time to return the child. I know it's too soon to ask—"

"that that won't be a problem, Reverend," the captain answered up front. His reply had been succinct. So succinct and upfront, it was possibly premeditated because the captain hadn't dithered, hadn't questioned, and certainly hadn't delayed. So much so, the captain's reply had caught the reverend at sea.

I shaporke's Osivie and his delegate of sick malnourished visitors did not make the journey home that day. Not that it was expected at their miserable pace.

"*Wo yhoro?*[13]?" one of the oracles asked the chief. It wasn't the first time he'd asked. Nor had he been the first one to ask it.

"No," the Osivie fumed, and not just the first time, too weak to exchange words with his oracles. He hadn't the energy to do so with the godskins, so god's foot! There was no way he was going to start now. Much of the journey still lay ahead; he wasn't going to squander that time arguing over nothing. His reply did nothing to halt the creeping feeling though. The feeling of being watched; it was the oddity haunting the oracles; signs in the bushes, like a forest of eyes, reading more like malice every time they plucked a leaf to read it; signs in the bushes,

[13]did you not hear it?

looming over them and growing quietly like a shadow every time. They didn't like it; this uncanniness of emotions building against them, sour emotions pent-up behind the camouflage of a placatory green forest, so they kept watching the trees, kept listening to the whispers of the wind and the forever green leaves. Occasionally, they'd finger out birds about their business, or monkeys as they skedaddled through the branches, but up until they burned off his wick, they really found nothing. Nothing at all. Nothing to prove they were in their right minds. Anyway what frustrated the Osivie in all this was how they rationed their steps. Walking a little faster won't kill them. Neither did he think it hurt the move of the gods—be it their turgid divinations of fate—to hurry things along whenever they required the procession to stop. These rites, rather this antediluvian testing system, was slowing their trip back by hours. "The walls are not yet cracked so as to wear me down to the god's swollen foot. If there's something then there is something, but if there is nothing then let there be nothing! There's no one following us. Can't you let it be and let's move on," he mentioned, thoroughly irked. In fact, he was getting tired of their suppositions. The former medium was the reason he made this trip. Even if his message had done them no good, wherever in Olokun's name the old Kiki was hiding.

He passed on his horsetail staff to his

granddaughter, passing off the burden of its weight as well, but the oracles didn't like the Osivie's attitude and so expressed their self-righteous indignation (and expressing it dutifully too) up until the moment the shadows begun to stir.

"Look," Jite said to her grandfather. She was the one who noticed it first. Or rather noticed him.

The crown of the forest, that is the forest's great canopy of leaves so high up over their heads, moved in ways almost impossible to explain. They literally moved shadows across the entire forest floor; shadows that grew darker by the second and, as a matter of corollary deduction, toyed with the sunlight that made it through to the forest bottom where they stood, vacillating light with darkness where it mattered most as would a forest-wide raffia mat. This unprecedented experience was as disconcerting as it was omnipresent.

"No, look!" she repeated to the beetleheads, pointing her finger at the only other child in their entourage of men, unable to understand what was going on with the Kiki boy for it could be said that the boy was crazy, or was at war with himself because he was scratching his body to bleeding and biting down on his own tongue until blood oozed down the sides of his lips.

"No, stop it! You stop it! Stop it!" Osate argued grudgingly as the oracles looked on in concern. He wasn't speaking to them, but he was definitely speaking with someone.

"Who is he talki—" the Osivie had begun to ask when the oracles hushed him and brought out their sacred leaves to chew. This was no ordinary boy, but then Osate turned to them and smiled. Quite the patulous smile, actually.

When the child spoke, he spoke with a voice that didn't belong to him, "*ose!*[14],"

He had spoken in a rich voice, but calling his voice rich didn't make it any pleasant. "The witchweed does not call the corn, father. We are not your fathers. We know you. What do you want?" the oldest of the oracles asked bravely even as Osate's smile morphed into what could be a frown.

"What do you want me to say?"

"Outcast! Taboo! We know what you are," the other oracles confessed, or performed, even as they spat masticated tobacco at him. Or it. Or her. Probably her for she sounded nothing like a boy.

Her frown was set in place now. "You know better than leaves," she taunted as she wiped the tobacco off his face (even took the time to help them chew it) as her voice, or be it his league of voices echoed, "we always come back! We always come back! You should have thought of that before you called on the Kiki! Nothing ever works."

"What does it want?" the Osivie asked his oracles, angst-ridden, "this obviously has something to do with the things you do. I don't want to be any part of it."

Osate's head shook almost like he was struggling with it, but then turned to face the Osivie, "*migwo*[15] brother," she greeted and immediately he recognized her (at least his sister's voice) from the night strangers came and took her away. She was only five at the time.

"You!"

"Yes me."

"—Us," the other voices corrected.

"But you died? They said you were dead."

"Only because you let them take me."

"They said you were never my sister," he responded in less than a whisper, beside himself with grief. Or panic. "You put things in my food."

"I never liked you too, sweet brother," she said with menace, the many voices taunting him (also taunting her) taunting what was once a filial bond.

"What do you want?"

"The fallen kernel does not offer the squirrel what to eat," he, she, or them answered in chorus, watching the Osivie hold his granddaughter, holding her tightly and protectively, right about the time the

[15]african expressionism
(a compound idiomatic word *serving as a greeting*)

first tiny ant dropped from the trees. It was easy for the priestess to brush the bug off her shoulders on having its puny legs tickle her skin, but it was not until the second and third ant fell that Jite realized what was already there. The ants drizzled down like rain and there was nothing none of them could do to escape being nibbled at. This peculiar army of ants had been sweeping mindlessly through the forest for days on end now, almost like a plague, and swarming faithfully, picking every blade of leaf clean on contact and sterilizing the forest floor of wildlife.

The boy Osate himself didn't look amused, or concerned, as he watched everyone else bump into one another and bleed from every orifice. At least not until he too was bit.

"Stop it!" he said to his siblings, a blister popping up immediately, even as another ant bit into him. "I did what you asked, so stop it!" he charged, but it seemed this time his siblings had some other thing planned. Something big. Something they'd been planning outside his knowledge for years because now they whispered to him morbidly, "we thought we told you we didn't need you to do want we want. It's time you returned."

Just bordering the outskirts of the third Village by the Hill, half of a day east to the lower grounds they had come, the captain fleered as his horse came up a lone footpath running uphill, "one would think by the 17th century, these mutts would use stones for houses," he mentioned, referring to the untapped basement rocks jutting from key positions on both their flanks. His lieutenants also snorted their disapproval; all four having to file their horses in a straight line behind the captain and the priest. The path couldn't take two horses side by side, a strategic advantage for the ilu-sango as it was a big disadvantage for the captain's men. Still, Ted and his boys came prepared, armed to the teeth with knives, machetes, matchlocks and a flintlock pistol—ready for a small war if things went south.

"Ted," Reverend Benedict called excitedly, his voice a tad elevated through the strain. The priest was appropriately dressed in expedition clothes for this trip, making his baldness and age more prominent, but in a good way; if ageing could ever be perceived as a good thing. "These homes are no different from ours at the fort. Or the stream bridges you freely use if the Ishaporke hadn't taken a liking to us."

"Meaning what? I don't owe these people, Reverend."

"No, no trouble, that's not what i meant, but i must

confess it makes me uneasy every time why you need all this weaponry?"

"Well then this will a good time to inform you, Reverend, if it's not too late already, that we have no relations whatsoever with this village, which is why I'll again advise caution. Do not be frivolous. Let me handle everything," Ted rejoined and looked uphill. It was one footpath. A winding footpath. The sole path in and out of Ilu-Sango. A footpath not only straddled by impassable virgin forests, but also interminable virgin forests. Something that wouldn't have mattered if this particular tribe wasn't so bloody belligerent because ever since the onset of British land expeditions into the Niger Cameroons, the Ilu-Sango had always been a very xenophobic tribe, with set beliefs, and chiselled warriors to carry out those beliefs, wielding arrows and machetes in one solemn order—arrows for hunting and machetes for outsiders. They were the tough guys and unfriendly to every other tribe. Big, hefty, dark blooded tough guys, with an uphill advantage, which was why the Brigadier had strategized reconnaissance and not diplomacy for the occupation of this side of the hill come future. "Of all the villages within the new protectorate, these are the ones to look out for," the captain mumbled uneasily, glancing at the child sharing the reverend's horse and taking the priest's ebony kid at face value, "I brought you here because I think if anyone can get us access up there, it's this boy. You say he's one of them. He is one of them, isn't he?"

"Winning trust is a gradual thing, Ted. You have to learn to wait for it. You can't just take it."

"Might surprise you what the Brigadier would say," the captain garbled, before leading the group up the path until the village came into view. From the distance, ilu-sango looked like a village of baked huts with dried foliage for roofs. The huts were from grey clay, some cracked, others hemmed up with kernel seeds to hold the clay firm. Even others had dark fibrous clusters or balls jutting out of their mud walls.

"What are those?" Father Benedict felt led to ask for there just wasn't a soul in sight from where they stood.

"Fuel for burning. The aborigines get it from the trees."

"If it's fuel, why do they wall their homes with it?" the priest asked again, pretty excited over this visit. The Captain could see that.

"I've never asked Reverend—if you really want to know, you'd have to ask them when you get the chance," Ted retorted, nervy now that they had gotten to the inlet of the village. There was an unnatural sway to some forest leaves astraddle the footpath, so Ted halted his horse. His lieutenants halted their horses too.

"Why are we stopping?"

"We are not alone, Reverend. I suggest we all stay sharp," he said, fingering at pockets of forest leaves in accusation, but when nothing in their immediate vicinity moved for a while, he nudged the reverend to look ahead, "—and because of those," he mentioned. There stood a delicate construction of mud tunnels across the herbage littering the grounds. One reconnoitred by ants. It extended yards before them, even a token into the village. "Fire ants," the captain informed, "Can be vicious little critters—could very well be the reason why there's no one in sight," the captain answered, saving himself a question not far from the reverend's excited chain of thought. "It is not pretty to see these critters swarm," he also warned, his meaning ambiguous, but signalling his cavalry divide. His lieutenants keyed intuitively to Ted's instruction, as the last two grounded their horses while the others prepped themselves for action. They were ready.

"You have to secure your boy as we storm across, Reverend," the captain advised, but was met by a lost look, so Ted squared their horses, and then lifted the kid off the reverend's horse and onto his. "Hold the ropes steady. Pull back when you're over the ants," he instructed as he slapped the reverend's horse from behind after taking the child. The priest held on obediently and it trotted right through the mud tunnels, unleashing a frenzy of ants. They also galloped across, the captain and two of his officers, before the fire ants flooded the pathway.

Now, though hostility had never been their intention, the intensity with which they had galloped into the village didn't speak well for the captain and the priest when they were met by fearsome warriors; each man wielding a stringed bow, a quiver of arrows, and a machete, and having a skin tone likened to charbroiled molasses. The darkest ever. The most intimidating of them was the one-eyed one because not only was he thick-set, he was wearing a stone-cut scowl and holding on to a backpack like a trophy. They didn't have to keep staring at him, but that was a backpack he was carrying. It certainly wasn't theirs.

the men stood a while, but after an unusually long silence of watching the godskins, one of the hunters asked elatedly, "Isn't he the one? the one we've been looking for?" he pointed at the captain with the child in his arms.

"Yes. The stream that one drinks from will never pass him by," Makanjuola grunted in response, "we will take him."

"But we must remember not all melons are the same, not all may have ill intentions. We must remember the village is dying," one of them suggested to his compeers, even if he'd hesitated in saying it.

"*bí ajá wo agbádá iná, tí àmtkùn wo wù j, tí ológìnní sán àkísà m ìdí, egb aperanje ni won ńṣe*[16]," answered Makanjuola before turning his damaged eye to him, pointing singularly towards the captain and child, "they bring him to prove their intentions. They are no different from the others."

"But—" he was already beginning to object when Makanjuola cut him short.

"—but nothing. It is the butterfly that chooses to fly the straight path that finds itself warm in the belly of the toad."

And so, even if they had been hesitant at first, lingering a little longer to contemplate their actions as they exchanged glances with these capricious godskins, the answer from the men of Ilu-sango was snappy, unequivocal, and impossible to miss.

As Elizabeth prepared herself for a wash after she was done, Un'ka Matulu took off his shirt only to pick up a machete and get started on the brushes by his quarters—brushes the captain's junior officers had either forgotten to cut or blatantly ignored. He ended his short exercise by the graves, even before the captain's soldiers were done mowing around the

---

[16]even if the dog dons a fiery robe, the tiger a bloody garment, and the cat merely girds its loin with rags, predatory animals they still are. **301**

doctor's personal bathroom all the way to the small stream. The captain had buried a dog recently and erected a wooden tombstone so close to his living space, he had to look past it, still none of it meant anything to Matulu since he had his charm. It didn't hurt him to feed the rotting trash in the ground to the thorns and thistles though, so he let those bushes be. Everything else within 5 feet of his sleeping quarters, the nurse diligently hacked down. It hadn't even taken him an hour to do it and was through before the captain's officers could wash off and rejoin fort duty.

The nurse sat into the grassy heap he'd gathered to rest his arms and dry up the sweat streaming down his body. When he saw Doctor Cambridge saunter to her bathroom ready for bath, she was behind a huge towel and lifting a pail of water—her skinny legs ever so distant from the protrusion that was becoming her belly—as she closed herself in the small stall with the pail. She smiled unevenly at him from the distance, the stall wasn't all closed off (the captain had built it that way) so she could spot the nurse and everyone else out there working the bushes from above the cut bamboo stalks that closed her in, even after she'd lathered her face and hair. The nurse was watching out for her privacy, she noticed, but Matulu had barely returned to sit in the heap when he felt a prick against his nape.

It felt like a twig had stabbed him, but when he got

off the heap, it was no twig because the sting hardened his nape to a palate and exacerbated in a pain too harsh and near paralyzing to utter. A pain that felt as if someone had literally jabbed a stitching needle down his cervix! The nurse wouldn't bring himself to scream. He didn't need anybody's help and didn't want it, but be that as it was, that one sting progressively cooked his throat, burning down his pharynx all the way to his heart. In fact, the nurse could no longer feel his jaw. Or his tongue when he bit himself. Conversely, a second sting sprung his dead jaw back to life and Matulu slapped the insect dead against his cheek, but now a pain shot up his face and exploded into his eyes in a migraine before he could get a look at whatever it was. His vision blurred immediately as all he could make out was fuzzy, or was it the unremitting buzzing he could hear? A buzz actively multiplying around him. Whatever it was stung again, and again, and again, and the nurse hadn't been at all conscious he let out a cry for help.

Elizabeth was there in a second, naked, all lathered up, and helpless. Her nurse had crushed a vespiary without knowing so.

On sighting the warriors and their machetes, Taiwo attempted to wiggle off the captain's grip but Ted held on stalwartly (the child being the only reason they were trespassing in the first place). "We've come to return this boy to you," he said with an uneasy smile, locking eyes with the reverend, very unsure what their bold intrusion might signify, but the warriors remained eerily silent, more concerned over the able-bodied intruders with their explosive sticks than they were with the hapless boy in their talons. They didn't smile back at the reverend or offer any gestures. In fact, their continued silence was almost deafening. Ted's two lieutenants squeezed their horses side by side behind the captain just in case, but when the villagers finally spoke, it was a language useless to them.

They spoke to each other in dialect. The one with the wounded eye looked the most threatening or influential because he was frequently pointing at the captain and the child, but the moment the reverend felt that fateful switch in dispositions was when the bruise-eyed man barked at the others. "What do you think they are talking about?" he leaned towards the captain, slightly dishevelled.

"You are the language expert, Reverend," Ted retorted, "that bag he slings across his shoulders is not ours. The French scout this hill—bastards!" the captain cursed.

The man of the cloth didn't notice the curse, but he noticed the bows and arrows aimed right at them when the men of Ilu-Sango attempted surrounding their horses.

Taye forced another escape, and violently, so much that the captain's horse grew unsteady.

"Let's not get ahead of ourselves here," Ted complained loudly as he struggled to latch on to the child and steady his agitated horse—all with one hand. The captain's second hand rested on his pistol, so his lieutenants drew aim, waiting coolly as they pointed their preloaded sticks at the aborigines, unafraid and awaiting the captain's simple command.

"I don't think they want us here," Reverend Benedict confessed, this visit obviously very bad judgment on his part.

"You don't say," the captain retorted sardonically, trying to gesticulate and surrender the child to the belligerent aborigines. He put off his officers, having them lower their muskets. "Allow me to drop him," Ted said calmly, but the moment he had attempted to, the wounded one hurled a machete at him.

The man had a good arm because if it wasn't for a concoct of luck and basic training, both Ted and the child would be deader than doornails as the menace of the flying machete forced the captain and child to the ground (and again to the captain nigh being trampled by his own horse!) In retribution, or self-defence, Ted's war face kicked in, and as if by reflex, the captain uncovered his flintlock pistol and shot the belligerent local through the pectorals. The man dropped like deadweight and like that, in the wink of an eye, the air was fired. Ted's lieutenants needed no instructions to open fire, so they put down these belligerents, dropping them like flies to the power of their muskets.

All that was left standing was the captain's men and a restive cloud of gunpowder.

"Mother of God! Ted, what have we done?"

"I am sorry this visit falls short of your expectations, Reverend, but you can't just exactly pick your way through this," Ted snapped heatedly as he got on his feet, wiping the mud and loam off his uniform. Very upset.

"What have we done?" Reverend Benedict muttered, gaping at the blood staining his expedition shorts. This was the second time the reverend had blood splayed against his outfit, though the reverend seemed to handle himself quite well this time around.

Ted angrily shoved Taye back atop the reverend's horse. "I've had enough of this. What you do with that kid is yours to figure out," he bellowed and mounted his horse as the reverend sat with his tongue glued to the roof of his mouth.

Father Benedict felt a twitch in his heart from all the bodies strewn across the ground.

The Captain beat his horse and they raced back, over the fire ants and back through the forest, the way they came, but they'd hardly even started off the hill when Ted lost one of his lieutenants to an arrow from the bushes. Only the captain and another of his lieutenants stopped to reacquire the body. The others hadn't stopped. They rode on because the path to Ilu-Sango they'd always known to be one-way, and it was nothing but downhill from there as Ted lost his second lieutenant to a machete from the bushes despite having failed in their attempt to recover the body of the first because the fire ants had begun to swarm, reconnoitring the body and flooding the grounds quicker than the time it would have taken the captain and his now dead lieutenant to lift the dead officer off it.

It had happened between glances. One moment her apprentice was fine and watching out for her privacy, the next moment the nurse had a pervading swirl of blackness about him. She'd stormed out half-naked with her blanket, armed with just soap and a soapy pail of water. Dr. Cambridge recognized the buzzing, watching the bees, or whatever it was, sting the nurse and watching him transfigure before her eyes; his head swelling into a formless basket.

When she screamed, two of Ted's officers heard her cries and rushed to her aid, but they stood a safe distance away when they got to the nurse, now relating his experience to some cicatrized bite wounds they'd incurred last week. When they noticed the nurse's head swelling out of proportion however, they took it a bit seriously. "Try using the pail, doctor," they advised, but Elizabeth was already out of breath. She hadn't the courage to do anything, so one of the officers stepped her soft wetness aside, and handling the soap and water, doused the nurse and wasps in it. Providentially, the wasps didn't put up a fight, simply making their way into the forest as Matulu fell to the ground convulsing; his head bearing massive boils and totally out of shape. Or proportion.

"His brain must hurt," one of them observed as the doctor checked her aide's vital signs.

"Help me with him," Elizabeth begged and they did as she requested—a wet and very well naked woman being hard to say no to. Even if she was pregnant.

She sought to band two cots together when they got to the infirmary because all the bedspace had been used up, so she left them standing there with Matulu in their arms as she tried to create more room by the old baby killer. The two practically shared the same bed after she was done.

"Thank you," she said to the men, before propping her towel and strapping it firmly in place. The compliment had been their cue to disband, but they quickly returned with a queer look or request about their faces. "What is it?" she demanded, a little less indulging now, but then she learned one of Ted's officers had fallen from his duty post. The man was now unconscious and his temperature was climbing like a rocket.

"Goodness. Not another sick one," she muttered.

"The Captain put him in charge of the fort," they explained to her as they hauled the sick man in.

This was quickly deteriorating into something else cause the captain had barely been gone an hour. She sought for her glasses. It would appear she'd be banding more beds together, but there's barely enough room in the infirmary to walk as it is.

Fleshy wounds are trivial being able to heal itself; be it a dart wound, a flimflam slit across the neck, or a sustained bite to the arm. It may take a day, maybe a week, be it a month or two, but all the flesh people can expect to be as good as new. Even the scars are easy to ignore, be you that lucky. Other wounds, as we see it, dig deeper into the soul. Wounds that follow one to the hereafter, like being pelted, or being stabbed in the eye, like losing pieces of your throat to a pointy stick, or being scorched alive (charred to nothing but the ash that hugs your bones). A disconcerting memory to walk you through eternity. A scar not easily forgotten, if you're of the type who comes and goes. In this world, we've come to learn pain is what you have to live with even if it is what we dread coming here. It is the earmark of the living. The intimate singular emotion by which you define yourselves and centre your lives, even if it eventually be lost to the tides of eternity. We who come and go, on the other hand, only see it as ample motivation abroad the shores of mortality (your mortality acutally), for what is any vengeance without proper motivation?

On the night the reverend and the captain returned with a corpse on a horse, the Kiki opened his eyes. Just his eyes. The rest of his body, however, refused to respond, finding himself paralyzed and flat on the bed; in the wan company of the sick and the only other ebony man in this god forsaken hut. They were the odds ones out; being not quite dead and not quite sick.

The oil lamps flickered ominously and the cotton draperies were a morbid red. There was also an acrid smell in this square hut, square in design from how these godskins build, but even if he couldn't figure out what smell it was, be it one of the many new smells that came with the godskins, it upset him that he couldn't pull together the strength to lift himself; to watch out for himself; to watch out for the others.

The ebony godskin that usually dressed like them was lying unconscious beside him. His head comparable to the breasts of a pregnant papaya (swollen in many places with nipples to bursting), it must hurt. Too bad no one informed the godskins to stay clear of guava trees.

From all the old Kiki could see, there was no one attending this red hut, but that's when the aura in the hut changed and something felt different. Tangibly different. He also couldn't feel it moving (the snail that was supposed to protect him from harm). His eyes darted about the tent in worry. It should have been moving, unless he no longer had the charm on him anymore. The godskins must have taken it away when they cleaned him up (surely they had just killed him) for now he could feel the shadows creeping in; that madness, that sickness, the evil growing all around him. The evil that grows in the shadows. Those shadows one can only see without the eyes. Without the light. He was without his charm, crippled in more ways than one, when not so long into the eeriness, he heard it (no, heard them), the very same voices from a hundred seasons thousands of nights ago, still mean sounding like little twitters just above his head. The old Kiki couldn't move his eyes to see beyond his paralysis, but he knew whoever was now breathing down his scalp was a congregation of one, just as surely as he knew they'd come for him.

"If you mark me, I will not forgive," a voice spoke. A voice unspoiled in menace.

Red was not your typical colour; the colour of blood, closed and uninviting, nor did this square hut feel like anyone would soon stumble to his aid. He glanced at the nurse sleeping soundly by his side, Matulu's breathing was calm and indifferent. Surely his time was up.

"As soon as abiku returns to the ground, abiku returns ash and not dust as told," the voice taunted as a small hand slid across his breasts. The voice now becoming a choir of voices.

"—He's so wormy."

"—and different."

"I barely recognize him."

"—All of them live to end up this ugly."

"No. Not to me—his face will always be real. To me."

Now that voice, that last voice, that female voice, he recognized. Not for its vengeance and ire, but its sadism. "Return! Depart," she whispered into his ears and thumped the old man across the breasts. Fortunately, he hadn't felt anything, but somehow he too felt she felt he hadn't felt anything so his eyes grew wet from angst, slowly giving up water. There was more.

"Look, he's afraid."

"—he's not afraid. If i know this one, he's not afraid."

"They are always afraid."

"—he wouldn't drown us if he was afraid of us," the others recounted in a fiery oxymora of admiration and hate. "He shouldn't be afraid."

"Maybe he's changed. He did have the mind to drown his own child just to be rid of us. You don't just walk away from that. See! No charm. He's old and slowly losing it."

"Maybe."

The child caressed the old man tenderly across the head and fumbled around the infirmary for a while, looking for something which always happened to be outside the old man's field of view. The Kiki couldn't see the child, but even if he spoke in the likeness of that old girl, the old man couldn't have been surer of it. This one was the boy he failed to kill.

The child sifted through a utensil set on the doctor's tray and snipped something together, still the voices sounded discontent, so he went rummaging through all of the weird awful-looking apparatuses in the red hut, but it was not until he rapped on a keg and it thumped that they sounded satisfied and came at him to do only the gods knew what, when footsteps suddenly came trudging through the entrance.

"Dr. Cambridge? Is anyone in there?" Ted asked as he flung the draperies open, but there was no one there. The child had dunked under and out of the huge cotton draperies before Ted could yank the curtains aside. The Captain saw the draperies flutter, but nothing to rouse his suspicion. If you mark me, I will not forgive, she had said, a voice unspoiled in vengeance all these years. So inadvertently, the captain had saved the old man's life without knowing so.

By NIGHTFALL Ted and his outing party had returned to the fort, two men less. Actually, two dead lieutenants sufficed in ironing out the captain's state of mind. Ted was as cold as lead. Atypically, the reverend was sweaty, ill at ease, and weary looking like he'd survived a trip to hell and back.

"Why is there no one manning the outlook?" Captain Book demanded as his horse pulled up by the gates. He jumped off his horse and had to let himself in as the only boys he could find were more concerned with the dead lieutenant he'd arrived with. "I left a man in charge, didn't I?" he demanded tersely, but the boys stood at loss for any suitable reply (a thousand concerns stalling their response). Only the capable ones pointed towards the infirmary. The dead officer had a gash parting his clavicle, and since Ted was less than hopeful the oxford grad could conjure magic in bringing a dead man to life he ordered his boys to keep the corpse from the pregnant doctor. His least need now was a civilian panic attack ruining whatever he could piece of a fort.

Reverend Benedict got down soberly and lifted Taye off his horse. Although they were all hungry and exhausted from the journey, the reverend nudged the child to the lodge and out of the captain's way.

The boy was ecstatic, the captain noticed that, as he also noticed the dogs had ceased barking. Even when the child whisked right past their cages. It made Ted fume, looking with austerity at the pellucid abnormality of his fort. The wind was strong and this place looked like it had gone to bed early (operating on skeletal personnel with hardly anyone doing anything!) "Who's attending the dogs? Why is it they don't bark anymore?" he grunted to stir up the air as some officers whisked the dead man away to the Senior Officers' cabin, where as agreed upon, the reverend would perform a quick clandestine ceremony. The Captain was irate and expressed it by picking on them, "what the bloody hell is going on here? I thought I left someone in charge? Where in hell are the others?"

"It's the quarantine, Captain," they hesitated to admit. "The doctor put everyone on quarantine."

"Everyone?" he retorted, but hadn't waited for an answer. The Captain handed over his horse and stormed towards the infirmary, "attend the dogs," he instructed (and stood in ire when he turned to notice the boys had refused).

"Doctor's not sure what's causing the fever, Captain," one of them had responded, afraid to fall into delirium like the others, but Ted cast them a livid eye. He needn't repeat himself.

Fortuitously, when Ted hadn't found Elizabeth by

the infirmary, the reverend drew his attention to the Junior Officers' cabin, where he encountered her exiting with an oil lamp; its small oil flame vacillating under the heavy harmattan winds. "You're back," she mentioned, as if startled.

"I demand to know what's going on," Ted required from four yards away, seeking to force his way into the cabin when he got to her. The Captain wanted to inspect his men, or find out what in hell they were doing in there, but Elizabeth kept putting her bulging tummy in his way.

"You shouldn't go in there, Captain. You don't want to fall sick," she said.

"Are they sick?" he requested, or demanded, as Reverend Benedict stole a peek inside the Junior Officers' cabin through a slit between the bamboo. The men were shirtless and limp, pushing their number to over a score of the captain's men, more than half the camp, suffering from The Madness disease.

"I'm afraid so. I just quarantined half your soldiers in there."

"When?"

"Just now. There's no more room at the sick bay, Captain."

"How long ago did this—?"

"About the time you left. They've been falling sick

since you've been away," Elizabeth replied and nudged Father Matthew away from the bamboo structure. "It's best you don't bathe around the others or use the stream water. And stay away from the dogs! They may very well be the reason Matulu and I are exempt from this thing—" she suggested, noticing now that the priest appeared shabby and glass-eyed. "Is anything the matter, Father Matt?" she asked.

"I'm fine, Liz."

"No, you're not. Not until you get out of those clothes and slip in something...something not wet and covered in dirt—is that blood?"

"The men in the sickbay, are they faring any better?" Ted butt in, out of concern or intending to steer her curiosity away.

Elizabeth declined and shook her head, not fully grasping whatever was going on between the two men, "Not since you left. I've even had to bed Un'ka, so now I don't have an extra hand to assist me with all this."

"I thought you said Matulu was okay?" Father Benedict asked.

"Oh, he's isn't the fever, father. Un'ka was stung by wasps."

"You mean bees?"

"Yes, i'm not sure, but I think they are the same

thing," Elizabeth responded slowly and Father Benedict felt a twitch in his heart. There seemed to be mucous building in the reverend's eyes and she proceeded to wipe it off, a bit concerned over his health, "he was stung while cutting the grass surrounding his lodge—grass the captain's men refused to cut."

"The hornet is a divine symbol of a curse," Father Matthew confessed, but Elizabeth hadn't thought he was serious till he said it again.

"Don't start this, father."

"That we couldn't return the child today proves it."

"You couldn't return Taye?"

"No Liz. Now I fear we've done a terrible thing."

"Say whatever you like Reverend, I know my conscience is clear," the captain said.

"No, I fear our misdeed is with the child."

"Leave me out of this."

"No listen. According to the book of revelations, I was taught the hornet is a symbol of a curse. A strong curse. I think that's what the old man has been trying to say all this while. The curse. The dreams are all so clear now."

"What dreams?"

"Whatever we must do to make things right—"

"—make what right?" Elizabeth hissed, clearly not

far from irritation.

"Elizabeth you are a child of the church. We actually know nothing of that boy," he said to her pointedly (as would a bigot) and for the first time the doctor felt a creepy rush exude from the priest. "I fear I am not one to perform an exorcism. Even if I remembered, we have nothing to exorcise him with," the reverend mentioned, deflated, and not so clear in his transmission of thoughts.

"An exorcism?" Ted scoffed, stirred by the words. "Like i said, whatever this is leave me out of it Reverend. Remember, it is you who brought the child into this fort. It is you who asked to keep him here. It is also you who asked we return him today. It's all been you, Reverend—there is no we here," the captain stated guardedly, though the reverend in some thread of reasoning did make sense of all the strange happenings over the past days. Not to count the bizarre visit by the Ishaporke only days before.

"I'm not one to disagree with the teachings of the church, father. I'd love to believe in something that helps me validate my faith, but not over trivial things like bee stings? People get bitten by bees when they trample a bee hive. People fall sick too. These things happen almost every day, Father Matt. It's nothing supernatural. Actually, it'd be a release to me if it was, but we can't let indigenous superstition tear down our walls of reasoning. If we become as superstitious as they are, how do you expect we enlighten them—if at all that is what you really intend for these people?" she argued suggestively, and a well placed argument if Ted hadn't butt in.

"What superstition?" the Captain grunted.

"The indigenes told the reverend the boy we've had for months now is in fact a spirit child here to torment them—an abiku—or something like that, but we've been over this before," Elizabeth explained exasperatedly. This time her indignation was directed at the priest, and Ted locked his lips.

"And you didn't see this local superstition as something I needed to know about before returning him, Reverend?" Ted asked, also directing indignation at the priest.

"I thought to do what was best for everyone, and the child," the priest confessed (and apologetically too), but even if Elizabeth might have cared for it, Ted didn't care for an apology. The Captain loaded his pistol and headed off.

"Where are you going, Captain?" Elizabeth asked impulsively not having thought much of it at first, but the captain didn't answer her.

"The child's own people did everything in their power to kill the boy today," Father Benedict confessed to Elizabeth, "they were even prepared to kill us to get him."

"Then they must really be crazy wanting to justify murdering a child for their selfish ends. Taye has been with us for months now and has done nothing but help since then." Elizabeth remembered the captain and his pistol. "What do you intend to do with that, Captain?!" she called after Ted.

"I don't care who that child belongs to. Or if what you're telling me is true. All I know is I lost two fine officers today because you and the reverend wanted to play Samaritan, but the bloody show's over. I hope you're satisfied because I'm ending this. That child is no longer spending a day in my fort!"

"Captain, if you punish that child for your mistakes then you brand yourself a coward!" Elizabeth bawled at Ted, hoping her words would get to him because she and her weighty womb most certainly wouldn't.

The Captain stopped in his tracks. He could feel a stutter coming, so he holstered his pistol, choosing to point an upset finger at the doctor instead.

It worked.

"I don't think killing the boy is the right answer Ted," Father Benedict mentioned and Elizabeth sighed in frustration, never having thought the day would come she'd prefer the captain's company to Father Matt's. It appeared today would be that day.

When Father Matthew returned, he returned to God and not the child in his lodge. He resigned himself to prayer in the termite infested chapel John had started and Ted had finished. The chapel wasn't the strongest of structures for it had a bug problem, knocked up from wood borrowed from the vast continental forest, wood subdued by rain, but it was by far the largest structure in the fort (twice the height of a man and running the walls of the reverend's quarters and the captain's combined). The brigadier had nailed a sturdy rood into the fifth beam over the altar, hung up for years and above any man's reach. The chapel was also barren, for aside the altar, there were no stalls (no stalls, no pews, no mats). Absolutely nothing. Mass was usually conducted on foot.

On the altar, sat a bible. Beside the bible, some holy manuscripts, a rosary, and water he'd once blessed in a piscina. Father Matthew cleansed himself, cited his rosary, and began by praying for the fort—then the captain's men, including the two they'd lost today. He prayed for forgiveness and for their souls to find their way to eternal light. Then he prayed for the officers at the infirmary, and prayed passionately when praying for Ted. The Captain needed strength and fortitude to bear loss. As he did for Elizabeth, hoping she was right. He prayed for Matulu. The nurse who had been stung by bees. And the Kiki.

His old convert and the only one who'd been so savagely mauled. He couldn't blame the old man for recanting his newly-found faith, hopefully the Lord would find it in his heart to forgive him.

When it came to praying for himself, Father Benedict prayed for faith and clarity to see through whatever was happening here, right now, on this new continent. At present his mind was cluttered, he knew that all too well, with things he could and could not understand; it was all right before his nose, even if it was vague. But when it came to praying for Taye, he hesitated. Father Benedict couldn't believe he actually hesitated to pray for the little boy; the one they'd come to know. But possession and curses were nothing new to the Holy Church, so Father Benedict willed himself to pray for Taiwo, and pray he did, up until the time he drifted off (he non-stop trip to and from Ilu-Sango bound to take its pound of flesh). The priest hadn't thought to bring an oil lamp into the chapel to fight the harmattan, or the darkness that comes with the night, but he'd been praying against the influence of local spirit beliefs—Abikus shouldn't exist, but if they did, then he needed the power to fight them (if in truth all land was God's land and this chapel was but a representation of God's holy church on earth).

About half an hour later, the harmattan winds woke Father Benedict up in the way the winds forced the bamboo and hardwood beams to creak and contort under its chill. The entire chapel was pitch-black. There was rumbling and lightning, but no sound of rain—the lightning outside telling of a storm prevailing over the fort. It was a dry storm, and one with loud rumbling. There was also a rising disturbance from the outside because barely after a number of flashes, he could hear a thunderous collapse of sticks and someone yelling fire. Most likely one of Ted's boys, but that was when the reverend noticed against thick darkness, the other someone standing by the door to the chapel; he stood the silhouette of a child, illuminated by lightning and an oil lamp in his hand.

"kaale o oko oluwa[17]," the child spoke and Father Benedict's heart raced on the spot, mostly because this child's voice didn't sound like any voice he could recognize, neither did he recognize what was just said even if he knew he didn't like it.

The child stood a third the height of the door and Matthew Benedict felt a twitch, a twitch he was now familiar with, and though the child had hidden most of his face as he approached in the dim light of the oil lamp, his shirtless silhouette was unmistakable. "I will not allow you take this child, Beelzebub," the reverend announced bravely, though finding himself tripping over his tongue when he said it.

"Put that silly toy away," the child said in perfect tense after the priest drew out his glow in the dark

[17]good evening, husband of god.

rosary; the child's one voice speaking in many voices. "You're not the first of your kind we've met. Or put away," they said, but they sounded aggressively defensive so he groped for the manuscripts someplace atop the altar. The voices taunted him even more.

"Look, the snake sees the hawk coming and tries to stand erect"

"—I bet you won't find what you are looking for, oko oluwa"

The child now lifted the lamp to aid the reverend in finding his manuscripts, but in angst and the dull illumination the reverend couldn't tell apart a recital hymn from what was holy scripture.

He, she, it, or they all snickered when they drew their light away.

Father Benedict kissed his rosary, his hands unsteady as he recited off the fragments that came to memory, "exorcizo te, immundissime spiritus in nomine Domini nostri Jesu Christi," he pronounced, dipping his hands in the piscina of blessed water the moment lightning sourced him enough light.

"I am not your demon," one of the voices answered back, and in Latin, but Father Benedict made up his mind to ignore as many taunts as he could. As he'd been trained to.

"The earth is the Lord and its fullness thereof says

your Servant. Hear, holy Father, the cry of the Church suppliant: let not Your child be possessed by the father of lies. I exorcize you, you unclean spirit in the name of our Lord Jesus Christ."

With his hands trembling fiercely, he whipped the water from his rosary in the air, hoping a little will fall on the boy, but rather than recede, the voices embraced him, drawing ever closer, ever bolder, not the least bothered or hindered by his exercise.

"You should not crow in another man's farm, holy book," they warned, actually a young female voice warned, resounding in its menace, "your sorcery will fail you here. This is our home."

"Exorcizo te immundissime spiritu, omnis incursion adversarii, omne phantasma, omnis legio, in nomine, nomine domini nostri Jesu Christi—da locum! Exi! Discede!" he commanded, and for a while it seemed he waited for something to happen, but there was only a clap of thunder. When the voices laughed, they laughed so contemptuously that the reverend forgot what to say.

The little boy lifted the oil lamp to illuminate his face, their face, or its face and their steps to the altar.

Father Benedict gasped! The water did get on the boy, and in several splashes about his ebony face, but that was all it did. "Taye!" the priest called to him, however the tide of voices that came after he'd said that bounced off the Chapel's bamboo beams in anger.

"Don't! Call! Us! Taye!!" they retorted, aggressively defensive. They had been voices much older, voices more belligerent, a voice expressing sarcasm and voices peddling malice.

Father Benedict's heart twitched again, beating violently, as someone from the outside launched the sirens in the fort, but even that couldn't drown out the voices. The many voices inside his head. How they'd found their way in there, he couldn't tell, but all he wanted to do was just claw them out (if he could, but he couldn't), so he summoned a louder voice, hoping to kill off the voices, "Hear, O merciful God, the prayers of the blessed Virgin Mary, whose Son, dying upon the Cross, crushed the head of the serpent of old, and entrusted all men to His mother as sons. Let the light of truth shine upon this Your servant. Let the spirit of holiness possess him and by inhabiting him render him serene and pure. Hear! O Lord! The supplication of blessed Michael the Archangel and of all the angels—God of hosts, drive back the force of the Devil! God of truth and favour, remove his deceitful wiles! God of freedom and grace, break the bonds of iniquity!! Hear, O God, lover of man's salvation!!—free this servant from every alien power!!! Come out of him demon!!!"

"Amen," the voice of a girl answered when it was

obvious he was done talking. Or chanting.

Father Benedict charged and cast the entire pan of blessed water in the air so that the water doused the child, wetting as much of them both as it could, but the child made his way up the altar, not bothered by the salt-free water running down his lips, "your god doesn't live here, godskin. Has no one told you? We have our own gods here; me—us—we, but they would rather burn me—us—we not worship me—us—we."

Reverend Benedict hadn't expected himself to reply, but he did because he hadn't expected the Abiku spirit to be so direct, but it was. "If you are a god, how come you speak of yourself in singular and then speak in plurality?"

"Omode to fe mo oriki agba a ni opolopo suuru, oko oluwa[18]," she taunted him, and so in coming to his senses he returned to his exorcism.

"Hear, o holy Father, let not Your child be possessed by the father of lies; let not Your servant be held in the captivity of the devil; let not a temple of Your Spirit be inhabited by this unclean spirit!"

"You know those are words you don't mean," one of the voices said, remarkably at ease when it said it.

"In nomine domini nostri Jesu Christi, exorcizo te, omne phantasma, omnis incursio satanae, in nomini Jesu Christi Nazareni te manifeste!"

[18]the newborn who wants to know the panegyric of the elders will need a lot of patience

"Mean what you will. The scarab does not forage on dung without carrying a smell on its back. We've seen the blood you shed, but this is our home. Not yours. They are ours. Not yours."

Father Benedict interrupted his interminable recital.

"I have shed no blood. I haven't killed anybody," he said to them and honestly, but they made sure he heard himself when he said it.

"The rocks at the bottom claim it keeps the water clean," they say, and the little boy now standing before the altar, slaps the sacraments away and boldly stares Father Benedict in the face. "The rock at the bottom claims it keeps the waters clean," he says.

"If you want to charge me with guilt speak plainly. Don't hide behind parables because I have nothing to hide," Father Benedict said, now letting go of the greater deal with his conscience not to contend with the child. Or children. Or spirit. Or spirits.

"You can't lie to us, holy book—you are a killer and a thief," the girl in the boy spoke up, charging at him violently and forcing the reverend to hurt his eye against the bamboo when she rocked the oil lamp (she'd been toying with light and shade in the chapel which kept the priest from seeing the exposed nail!)

"I have killed no one. I covet nothing of yours," he

fought back while trying to hold back the bleeding, though he couldn't explain why his mind against his will kept running to the earlier hours of today. He never held a gun, so why should he be blamed for being there?

But the child froze in the grease-lit chapel, almost as if shocked by the news, "the eggs may look the same, but a bird will always be a bird and a snake will always be a snake," his rich deep voice echoed, echoing with the rumble of the storm outside.

"I have done nothing of—"

The child huffed and the oil lamp snuffed itself out, only to come back on again like the working of a miracle.

"Liar!"

The girl in the boy had returned, this time scratching Father Benedict herself. She was the aggressor. She was the one who really wanted to hurt him. "The hen is not so busy as to forget her eggs. You let them die like you let her die! You knew yet you sent her away anyway! You are a killer!" she said maliciously and immediately Father Benedict realized she wasn't speaking of today.

A speck of sawdust and a few mites fell onto his expedition clothes when he realized he let them back him up against the chapel beams. Now that he had no more space to back into, the voices came in torrents, chortling, taunting as the mites bit into the reverend. "What?"

"Why?"

"Now you have nothing to say?"

"—tell us"

"You knew about the infestation"

"But you sent her there to die anyway"

"—confess"

"You knew"

"You knew she was sick"

"but you left her there to die"

"—you godskins kill to save your miserable skins"

"—tell us now"

"How well are you saving your skin, godskin?"

"You've wanted"

"—everything since you got here"

"—but their lives are ours"

"not yours"

"—thief!"

"You've coveted"

"affixed your eyes on"

"—everything since you got here"

"These lands are ours, not yours"

The child now stood before the bald priest, watching him squat in guilt, "you cannot cut into the source of your own destiny because my current is just too strong"

"—killer"

"If you won't admit it, we will admit it for you."

"—you're like him with the hat"

"Yes, he's him with the hat"

"—a killer and a thief."

"No! He's worse"

"—he's a killer, a thief, and a liar, for lying to himself."

"Taye," Father Benedict called affectionately, seeking to reach for the child within the voices (a boy trapped in darkness according to all he was taught to believe).

"I said stop calling us—me—we that!!"

The reverend's heart twitched again and they watched him fall faint. He had a bad heart and so he, she or it just left him there. Besides, the termites were done eating through the fifth beam. It was the one beam in the chapel holding the rood in place, so soon enough after they left, its nail-work buckled, and swiftly the entire weight of the rood came crashing over the priest (swinging down actually) to hang itself the improper way before falling over.

More lightning crisscrossed the skies but less thunder rumbled; the signs were clear, the eye of this storm was yet to pass.

The curtains rocked back and forth from strong winds, withering the lighting and lanterns in the medical tent. "We don't have much left," Elizabeth spoke as she reorganized the lanterns hanging from the skinned tree posts. "Horrible. Father Matt is always with praise about the indigenous tribes. They are really gentle folk. It surprises me they would attack you," she garbled on as Ted watched her talk. He watched solemnly. The Captain wasn't for any talking tonight. The infirmary stunk heavily of disinfectant and kerosene, and it didn't augur well that two of them still took up space in his infirmary, perpetually robbing Her Majesty's soldiers of the meagre resources she was speaking about. None looking any closer to death. A bloody stalemate. He took off his hat and slapped it back on, a bit restless, no, infuriated by the doctor's overbearing sensibilities. "Something's changed in here. Captain, did you say you heard someone when you came in earlier?" Elizabeth asked mildly when inspecting the trays and some medicaments out in the open, but Ted moved to examine the extent of their condition. They were all still unconscious, and seriously burning up.

"He's been that way since you left," Elizabeth said

on noticing the captain's interest in her aide, only for Ted to waltz past like he cared not for the nurse, or her conversation, so she went on to inspect the curtains and fasten them to nails to keep the winds from bludgeoning the helms into the faces of her patients. "At least the jerking has stopped. I'm hoping it's a sign your officers will get better," she remarked, but that was when the captain broke his silence.

"I was under the im—impression they would no longer be here when I returned," he uttered, not acquainted with bottling things up.

"And what gave you that impression? I can't just toss him out in the cold?" Elizabeth countered, fingering the captain take a look at the strong winds wilting the lanterns, "—and you needn't refer to one man as they, Captain? Unless you intend I send our own nurse out as well?" Elizabeth intoned sardonically, but Ted had found no humour in it. As humourless as she'd found it when she discovered he'd actually been serious. She turned on a frown. He was as predictable as he was incorrigible, but like always the doctor wilfully chose to ignore his lack of tact and went right on to inspecting Matulu's boils. Matulu's head had shrivelled to a redeemable size, so she sifted through the medical trays for an experimental bottle labelled ACTH. It should suffice in knocking off his sedation. "He'll have to get better first if you want him out," Elizabeth spoke up, referring to the baby killer taking up space in her infirmary as she injected the nurse. It was then she noticed the old man with his eyes open—her first positive response in days. She almost cheered but the elation was short-lived cause she'd rather have the lunatic rot to the afterlife, had it not been for the oath she'd taken. "In the least Father Matt would be happy to see his butcher friend awake. Congratulations Captain. You will have your wish," she informed duteously the instant she was done with Matulu. She left to find the priest.

Ted also inspected the old man, but solely out of curiosity. Or optimism perhaps. Although his amputated arm was a mass of dried blood and bandage, his breathing was steady. And conscious. He was a resilient old man, this one.

Elizabeth returned to borrow an oil lantern from the tent, or maybe because she was unsure whether to leave the captain unsupervised, but Ted himself hadn't looked killer keen being left with those he couldn't stand in the first place, so she ended up leaving him there.

the starlit sky did nothing to lift the darkness over the fort, or stop the stormy winds blowing in from the East. It was breezy, with the howling of trees, creaking bamboo, and roar of approaching thunder. Underneath it all, Elizabeth thought she had heard someone scream fire. But, that was just a thought. Besides, the night was breezy and she couldn't smell a thing. She made her way through the dirt road to the priest's quarters. All of Ted's able officers were on watch this night, supporting the personnel doing rounds about the fort (so almost too frequently they ran into her with their torches), almost as if they had reason to be on guard tonight. The evening breeze intensified, threatening to rob her of her clothes and snuff out her lamp before she got to the small lodge. When she did, the doctor also noticed no one occupied the West Outlook (even if Ted usually had someone up there), still she didn't give it much thought and she eased into the Mission School. Now just before she did, Elizabeth thought she'd seen another oil lamp exiting the chapel—someone hitting the dirt road swaying a lamp recklessly through the darkness. For a moment there, whoever it was seemed headed in her direction, so she had waited for him, but when he too spotted her obscured lamp in the dark, he slowly started away. When she inquired for the father from him, he took off fleet-footedly. Like a wild cat. An odd thing to do. Very odd. But that too she hadn't given much thought since whoever it was, was clearly not the old man she was looking for (on account of his agility and speed).

the child lit two candles and was half through eating the special roast reserved for communion when she came in. She stood aghast. He'd been sifting through the reverend's personals beneath the small altar table. "What are you doing?!" Elizabeth inquired, hurriedly shearing the boy off the priest's sacred things. The locker beneath the altar was open. "How did you—never mind. That's communion bread, you shouldn't eat that!" Elizabeth stated (quite troubled the priest would find out) and snatched the bread from Taye, but her manner had startled the boy, and so on spotting fear imbue him, she calmly tossed the bread back into the locker and held his face in her hands. He looked lean and famished. "You must be hungry from your trip. Do you know where the reverend is?" she asked, but a question she knew would foster no answer. She tugged the child playfully by the cheeks, "let's see if we can get you something to eat beside the reverend's bread."

She walked Taye out (the new kitchen was just along the path because she'd passed it on her way here) but on exiting the reverend's lodge, they discovered a soft orange glow rising from the direction she'd only just come. And a whiff of a very peculiar smell in the air. It was the smell of burning wood. Soon enough Elizabeth heard gunshots, and immediately was very anxious, or befuddled, as she clutched on to Taiwo, shielding the child for safety (inasmuch as she used him to shield herself). The stormy evening breeze only intensified the yellowness of the glow; a glow peaking in glints of red in the gun battle soon to follow.

fire didn't augur well for Fort Willy. A fort pieced together mainly from wood, sack material and iron mesh. Ted dreaded the outcome. His officers had rushed into an ambush of arrows and flying gourds (apparently losing two of his finest wouldn't be all he was to lose today), as flaming arrows lit the sky like falling stars and charred anything unlucky to be bound to wood or sack.

The Captain's officers called to the captain from across the marching grounds as Ted watched the commotion. They had oiled their muskets and were fully armed, but had been handicapped by the ever-growing wall of fire around them. The wood that made their perimeter burnt like a furnace, shrouding their foes in a visor of smoke and blackness (fighting through this would be fighting blindly because their enemy could blend easily with the night), so as always the captain had to think on his feet. The big gun from the Northern outlook was loud and disorienting; and the damned thing sounded even slower at recurring shots. "Doesn't anyone know how to operate that bloody thing?" he bellowed at the outlook. Obviously the noise upset him, so one of the senior officers forfeited his horse and clambered up the structure whilst the captain galloped to the training grounds. There he found just one officer working to set the dogs free. When they'd managed to set the animals loose, Ted raced back only to find the junior officers' cabin on fire! (And with the staggering way the winds bounced about) A fire only minutes away from the doctor's lodge. And the infirmary. "Put that out!" he ordered, even if there was a limit to how many buckets of sand and water a handful of men could work. He quit the horse and rushed into the smoking cabin, shoving two or three of his younger men further inside. "Get them out! Get them out!" he barked as he grabbed at sick men, puking and peeing all over him. It was obvious. They were shorthanded, overworked, disorganized and dishevelled. The Captain knew that. This assault had them stretched thin, his officers could see that. Unfortunately, so could their assailants as more arrows and flying calabashes followed.

It was then he saw them; the ilu-Sango overrunning the perimeter, a good number charging in through the gates and in more numbers than the dogs could tackle. The big gun stopped shooting as they skewered the officers operating it clean through. Each fell from the outlook with a spear buried in their loins, and so the greater number of Ted's officers moved to stall their penetration, only for the generator to explode in a bitter smack of fate bringing the entire outlook over their heads in a golden display of fire and light. Ted panicked in the bedlam and slipped out his flintlock. The Ilu-Sango were taking his fort apart, but they had either come for everyone or just someone. He had little time to figure that out, so Ted sprinted for the reverend's lodge; all doubts resolved in his mind.

lizabeth returned Taye to the safety of the reverend's lodge the moment she heard the gunshots and snuffed out all the candles save her lantern. He grabbed her hand fiercely, almost possessively, not wanting to let go, but she had an infirmary filled with sick people who needed her assistance. "Stay here," she cautioned warmly, kissing him on the forehead and trying to force him to sit on the reverend's bed. Strangely he was much stronger than she had realized, so she let him be; his ebony complexion helping him blend elusively into the darkness.

"Stay," she cautioned again as she closed off the Mission School with whatever her hands could find. The noise and turmoil seemed to be coming from the east end where the lights glowed. There was no clamour westwards. Not yet anyway. Nor did anything appear to be happening towards the South. So, since there was no shorter route, she gunned for it; tiptoeing and second-guessing her every step, guardedly making her way to the infirmary, creeping as fast as her legs could take her.

Her heart skipped a beat when she encountered a man jogging her way through wild brushes. "What's going on?" she asked, after recognizing the man was with a hat in hand.

Ted parried the question. "I need you to get my officers out of your infirmary!" he said by the time he got to her, trying to conceal the flintlock while jogging past. He was whispering. "Where's the reverend?"

"I don't...I don't know. Are we in danger?" she asked quickly, on spotting the gun.

"Get my men out. Where's your aborigine boy?—the one we brought back with us?" Ted huffed, like he cared not for an answer.

"I found him at Father Matt's quarters. If you're going in that direction, you'll need this," she slipped him her lantern, "...I left him there to keep him safe. Why do you ask?"

The Captain jogged on without an answer to boot.

"What exactly is going on, Captain?" Elizabeth complained bitterly, again, with a hand over her belly, "Look at me! You don't really expect me to move all those sick men by myself?"

"Do what you can until I get there," the captain

answered from the distance. "And make sure you keep your eyes open," he added, though it hadn't been his intention to frighten her.

By the time Ted got around to the reverend's lodge, flying gourds were coming from that direction too. The ilu-sango invaded like roaches, charging under the cover of night and coming at the fort from different angles—subterfuge, they might have been primitive, but they weren't stupid. This was a tactical attack. In a streak of irony, this was also the very same stratagem the Brigadier had documented to subdue the hills, and French, had the opportunity arisen. The West Outlook was now empty, or open to the intruders, as Ted's boys had deserted one end of the fort to fortify the other. They continued to hurl their clay calabashes at anything they saw; the combustible oil in those gourds, every bit similar to cooking oil, had been what inflamed the fort like match to straw, devouring the entire chapel in unimaginable heat. Ted's personal quarters had long been decimated to ash and rubble. Now the flames had moved on to the reverend's quarters, so both the priest's quarters and the chapel were touch and go. It was either one or the other, he hadn't the time to go through both so the captain made his choice, but now when he busted through the Mission School, the lodge was empty. The bloody child had slipped out. Not that Ted could hold it against the boy for the air was stifling and filling with smoke; with red oil dripping from the sack cloths above, staining his cotton shirt countless times. He could literally feel the fire spreading as the heat drew closer.

Now the second generator, the one at the West Outlook, the one that powered the Edison bulbs, ignited like a torch and with it the lights went out; not that the lights had been of any use, the Ilu-Sango having damn well lit up Fort William like a fire cracker. And with the billows to prove it. A lot of heat was making its way now from the chapel, so Ted tried stealing a look into it through the crevices in the bamboo. Even from where he stood, it was hot; extremely hot in there. He couldn't make out a thing outside fire and smoke. So when the West Outlook came crashing into the chapel and most of the structure caved, it served as Ted's cue to get out or he'll be trapped by the flames. Luckily, the flames lit up his surrounding just enough for him to notice two chiselled men from Ilu-Sango slipping past the west perimeter with machetes in hand. When they encountered the captain, they also encountered his flintlock pistol as Ted shot one dead, but was forced to maim the other in the shoulder with a rusted nail. A nail he found in the dirt after a brief scuffle when his pistol turned up empty. He stabbed the man dead with a splinter of bamboo just before the

Mission School came keeling over, and then took his time watching their bodies burn. In one night the ilu -Sango had brought down what had taken him years to build, so the captain quit searching for the boy. He was livid. Oh, Ted was as livid as a hornet.

W ake up—"

It wasn't the sirens that woke Matulu up. Or the warring outside that stirred him from sleep. No, it was that eerie dialect. One that stirred the nurse even if the boy's wrath wasn't directed at him—yet.

Matulu found him by his bedside; a boy he'd once thought he'd been familiar with, now having pupils coloured in blood and speaking with a congregation of voices. He had shut the old man's nose with one hand as he towered a jug in the other. There was this perilous glint in his eyes; that glint that made him look like he was enjoying what he was doing, so Matulu shut his eyes pretending to be asleep. When the boy uncapped the keg, the immediate and acrid smell of kerosene ran up the nurse's nose. "You marked me," the voices said, downing the first litre over the old man's nostrils and the old man's body buckled like a generator in response. If he didn't feel anything, they knew he would feel that as they chortled and watched him gurgle up kerosene, before turning to the nurse, "I know you're awake," one of the voices warned morbidly, speaking clear and precise Bantu at the boil-afflicted nurse. The boy's wordless stare was enough to jolt Matulu off the bed and running, wobbling out of the infirmary and almost knocking Elizabeth over when she tried stopping him. Besides, the tent had caught fire.

The doctor tried to latch onto him, "you're recovered!" she said, but Matulu was just out of it; out of wit, out of balance, mumbling a whole world of Bantu gibberish. She tried to examine him but he shoved her away and took off, almost as if he was trying to outrun his shadow. She held her belly, fortunate he hadn't hurt her. Maybe this was another episode of delirium.

The dire smell of spent wood reached her nose and she hurried into the medical tent to find its sack roofing in flames. Ted's sick officers were lying with luminous faces under its brilliant burn as the fire quickly spread abroad the sacks and down the curtains. It was fierce. There was no way she was going to be able to save anyone in the little time it would take the flames to sweep over everything, but there was also that awful smell of kerosene she used to fight off the mosquitoes; kerosene which might have been responsible for how quickly this fire spread. In fact, it was too pungent. Almost like someone had spilt it or something. It was then she saw him, Taye, playing a dangerous game of doctor by helping with the sick and ignoring the crown of fire building above them. His ebony face stood resolute under its golden glow, hardened like marble, in that one selfless desire to help, but it was not until she watched him flush a jug of kerosene down the old man's nostrils that she saw him in the real light. Taye wasn't playing doctor. Or playing at all. Her guess would be he'd set the tent on fire because he was mumbling something to the old man. Almost as if he was singing. "When Abiku returns to the ground, how will abiku repay what abiku owes? So you will drown, you will burn, but how will you ever return?" the voices muttered in dialect, even as he downed another jug in callous routine. Again, the old man's body convulsed mechanically and Elizabeth could sense life fizzle from it. All she could make out from his weird song was that word Father Benedict told her—Abiku. She called to him, terrified, in doubt, and confused, even bellowed at him trying to get his attention, but he wouldn't stop. Each time the jug was empty, he refilled it. And each time he refilled it, he down it right into the old man's nostrils. The old Kiki's body stopped responding soon enough, as excess fluid spewed from his mouth and his chest fell lifelessly. Even then, he didn't stop. He just didn't stop. Elizabeth panicked in disbelief, even then he didn't lift his head to her. She locked her fists, blind with rage, never really recalling charging at the boy. She shook him as she would an adult, inebriated with anger, and regret, as the old man lay dead, "Taye! Taye! What are you doing?—what are you?!!"

"Let us go," it, she, or they bawled at her and Elizabeth nigh tripped herself in disillusionment. They were bold, cognitive and precise words from him as he stared at her with vacant eyes and pupils black as coal. His first words at her.

He had a charm about his neck; a live mollusc, greasy and icky.

"Where did you get that?" she asked, unable to understand how he'd been hiding it from her all this while; frozen, unable to think, unable to run, unable to even tremble. She just stood there discombobulated and helpless. What else had he been hiding?

The child frowned bearing an eye for malice and Elizabeth could hear a baby crying.

"I like this one"

"No surprise there," another entirely different voice said as the little boy pointed a finger at her. "Go home!"

"—don't hurt her!"

"She's not one of us"

"I don't want to hurt you Elizabeth," a boy voice said, a voice familiar to her.

"Osate?" she asked in disbelief.

"—Don't put your apple in our basket, godskin"

"Kill her!"

"No"

"She's one of them. You have no mangoes here, Elizabeth," a girl in the boy spoke and all the voices went silent, watching Elizabeth watch them watch her. His eyes were now bloody; not bloodshot, bloody, and at that moment it felt like the carpet had been ripped from right under her. Father Benedict was right. She had known nothing about this child. Or his many persons. Or talents. Or friends. It was so implausible that she had forgotten about the fire, the heat, or the captain's men. The charred posts gave in, and the entire medical tent came crashing down in a curtain of fire, sacks and burning lanterns, and so everything that could burn burned right over Elizabeth.

A man wearing a hat was the first person she saw after that, pulling her from amidst dirt, bone and soot. Everything and everyone in the infirmary had burnt. Either to the ground or to the bone. Her eyes were covered in dirt or ash when Ted pulled her from the cover of the wrought-iron cabinets that had spared her life. And at first, Elizabeth Cambridge couldn't speak or cry. She was hardly conscious. When Ted touched her belly on the other hand, she unconsciously arrested his hand. The doctor would be okay, so Ted wrapped her within his jacket and lifted her to open grounds (much safer grounds) by the kitchen. She jolted when he attempted to clean her up because her right arm hurt—a bantam portion of the hand having been sizzled by oil. Ted frantically searched through the debris for something, but had to make do with the broken bottle of vinegar he'd found. The Captain doused her burns. He also tore through his inner shirt to have something to wrap around her wounds when she fought deliriously, "Don't—it's—don't—" but Ted could only hold her down. He didn't know how to pacify her for despite that she'd been covered in ash, he'd been covered in blood. No, more like bathed in blood. The blood wasn't his though, and luckily so. "You're alright," he tried to say to her, or could have said to her, but he just braced the arm with a stick, scanning the entire fort with a vigilant eye, on the edge and look out. Everything lay in embers or charred. And the stench! A bloody nightmare. Captain Book shed a vengeful tear. The Ilu-Sango had left the fort smouldering in their wake. Ted's officers were either dead, buried under the char alongside arrows and machetes, or isolated, lost in the forest somewhere, for the fort was deserted and completely quiet. Same thing when he tried locating the reverend, above and beneath the debris. The chirping of crickets and cackling of half-spent wood was what was left. They had gotten what they'd come for, if this was what they'd intended. Fort William had been razed to the ground, the Ilu-Sango scoring one at their moment of weakness. Elizabeth was gibbering again; gibbering now something about the boy, or was it her hopes to save him, or get him back, obviously suffering from shock. It was more than likely the kid was somewhere under this rubble (if in fact he hadn't been taken). She was still struggling with shock when something rambled through the bushes though. In actual fact, her boy stepped out of the forest. He had two of Ted's dogs with him and a snail tied about his neck.

The child was also naked. As naked as the day he was born. It would seem this night was far from over.

Beware the bird that shows up at night. We know it as a bat, only born differently. And beware the cockroach that travels by day, we say it carries the sun on its back for a reason. Not understanding this paradigm as what separates you from us is why your misery tends to breed more misery. Even so, it is just as wise to seek to understand the warning behind the mystery because for all we know a leopard never trades its spots. It may sound as a cliché of an adage, but not so much as the reasoning behind it, the reason being if one ever really ventures to, what you now have are two leopards harder to spot.

t he little boy only stared at them. After everything that had just happened, he stared eerily on and the captain felt a chill in his bones. There was something he couldn't place. Something oddly wrong with the way the child just stood there, watching them with vacant eyes, and waiting, waiting comfortably around the dogs—her Majesty's very own dogs if Ted was to be seeing correctly. Ted lifted Elizabeth in his arms. Surely this night was far from over.

"Come, I need help," Ted called, his mouth dry and

tongue parched, sticking stubbornly to its palate and refusing to wet itself, but the boy seemed at ease just watching him stand powerless and helpless. Almost contentedly. The Captain was handicapped with the doctor in his arms so he called again, "she needs help. Are you bloody listening?" he said when he remembered the reverend was one for these peculiar arrangements, trying to shear his mind off the broiled flesh and bones he'd nigh tripped over around what was left of the chapel a few hours ago, but he didn't have to wait long to realize the boy standing before him had no intention of reciprocating the assistance or attention they'd showered over him the last number of months. The Captain oppugning his convenience tried reaching for his holster, yet by the time he could pull out the flintlock to gun down the little ingrate, the child had disappeared behind the bushes—leaving just the captain and the captain's dogs behind. "Pickaninny!" Ted swore after him with Elizabeth in his arms, before whistling fondly to draw the attention of his dogs, and their attention he got because they came charging at him; charging at the captain like feral dogs, rabid and out of control.

By the time the sun came up the flies had begun to settle, hovering in hordes over the fort and indiscriminately over the corpses of man and beast. The Captain wouldn't have felt the fly dancing about his lips, if something or someone hadn't kicked dirt in his face. He could barely make out the two images across from him, his sight a little blurred, reacting terribly to the morning light. He blew off the fly and dirt trapped between his lips. Matulu was building a small fire a few inches from his bare feet, and Elizabeth laid a wet towel across his forehead. She smiled down at him. Her wounds cleanly dressed. The doctor was clad in a happier colour of clothes and for one very short moment Ted wanted to believe the indelible memories he had of the previous night were only half-dreamt thoughts and over-baked imaginings; and he just might have, had it not been for the flies swirling over his head, the inimitable smell of spent wood, and the pain pulsing through his leg.

"Un'ka, he's awake!" Elizabeth intoned and Matulu hesitated a moment, but in the end the nurse just ignored the captain. "Captain? Captain Book? Captain, how are you feeling?" she asked warmly, "I feared...your temperature's been climbing."

Ted's mouth was still dry. He muttered something but she couldn't hear it. She signalled to Matulu and the sore-head aide handed her a small water bag. She nursed a tenuous smile as he left, scouting for flies as he was scouting for resources.

She carefully fed Ted the water. With his tongue

moisturized, the captain spoke up, and quickly too, "what's he doing here? Son of a bitch!" he grumbled, casting a petulant eye at Matulu to the doctor's surprise.

"He's the one who found us," Elizabeth remarked in displeasure. She flipped the towel on his forehead to its wetter side, "he fixed your leg. He saved our lives—probably shouldn't have," she grumbled back.

Ted lifted his head to find his leg and elbow bandaged properly and neatly. Still, the fort remained smoking, a nest of flies, and charred over. "No, I saved our lives—I saved your bloody life, dammit!" Ted retorted sorely before laying back his head to rest. "You don't remember last night because you were delusional. I rescued you from under a mound of tables and debris before you suffocated. I'm the reason your bloody African found you in the first place." The Captain ground his teeth. "—and you're the bloody reason I'm wounded. Bloody canines!"

Ted had squeezed the trigger, but the gun refused to go off. The flintlock refused to go off because it was empty. Either empty or grimy. He dropped Elizabeth in the nick of time to handle the splintered bottle of vinegar—the shard his only defence when they leaped at him. Without explanation, the dogs had ignored Elizabeth but tore at Book. He'd stabbed both dogs to death. The first one quickly, right under its belly, letting the animal rip its own guts through the shard as he fought it off. But the other one, the one that bit him at the elbow and hamstrung his ankle, he'd driven what remained of the hardened glass square into its head. He used the torn pieces of his shirt to secure his wounds. It was bound to get infected, the captain had realized that, but that was on assumption something else didn't get him first. Elizabeth was still in shock that night when Ted collapsed right beside her, too exhausted to care.

Elizabeth noticed the flies and dogs; the dead dogs attracted the most flies, their mortal wounds still fresh. "Thank you," she said gratefully, but after that said nothing.

The Captain sat up when his vision evened out, his leg hurting, "how did you come about these?" he grimaced, examining his bandages and the little dressings adorning Miss Cambridge's face.

"He did...when he came for me," Elizabeth answered succinctly, pointing to the sore-head nurse scavenging through the grime. "He'd found some of our things still packed in the training grounds. A few boxes didn't get scorched."

Ted's eye glistened with intent.

"But just the wardrobe," she explained. "Un'ka packed our wardrobe in the steel boxes, and a—" she pointed to the sanitary dressings on her face, "a few of the toiletries."

Matulu dislodged another horde of flies to unveil the carcass of a large animal. In the day light, Ted could see past the char and grime to the full extent of the burn. That was Zachariah they'd burnt to a crisp. Ted could recognize the horse from the size of its horseshoe. They'd burnt his horses. All of Her Majesty's Graces burnt and buried by the Ilu-Sango. The nurse held on to his nose and charm before scuttling to his next gathering of flies. He could probably make out the corpses of the captain's men in the charred remains if he wanted to. The Captain shed a tear. "Why the bloody hell is he still searching?" he fumed now raising his voice at her (or at them) so Matulu suspended his search to watch the captain intently from a distance. He didn't want any trouble.

"I begged Un'ka to search for Father Matt. We haven't found him yet," she stated, her eyes now pinking softly. She lifted her head skywards to keep her tears from falling.

The Captain turned his head away. They didn't speak for an eternity.

"Tombs are what you uncover in a graveyard," he confessed, long after his tear had dried, helpless when it came to mincing words. Elizabeth was close to crying but she didn't.

"What I saw yesterday Ca—"

"I don't want to remember," Ted cut her off. He tried getting up but his thigh hurt.

She looked around. The forest remained quiescent, verdant, and puissant, aloof to their plight in its serenity. It remained stunning, and brazenly so, concealing all evidence of the horrors of last night. Even the birds were still chirping, with the sunrise feeding golden rays through cirrus-bathed skies, revealing silky threads when the light filtered through overnight spider webs. The skies towered brilliantly over her in such azure blue that could steal your breath away. Oh! This continent was that good a deceiver. "First time I arrived here I'd thought—it'd looked so inviting—" Elizabeth had begun to say.

"It's always looked that way. Didn't mean it was inviting," the captain snorted whilst whisking his towel at the flies buzzing about his injured ankle. More flies were beginning to settle on him, so he forced his way up. "We can set camp at the docks. It will be the safer and faster way to get you out of here," he said, but this time he'd spoken not for her sake, but for whoever's baby she was carrying.

"Thank you," Elizabeth rubbed her belly tenderly, and sought to help him in standing erect. By the time their heads were close enough to touch, Ted asked, and a bit too curtly, "is he the father?" but that was the moment Matulu ignored the grime and the flies, and came running towards them.

The Captain offered the nurse a friendly hand, but Matulu openly ignored it. Whatever he said in Bantu was reason enough. He'd pointed at the forest in the direction of where the chapel used to stand.

"Voices," Elizabeth explained on the hinge of panic.

Un'ka Matulu hurriedly stamped out the small fire and tried picking up everything that might give their presence away.

Ted grabbed Matulu by the collarbone. Although he was hurting, the captain generously handed Matulu his compass. He pointed in the direction of the docks. "You lead but make sure she gets there!" he worked a voice in command, or in the order of a threat, so Matulu shouldered off the captain's hold. Ted was in no physical condition to work up orders. Or threats. Or whatever. Still, coming from Ted, the compass was a kind gesture. One showing egalitarianism. And if Elizabeth had seen it, she just might have been pleased to witness the shift from the captain's usual jingoism.

Matulu worked Elizabeth's feet free of shoes and aided her through the charred perimeter and into the forest. She let him know when they were into meaningful cover that she'd be able to continue by herself and stay camouflaged. She prodded he head back for the captain, but the nurse had been reluctant to leave her unattended. She entreated then insisted, so he did. Un'ka Matulu returned to assist the captain, but did so his way; he shoved his water bag at Ted, who was at best wobbly on both knees. The Captain fell like a log back into the debris, and grime, with a pain that shot up his thigh letting out a deep guttural cry—a cry Ted muffled on a whim. Ted glowered at Matulu, but Matulu snorted, "fuck you," literally forcing the words out his mouth. He spat at Ted, raining down curses in Bantu. By impulse, the captain threatened the nurse with his defunct pistol and so the nurse took his time to smirk before running after Elizabeth. His message was clear; the captain was on his own henceforth. And remained on his own when three chiselled men of Ilu-Sango emerged welding machetes. Just machetes.

"Where's Ted?" Elizabeth asked out-rightly when she discovered Un'ka was the man hacking her way through the forest, but the explanation he weaselled out was something off the words Horse and Sail in Bantu (an explanation that sufficed when she saw the captain's compass he was so proud to show off). They hacked their way South through the forest until Un'ka recognized a trail through the forest, more like a footpath overrun by thick zealous grasses, and so generally meandered their way towards the docks. But after making headway, about half a mile or so, Elizabeth fell abruptly, falling facedown and flat to the ground. Matulu panicked having failed to break her fall. He picked her up almost immediately.

The bigger shocker, however, was when she came back up she felt perfectly fine. "I'm alright. Something broke my fall," Elizabeth stuttered, slightly bemused by what could break her fall. Un'ka placed a hand on her womb, and she did same. She was truly fine, but it didn't matter to Matulu how fine she felt to argue as he took off his charm of bat wings and landed them over her neck, speaking some words in Bantu (be them prayers) at her.

"No, it's yours," Elizabeth objected languidly even as she allowed him string the voodoo charm around her neck. He showed off another charm he'd hidden from sight, another red string around his biceps, and she smiled gratefully, taking relief in his protective eye over her. She checked herself again to make sure she was fine, and then she and Matulu searched through the grass to find out what broke her fall, only to discover a congregation of maggots and decaying flesh; fully developed maggots feeding on human remains.

Scouring through the grime of what was once his fort, the Men of Ilu-Sango were doing a sweep of the littered corpses underneath the char and debris. Some of the corpses they tossed aside like refuse while others they hauled off respectfully. Yet every time they took their eyes off his direction, Ted crawled an inch towards the perimeter gauze. The soot he'd powdered about his face and the dirt on his uniform kept him alive, aiding him within the dirt and ash. The rest of the time, the times they were looking in his direction, Ted took to mending his busted flintlock with the intention of nursing a bullet for the Bantu. The pistol was indeed grimy, inasmuch as it was empty. It'd skipped his memory that he'd exhausted the gun shooting at the Ilu-Sango last night, but now that he found it without purpose, he'd decided to find new use for it. Ted catapulted the flintlock in the air, intending it a mighty distance from him. It ended up not too far away however. Still it was far enough for the captain to gain grounds perchance the men of Ilu-Sango took the bait. They took the bait. The men with machetes went exploring whatever made that clunking sound and the captain inched for forest cover, making it to the forest unnoticed, and in the nick of time too because not long after one of the Ilu-Sango came across a partly extinguished flame; the others finding an uncapped water bag, and this overly weighty footprint across the grime. They had made the captain on the run.

Had it not been for the child's snakeskin attire, the putrefying delegate of bodies would have been impossible to recognize; eaten to bare bones and rotting masses by the maggots wriggling about them. The reaction from Elizabeth and Matulu was an impulsive one, in addition to being inevitable; Matulu vomited over the bodies and Elizabeth puked into her hands. She couldn't see properly as her eyes flooded with tears, only to discover those very hands stunk worse than her vomit. Even if she hadn't noticed it when she fell, she noticed it now. There was blood on her hands; congealed and redolent blood. In fact, it not only stained her hands but stained her dress as well. The doctor forcefully tried to get the blood off by thrashing her hands about but Un'ka grabbed her, to stop her from hurting herself. He clasped her hands tightly around the voodoo charm.

Everything would be fine as long as she had it on her, so she gave it a shot and tried to think positive thoughts, as well as breathe, but she just couldn't keep her mind from straying to the fire of last night. Or the images of the old man lying dead in the infirmary. Or the many voices of Taye or was it

Osate who'd threatened her. Just one too many voices that belonged to that child. A flood of memories came back and it was all too much. She panicked and ran; hyperventilating and stumbling over more bodies as she ran, which certainly didn't help. Still, Elizabeth ran headed anywhere other than here. Or there. Heading no place and in no known direction. Running aimlessly, minute after minute, through hard and soft blades of grass, wet soil and dry ground, barricades of epiphytes and cobwebs, over fallen trees and past monster roots until she was forced to depend on her wits; the doctor had stumbled into a neck of cocoa trees. These trees confronted and confounded her need to run because a cocoa field was not just any field. There North was west and West was east for everything looked the same down to the last litter. It was everywhere being nowhere and nowhere being everywhere, so she squatted by one of the many cocoa trees and cried her eyes out, lost, for the most of an hour.

After she was done crying, she nestled herself in the pacifying ambience and symmetry of the field, watching foraging insects do their thing to the cocoas, birds on the lookout for worms, and a beetle parade itself about, finding interest in many things, one of which included her hair.

In that moment of peace, the doctor almost found her smile back, but then she noticed some movement behind the trees. He'd finally found her and was coming in a beeline to get her out. "Un'ka?" she ventured to ask, but unfortunately it was not Un'ka and so right off the bat, she was on her feet fumbling for anything to arm herself with, "who, or what, are you?" she shrieked and all the birds who'd kept her company in the field took to flight. "Stay away," she threatened, arming herself with some of the cocoa pods she could pluck off the trees, even if she hadn't meant it. She hadn't meant it because it looked like she hadn't meant it. So he came at her, as the crow flies, even after she hurled one of the pods at him. Actually, at that moment, after she'd hurled the pod, the baby in her womb kicked back at her (almost too aggressively in fact) and that startled her. Elizabeth faltered, dropping all the pods, with nothing in mind but screaming for help; even if there was to be no help because only the monkeys in the surrounding forests screamed back at her.

Matulu couldn't find her. There was no point straying off the main trail if he knew not where to look, but that was until he heard the doctor scream and a troop of monkeys in the trees squawking after her— her voice stemming from the cocoa field he'd been skirting for more than an hour. He was hesitant at first primarily because large snakes were lovers of littered fields, aside the greater danger of getting lost in something so symmetrical. Still she was all he had and so Matulu bravely charged through the cocoa trees with his machete in hand, careful not to disturb or sink his foot into any holes camouflaged by all the litter. When he spotted them, the nurse charged at the child, much against his will to give Elizabeth a chance to slip away, but Elizabeth hesitated and so a scuffle soon ensured between the two. The boy fought Matulu's grip as he'd fought the captain's much earlier (to the expense of the machete Matulu was wielding). The child was strong, much stronger than Matulu could ever have guessed. In fact, now the nurse wasn't so sure if he could keep the boy restrained for long, which is why the word curtle ax was the only direct translation of the request he made off Elizabeth in Bantu.

She had noticed it too, the cutlass in the litter, but the look in the child's eyes was so paralyzing that she couldn't think while looking at them. His pupils bore tremendous desolation.

Matulu tried wrestling the child against a cocoa stem, but when the boy slipped his grasp in that eternity found in every second, he panicked and yelled at her this time to save their lives. There was now contempt in his voice, so she wrestled her fear and scrambled for the cutlass. To the doctor's surprise, the feel of the machete stilled her nerves. She inched closer and stretched the axe to Matulu, but handing him the axe was not what the nurse had in mind. Matulu had intended for her to use it! (Actually he'd never said so, but it was just one of those things people feel without having to spell it out)

Elizabeth paused in horror! She didn't think she could bring herself to do it (even whilst the boy rammed the nurse again and again into the cocoa tree to loosen his grip), but Matulu was adamant, already bleeding from the scuffle and so she towered the machete over him as would an angel of the Renaissance poised to strike down a demon.

In that moment, that fleeting pass of air, the child stilled his struggling. It was a moment they shared. A moment that stilled her heart from beating. Elizabeth stood staring into Taye eyes and just couldn't bring herself to swing it. She bailed with the machete. A decision that turned up unfortunate for Matulu for the boy let out a deep and intense cry and resumed fighting with the very strength of a gale. Matulu broke free the red string he'd tied around his arm, attempting to strangle the child with it, but the boy bit into him—a deep cavernous bite! Although it stung, the nurse refused to release the boy, or succumb to the pain (and bleeding) as a matter of life and death. In fact, he would have succeeded in choking the life out of the boy if his leg hadn't slipped into one of the holes beneath the litter and a sibilant predator hadn't taken him by surprise. It wrapped itself around his leg very quickly with the power to crush it and the child had found his moment to break free. He left Matulu asphyxiating under the nipping crush of the huge snake till he was no longer breathing. A slow but certain swallow soon to follow.

With the pace he kept, Ted's ankle had begun to swell. He could hear the thickets crackle not far behind and so had a stone guess those on his pursuit. He didn't have his hat on, but if he was to survive this he was going to have to think on his feet. Ted's left ankle was sour (probably infected) but with his would-be assassins only a wall of bushes behind, the captain contemplated refuge in the trees. To end his contemplation, he speared himself under a thicket of cocoyam leaves (it was hardly desirous but clearly less onerous), and to the fortune of his divagated wit, barely a minute after he'd concealed himself, stormed past the ilu-sango wielding blood-thirsty machetes.

Ted spent the next minutes blowing vigorously down his shirt, but even he couldn't cool off in the heat building beneath the broad cocoyam leaves. On the contrary, blowing himself made him more uncomfortable. It was as the doctor said; he was burning up—and something hurt, not just the hurt from his ankle, or elbow, but a hurt from inside his head. The pain pulsed with a heart of its own; shooting up one half of his face, slowly morphing into a migraine.

There was also a snake, a little brown one, sharing his hiding spot but Ted had thought better not to kill it when its smooth svelte body slithered over his arms (it had been so lithe that when it finally slid by he'd never even noticed it was gone). In a stroke of providence, the men of Ilu-Sango returned a second before the captain concluded it was safe to come out of hiding. They spoke in local dialect but their voices sounded perplexed. It was obvious they were searching for him. The Captain of Her Majesty's Royal Niger Company quivered to the idea he was going to meet his end lying in the mud of a foreign country and at the end of a savage machete. The pain in his head intensified suddenly, pulsating with the force of cannon fire, but the captain kept his eyes open as the Ilu-Sango sought through the bushes and cocoyam thickets with a critical eye; the sap of which Ted would soon come to realize itched far worse than a mosquito bite. Before the men of Ilu-Sango could scout a meaningful portion of the cocoyam foliage, they heard the echo of a voice and the squawk of monkeys a good distance away. They headed after it and almost immediately the captain relieved himself from the dirt. His double vision had returned, but Ted couldn't linger to even it out.

Elizabeth needed his help, though he wasn't sure how much help he could be because his lips were dry, the left half of his face throbbed like a piston, and his ankle hurt. Even his hands were shaky—that was new.

lizabeth heard his cries before she could fully balance the weights of what favoured the greater good. It stilled her dilemma for a moment, freezing her in her tracks. No cries followed after that. "Un'ka!" she hollered back compassionately, but with a voice incapable of the bravery required when something ruffled the bushes (or some kind of bramble) behind her and she jerked away. Anxious and on the edge, she timed the machete at the bush only to discover a litter of grass-cutters take to their heels. She immersed into herself by muffling her cries and squatting, only to realize the mud wetting her dress and oozing through her feet was atypically soft. In fact, the leaves were a lighter lustre! It was her silver lining in dark clouds, for now she could see the bamboo plants! And though she hadn't felt any mosquitoes, that could easily be explained because of the tension she was feeling. On her own, Elizabeth had already concluded she had missed her way, having been on the run for so long, but now on getting to realize she'd been running in the right direction she couldn't be more elated. She hadn't heard the trickling of a stream, so her guess was the docks were just around the corner. Elizabeth disrobed into her white undergarment, not letting her blood-stained dress linger a minute longer. She fought off the mosquitoes hovering over her head like a miniature tornado but had barely recovered the machete when someone tugged against her underwear. It was much too private a touch so in swinging the machete, she attacked whoever it was. She'd mauled him, Taye. It had been Taye, as she turned around, but she'd swung the cutlass in reflex not deliberately intending to cut through the boy the way she did.

He died instantly, his head giving way as would an okra pod, splotching her undergarment a vivid red as he dropped to the ground dead! She dropped the machete, watching his body convulse mechanically, but then, when the doctor remembered to run, ran too fast to hold her balance, haunted by a fragmented conscience and what was slowly becoming her fragmented mind. She couldn't escape the guilt, or tears, or the blame it shoved down her throat as she ran, so when she encountered The Lady Anne at the mushy docks waiting as the captain had envisioned, tears welled up in her eyes at this one palpable means of escaping the inhospitable jaws of the Niger. Or the unfathomable terrors she'd witnessed here. She didn't linger, no, Elizabeth hurried so quickly for its boarding planks, so imbued by emotions outside her control, that she hadn't seen the root that caught her foot. The doctor fell. And splat on her belly, she fell.

 resurrected

"Elizabeth," Ted had called, but all she had seen was a stranger's soiled face. Elizabeth had been out, unconscious, and falling in her dream with no one to rescue her up until the captain lifted her face off the mud so he didn't take offense when she scratched at him like a cat having fingernails for claws. "Eliza—bloody hell!" he cursed, wading away in hurt, "it's me, dammit!"

With immersed roots and a pie of mud on her face, Elizabeth could barely see. Both her arms had sunk all the way to her elbows, sopping whatever remained unstained of her flowing underwear. "oh Captain," she heaved, lunging at him, hugging him tightly and crowning it with a muddy and balmy kiss. Finally she'd returned to her senses—or not, as he helped her to her feet in the cushion of mud she'd fainted on.

Elizabeth staggered, almost slipping a second time, so he threw an arm around her to help her out of the soggy mass. There was a bold imprint in it that promptly filled with water the moment he got her off. Had the inlet overflowed its banks, she would have met her end here upon this chocolaty bed of death.

The captain wiped her face clear. "Where's Matulu?" he asked promptly, but she looked to the planks. There was no one in sight and The Lady bravely sat where it'd been docked, unmoving and confidently towering over everything, so he couldn't blame her if she just couldn't wait to start for it. Her eyes bore holes, there was this tortured vigilance about them, so they waded through the cohesive mass to get to the planks, but when he got her on the planks, the captain couldn't help but ask again, "where's Matulu?" he asked, tense and petulant (for he'd been nursing a foot, a migraine, and a grudge since he and the nurse got separated).

"I killed him," Elizabeth confessed in disillusionment, finding her voice now that they had gotten to The Lady. She looked around quickly. The captain too was quick in looking over his shoulders, vigilant for any who would follow. As before, there was not a soul in sight. "I killed him," Elizabeth repeated and despite sounding pretty off the wall, Ted was content to leave it at that. "That bastard deserved something worse—a fate they all share in this bloody continent," he muttered but then hesitated. Something was off about the boarding planks. All of the planks had been set for loading. Or offloading. Something highly unusual especially since there was still no one in sight. So he called to The Lady Anne to confirm his suspicion, but not a soul was aboard the ship. "We must wait," Ted said dryly as he drew the doctor closer to himself. They watched The Lady sit peaceably in the distance, rocked by incoming waves and sitting lifelessly for a ship always on the go. The more they watched, the more the captain was convinced her sails were busted, her hawsers were loose, and The Lady Anne had lingered for days on end without command. Or any trace of activity. In all likelihood, She had never departed the shores of Africa since his last loading. (but if that was true, it meant his last shipment never left for Bristol too). The captain grew nervous. "Where are they?" he kept asking himself though he feared what his answer portended.

It was about that time the doctor freed herself from his embrace. "You have the fever," she let him know, having taken the moment in the minutes they'd spent together to observe him. Ted's hot breath, burning temperature, laboured breathing, and cold body flashes (in addition to the sluggishness of how he moved) weren't all symptoms she could appropriate to causalgia (effects from exposing his swollen ankle to the mud and elements for so long), but there was just no way Ted could allow himself to believe that (certainly not here! And definitely not now!) Surely she must have misdiagnosed, yet aiding the pregnant doctor board the ship was the last thing the captain remembered doing before losing consciousness.

She hadn't objected when they seized her, dragging her like game back into the forest. Strangely, the godskin wasn't threatened by their manhandling. It had quite the opposite effect. She cherished that they were moving her away from the docks and deeper into the forest, always looking behind as if something was after her. After them. Elizabeth's face was flushed pink and overwrought, bearing on the fringe of insanity by the look of her. The two warriors only stopped dragging her along when they reached a neck of the forest, the low grasses there having just an anthill at its heart, so it was a conspicuous and relatively safe opening from the openly aggressive canopy of darkness and vegetation extending throughout the forest. They let her go, but only to bind her hands and bind her to a tree.

"kini a maa se bayi?" one asked the other, an uncertain look in his eye, "were leleyi. Sho ri?"

The other sneered, sizing up the white woman as they pondered what to do with the laden female, "a maa duro naani."

"ha. arabinrin toloyun? ti o ba sise nko?"

"ti o ba sise, pa," the other antagonized because his intentions were clear, his mind stalwart to the task at hand, but his colleague turned his machete to its blind side.

"ki lo so? Arabirin toloyun?! emi o le paa o! egun

leleyi."

"ti o ba sa lo nko, kini o ma so ninu oja? oya, so arabinrin yen kia kia."

These men had bound Elizabeth with raffia palms against a kernel tree, so as agreed, their plan for the foreigner and her unborn baby could wait.

the captain had fallen off the boarding planks leading up to the ship and splat into the mire before he realized it was because Elizabeth had swiftly withdrawn from the ship, witlessly racing down immediately after boarding. He was fortunate however that the mud and water had broken his fall, but possibly his back as well, having a type-A class of pain cringe up his spine. Ted literally worked his nerves out of the mire to the lower ends of the boarding planks and latched on to them for dear life, spewing dirt and root nodes out of his mouth. Elizabeth was nowhere in sight when he recovered his place on the planks. He called out to her twice but there was no response. He'd lost her. The Captain felt a chill inside his bones; the water and mud he'd fallen into doing him a far greater unkindness than the pain feasting relentlessly on his body and limbs. He was too weak to use his legs so he crawled with his arms, shivering all the way for the cover of the ship and the genial resources The Lady Anne stood to offer, but when he clambered on board, The Lady Anne was but a morgue of cadavers (and that was what had been her pursuing shadow!) The ship was brimming with the bloated remains of what had been his export; an export of new land slaves, slaves in shackles and wrought-iron dog cages bound for Bristol.

It also held a colossal stink for not only the dog cages harboured the dead—a litter of Her Majesty's officers also graced the decking, some covered in blankets, others naked for the flies to feast on, but everyone aboard The Lady was either bloated or festering, and to unreasonable proportions. There was also vomit everywhere, mouldering vomit, aggregating in the huge stink and filth that consumed the ship.

It was filthy, yet Ted had no alternative. He had to crawl through the mould to the starboard side, barely having the strength to avoid the slime that could be avoided, heading resolutely for the ship's pilot slumped by the wheel. The man wasn't bloated but had sputum and phlegm dried against his bluing mouth. He was snuggled in a blanket with a bottle of gin, but that was before the captain robbed him of property, finding new use for the blanket and gin since the dead could bear no grudge. The pilot had a note sticking out of his breast pocket and Ted slipped it out. It read *To Captain Thomas Edbyrte Book of Her Majesty's Royal Niger Company, In The Name Of Her Majesty the Queen of England,*

Head of The House of Lords, and Protector of the Seven Colonies: The Slaves Are Sick. We Too Have Taken ill. We Request Your Assistance And The Aid Of Your Resident Medic. Bring Her To Us As Quickly As She is Able. Signed—actually he hadn't been able to sign his note, but if the captain could laugh through the irony of it, he would have (had he the warmth and strength to do so).

He quaffed down the bottle to protect himself the best he could from the cold building within him, cleaning down the lips of the bottle every time he drank from it. Ted's back hurt, his limbs were limp, and his head pounded like pestle to mortar. Even his vision was blurred, but that was partly to the tears cascading down his cheeks because he pretty much figured at one time they'd all been as sick as he was now. Somehow, he was never destined to escape the jaws of the Niger. Somehow, he was destined to die here; a loner's death, in a foreign land, with no help forthcoming. That was the impression Ted had had when he emptied the bottle (but that was the impression he had).

By the time he came aboard The Lady Anne, he came dragging a blood-stained machete—Elizabeth's blood stained machete. And like all things the captain had been slow to notice, having drifted to the numbness stealing his body and into the arms of Morpheus (mostly to escape the pain racking his skull) the boy stood a presence impossible to ignore, just standing there by the port of the ship, wielding a morbid stare and a portentous machete. Ted squinted at the child because the machete shimmered in the light, as did the entire ship, for both his pupils had fully dilated; flooding them with visual lies and lucent imagery.

"You again. Come boy. Kill me," Ted said dryly, barely able to part his caked lips, not sure if what he was seeing was an apparition. Or a real person.

The child carved the ship as he came to the captain etching a bee-line into the floorboard with the razor end of the machete, a machete as sharp as the scowl etched across his ebony face, only for him to poke the machete against the captain's forehead, and then looking Ted in the eye, spoke to him with a feminine voice, "I want them to suffer for what they do to me. Why would I fancy your blood, godskin?" she demanded tastelessly and in perfect tense before a flood of voices took over, resounding in mockery and derision, "he has no heart, this one"

"he's the water in the coconut"

"—caged them like dogs, he did"

"it's playing apple against mangoes"

"—poor fool, no one told him"

"we are gods, but no one ever calls us godskins"

"—this one reminds me of holy book. It's good we kill him."

"—he's the water in the coconut, why kill him?"

"oh, let him be, surely we've had enough—"

"—he's the water in the coconut, why let him be"

"poor fools look like balloons—"

"the other one's not dead, yet"

"—too bad they all die."

Ted looked up at the bloated corpses around him (at the entire cargo ship with aborigines incarcerated in his bastion of shackles and wrought-iron cages). All must have suffered from starvation and dehydration, like he endured now, as the daylight toyed about them, animating their corpses into ghouls clamouring for payback—be it payback in kind or payback in blood. The child stared at the captain without blinking, his morion jewelled eyes vacant of expression; void of pleasure, or scorn, expressionless, bereft of loyalties. Ted lay there, dry as limestone, as the boy towered the machete over him.

In bringing it down, and swinging it violently, he carved up the ship's pilot by Ted's side until he'd carved right through the sternum to the officer's heart. He left the captain alive though, trudging off The Lady Anne the same way he'd come, with blood and an uncertain smile adorning his face.

"Kill me," Ted pleaded, but the child took his machete with him. "Kill me you pickaninny!"

"Why the haste, Thomas?" the girl in the boy said.

"—you'll get what's coming to you"

"it was never our intention to kill you"

"—you caught the malaria all on your own," the voices chuckled, leaving the captain aboard the ship to his comeuppance.

So, dusk met Ted alone with his conscience, even if twilight couldn't because one of them, the sinewy one-eyed man from Ilu-Sango, finally encountered the captain helpless aboard the ship. As expected, he did what his brothers would have done. He drove his machete squarely into Ted's skull, having it be recompense for the scores rotting inside his bastion of iron cages. "omo ale! aa tii paa, sha," was all he said before he left, his breasts still hurting from Ted's stick magic.

i t came for her by twilight. Even though it had taken all night, it came for her by twilight. The plan was to leave her bound at the neck of the forest where the grasses grew low, in a place there would be little resistance. Unlike last time. So he came with a machete in hand, having skirt the neck of the forest for hours to be certain she was just the one; she was just the one, so he came as naked as he was the last time, lifting her head with the machete and making a face at her, "we told you not to put your apple in our basket."

Elizabeth screamed with no one to hear her. The raffia palm was a coarse tree. The tree and its threads were meant to hurt if she struggled, so all she could do was cry. "Don't hurt me. Don't hurt my baby. Please, I beg you. What do you want from me?!!"

Now, being that she mentioned it, the boy placed his spiny fingers against the doctor's womb and Elizabeth quivered at his touch. He took pleasure in feeling her, she could see it. Even down to her thighs. She sobbed helplessly. "Please, allow me go— allow me go home!!" she cried at the top of her voice, begging to be freed and it seemed it worked because the child stood amused by her begging.

Only one voice answered in the end, "home is here, Elizabeth. It's alright to giggle," a boy in the boy had said, yet that was enough to exhume a memory she'd repressed for almost a year. One that refused to stay under.

"It's alright to giggle"

"—t's alright to giggle"

"it's alright to giggle, doctor!" the voices seemed to continue in her head. More voices. Many voices.

NOW, Cape Bedford was situated on the edge of the

African continent, proudly overhanging its southernmost cliff, and just one of the many colonies made possible by Admiral James T.T. Bedford, whose grandson Elizabeth would come to know as Seymour Bedford, Admiral S.T. Bedford, or the Admiral as the others knew him. He'd always been nice to her—always checking up on her at the Cape, always keeping his officers in line, and always one to converse. He was the perfect gentleman. So on what would end up being her last night at the Cape, after all the indigenes had retired, the doctor accepted his invite to share a drink at the infirmary. It was a nice night and Seymour spent it bragging about his escapades in the Cape and how he'd go about winning over the Bantu tribes behind colonized frontiers and yonder. He knew them as hostiles, but he wasn't moved. There was little that could stop the Admiral once his mind was set. He was brave, audacious and daring, Elizabeth knew, which also served as his Achilles heel. He wasn't at all a perfect man like every man she knew (a subordinate had once reported the admiral's control issues to the mainland once), but he was by far the closest (even if it was rumoured Seymour had had that man discharged).

"So, they say you'll be leaving us for your next assignment?" he'd said to her, with a voice of steel for one so young and that ever so charming smile. He was always one to keep long hair, as he winked at her and she smiled generously.

"Yes. I'll be leaving. That will feel like a real assignment, you've made this like home to me," she'd answered him, now fingering the narrow drinking glass he had given her. She'd let off a more than generous smile, and with alcohol at the tip of her lips, she couldn't tell how much more she would let off. He had been sitting by an open window, someway drawing closer to her as he showed her the stars. The stars had lined themselves so perfectly that night, that this time she could make out Sagittarius and his elusive arrowhead the Admiral had infinitely failed portraying to her prosy company from the cabin window many times before.

"Home is here, Elizabeth. Sure you're not going to miss any of us?" he'd asked then caressed her hands from across the table. The doctor wasn't one to giggle. Or hoard the silly smile smack between her freckled cheeks. "It's alright to giggle, doctor," he said and she nodded. Or blushed. Whichever came first. Elizabeth had never been with a man before, but she thought the admiral knew that. If it would concern him, that is. He was always so nice. She had stroked his hair a little too tenderly and he kissed her on the forehead for it. She had always wanted to do that, ever since the first day she'd arrived at the Cape and seen that flowing golden hair fall out his hat. She never knew how he always kept it so kempt. So organized. So disciplined. He motioned further and took the audacious step to kiss her on her lips, and was surprisingly gentle at it for a man she'd known to be toughest of the men she knew. The admiral also had soft hands, she learned that from the way they glided about her hips, and lips, when he pressed into her. He kissed her again more audaciously and fully into the mouth. She could hear the tumbler break when it dropped from her hands, and the table and cabin chairs crash into oblivion after they hit the floor in excitement, but it was awfully breezy in there and the cabin doors were very well open to any who would enter.

She hadn't remembered when they were by the medical cabinets, or when he had her by the walls, working his fingers up and down her blouse, through her lingerie, over her breasts and now under her pantyhose, cushioning her thighs with his soft warm hands—god, he was quick. Or maybe that was how lovemaking was meant to be. The only time she hesitated was when the stretcher cowered under their collective bodyweight, barely providing the support they needed, so she thought better of it—this was not the best of places for this, but when she said no, he continued to press into her. It appeared he hadn't heard her, so she kissed him back and tenderly tried coaxing him off. Instead he kept kissing, repeatedly kissing to keep her from speaking. He wouldn't be coaxed. She shoved him off but playfully, "Seymour?" she chided only for the admiral to yank her by the buttocks, spin her around forcefully and sprawl her legs against a cabinet. The next she felt was a sharp pain and him inside her—the intensity of the pain had taken her by surprise, even though she'd been well informed that was the way these things went, but besides the confusion and fear, she really hadn't been able to figure if the Admiral needed her express permission to have relations with her having led him on this far. Still, she tried fighting him off but he seemed to exert himself even more, ramming her against the cabin again and again until it turned to a struggle. She scratched the Admiral in the face and couldn't be certain what would have transpired had one of the indigenes not come to her aid. Matulu yanked the admiral off her and sent him flying into the stretchers like a wad of hygiene paper. It was an awkward moment they were forced to share with the Bantu, but his action alone was sufficient to reset the Admiral to normalcy. Immediately the Admiral sought to apologize, but Elizabeth shrivelled away from him. She stood utterly terrified so he exited quickly, and humbly, not able to take back what he'd done for the graze across her forehead was starkly visible. As visible as the blood trickling down her thighs.

The nurse in training offered to see to her wounds, but Elizabeth made it clear she could handle herself. She was grateful he showed up when he did though, fortunate he'd come to lock up the infirmary.

"WHOEVER carefully dismembers an ant, will see its intestines," the voices taunted, snapping Elizabeth to reality, "—the gourd is broken"

"—he used you"

"and left you with his baby"

"My baby! Please don't hurt my baby," Elizabeth cried, but a brute voice cut her mid tense.

"—stop saying that!"

"Liar!"

"you do not want your baby—"

"No!" she sobbed.

"—ooto oro bi isokuso ni," the voices boomed at her and the child faced the machete razor side up, testing the blade against the stringed bat wings hanging from her neck. "—this does nothing," he growled, or rather she growled, as the voodoo charm dropped to the ground and Elizabeth groaned from an abyss of despair. But just when he was about to cut her open and relieve her of the little godskin growing inside her, a twig snapped within the bushes. The men of Ilu-Sango who had her bound to the kernel tree had returned with a corpse of another child. They threw this child to the ground for them to see. Or for her to recognize. And she did, panic fraught.

"Mo ri oti ri ikeji me[19]," he said to them unflinching at the corpse of his exact other, the one whose head had nigh been split in two not too long ago. Still the men had banded the halves back together with some kind of rope (or raffia) and strung him up like firewood. They were to have this one bound for the fire too, as the oracle would so desire; this one, being the twin that slipped their grasp the last time they thought they had him. The two men threw fermented wine at him, and then circled him with machetes in hand.

This time they knew not to handle him lightly.

Kehinde returned his gaze to Elizabeth, not perturbed by their sudden interruption, "I should thank you for freeing us of him," he mentioned to her.

"—we by ourselves could not kill the runt"

"being that we share a mortal soul"

"—even if he did protect you,"

"but you you've angered the goddess"

"—and we are the incarnate"

"I like Her even if I hate him"

"—we warned you not to put your apple in our basket"

"—you—elizabeth."

"—or should we call you Liz"

[19] I see you've found the other me!

Elizabeth fainted on facing the truth; she'd killed the wrong child (no, she'd murdered him!) Fortunately for her the indigenes nabbed Kehinde before he could split her in half much the same way she'd split his other in half much earlier. She had a price to pay for she'd aroused more anger and hate by that action alone than her blood could ever hope to repay, but the indigenes won't let him offer her (to the Goddess). They bound him by the arms and legs. She had a price to pay (to Ibeji), but they stapled him to the ground spinning gin-soaked raffia all around him. He refused to yield and would not be bound a second time, and so the anthill obeyed the incarnate when it erupted bullet ants like a miniature volcano. The little critters began to swarm, swarming progressively from the anthill, and swarming in every direction. Ibeji was in fury. She was on their side.

"oya tete! o ti fe bere o,[20]" the hunter that had the child subdued by the head cried, but now the voices cawed out like crows to an unkindness of high flying birds, and quickly (like in defence of their own) a black kite with white breasts swooped down into their midst, and vengefully poked at the eyes of the man who was first to look up at it. It flew away before either man could kill it, so hurriedly they pressed themselves upon him. In effect, driving the outcast further into the earth and trying to keep him subdued.

[20]do it quicker. It is about to begin.

When the sea of termites caught up with Elizabeth who was unconscious and helplessly bound to a kernel tree, a comforting breeze travelling through the neck of the forest in a subtle rustle of leaves blew up from under her. It was a strange breeze and very conscious too because each time it blew, it blew the ants away just enough for them to reroute their swarm around her in some strange obedience.

The first of two men to misplace his foot was the one who suffered the gravest injury. He fell into the swarm of bullet ants and immediately they overwhelmed him, sending him scurrying in every direction clawing at his orifices and haemorrhaging badly. The other man took to his heels, but the kite came back, and with it an unkindness of its brothers, making certain the hunter had no escape from the black sea of death.

When Kehinde got to his feet in the end, only Elizabeth was left alive against the raffia palm, so he picked up the bloody machete to pick up where he left off. He took one good swing at the godskin (making it his second swing today), but his harmful intention alone was enough to send the machete flying far away from his grip. He'd aroused the attention of something powerful. Something present, omniscient and unseen.

Whichever Loa it was, it wore no colour as it clawed its way up from under the ground. The incarnate stood the form of a tree with fingers and a man with roots. It held the face of an old woman, yet the genitals of a young man. Its head was downside up situated comfortably between its thighs, but its genitals stayed perched above its shoulders with no care or regard for this world.

Kehinde looked to the spirit as one would a mirror. It was not in the nature of a Loa to meddle in the affairs of the simple. Not unprecedented, however. These higher spirits were highly unpredictable when resurrected, and far from pleasant, "which of who are you—" he demanded at the time the voices bragged, "we are your incarnate"

"—we shed more blood at childbirth"

"more blood for You than their worthless human money can buy—"

The Loa didn't seem to mind (or acknowledge) these lower spirits, all this Loa did was stare at Elizabeth obsessively, only for them to observe how the termites shunned the godskin, almost like a plague, as if they'd been instructed to make their way around her. Actually, a gentle breeze had kept blowing them off.

"—he's not of us," the voices confessed, piqued by the Loa's continued silence, and its nestled attention.

"—who of what are you?"

"—why have you come!" they screamed tersely, in a violent gesture of dominance, but the Incarnate screamed back, screaming a loud inaudible scream, a scream incapable of rousing Elizabeth, or any human ear for that matter, but loud like a dog whistle sufficient in dropping Kehinde to the ground in a violent convulsive fit, much till after twilight, when the third hunter came by.

Makanjuola encountered his two dead companions by the neck of the forest after returning from setting the unholy ship on fire. He also encountered the two outcasts, and yet another godskin bound by raffia to a palm tree. Of the outcasts, only one was truly dead. The other one, the troublesome one, was in a paralytic fit, though he was strong enough to speak, "do not—hurt—what you—can't—kill!" it threatened, but he had permitted the mistake before, so this time he preferred to return both outcasts already prepared for the ritual—he ignored its toothless threat as he undressed them both and then driving his machete through the child, quickly ended him before anything strange happened. But if by anything strange he chose to ignore what he might have perceived to be voices in the wind or from the trees on his way home, then their threats bore no relevance, "we will wait—for you"

"—come next life"

"if we—do not meet you—ever again—in this life—"

"don't be late"

"—we won't be late."

Still, the hill would be a much safer place after the offering. That was the way things worked.

*E*lizabeth had her baby in a hut with the aid of the Ilu-Sango. The child had come as they'd expected, and in the same manner they'd expected, just as they expected The Madness to halt its torment of their village. The only thing they didn't expect was why the godskin wouldn't stop bleeding from her time of delivery. Elizabeth had tried all she knew as a medic to no avail. They had little resources in the new continent, but her strength waned, and she lay sick now, limb and dying in the delivery hut, so she allowed the strange man painted in white, the one they referred to as babalao, to quote prayers and say incantations on her behalf. He marked her face with chalk and quickly moved to prepare a fireplace to save her life. The men of Ilu-Sango had strung up charms to the Deities and sprinkled cowries about the big fireplace, but the women of Ilu-Sango who'd once been so helpful till the day of her delivery wouldn't even come near her until after the ritual, so the one eyed hunter who'd saved her life once was the one they'd sent into her hut to save it again. He came for the offering and Elizabeth handed over her baby without hesitation. There was little to no harm a baby could bring, but to immolate the little godskin, it had to be encumbered with palm wine and rubbed with oil so it won't escape the fire by finding a way into the others. The one eyed man placed the baby over the fireplace, and at the babalao's command, the men of Ilu-Sango lit the firewood altar from its ends. The fire devoured the wood quickly, but not before the French raided the village. They shot the men and brought down the pagan altar. They captured some of the women and children present and took many of them away as they could.

"Commandant! Mon commandant Pimsleur!" one of the French men howled while they were yet taking the burning altar apart. The man rescued the helpless waif, bringing it to the commander, "la enfant."

"la tribu froid, celle-ci. Les sauvages," the commander grumbled when he took the baby from the soldier, thoroughly vexed, "il doit être du les Anglais à l'ouest de nous."

"La femme! Mon commandant! La femme!" another soldier yelled a little while later from one of the other huts afar off. The commandant rushed to the hut. They found Elizabeth almost passed out in the hut in her underwear. The commander's hesitation was one of fear. It appeared she'd been wearing that very undergarment for months. "Docteur!" he called, they had a medic in their midst, and immediately had his officers try to put something befitting on her—something less sickening. They discovered she was bleeding, so the French officers also screamed for the medic, "docteur!!"

It hadn't taken long for the medic to arrive and examine the extent of Elizabeth's injuries. He shook his head, "she'll barely make sunset, not to talk of the six-day journey back to camp, mon commandant," he declined. "Elle sera mort d'ici là."

"Mon Dieu!! God help the English—vers l'ouest. Nous nous entraidons. Allons-y!" Commander Pimsleur announced as the medic examined the little child the commander had bundled up using his officer's jacket. The baby had a bold scar to the right side of its head and ear. It appeared as a fierce imprint, but the medic ruled it as a birth scar, and not the inflicted injury the commander had resolved it to be. An anomaly, yes, but a birth deformity nonetheless. The baby wasn't singed; he was still covered in blood and amniotic fluid, so it was nothing to be hot and bothered about.

Titles by Nigeria's phantom publisher.

GENERAL FICTION

THE BEDSIDE AND CAMP FIRE SERIES

Request for your favorite titles and our newer books at your local bookshop or visit your online retail bookstore.